# WENDIGO ROAD

## DOUG GOODMAN

SEVERED PRESS
HOBART TASMANIA

# WENDIGO ROAD

For my wife and son.

# CHAPTER ONE

The plane cabin was filling with smoke.

Oran tensed in the makeshift seat. An old Metallica T-shirt was stapled to a board, creating his suit cushion. *Metal Up Your Ass*, the T-shirt growled defiantly. It was a manifesto statement. Oran Old Chief would've laughed if he didn't worry he was being slowly choked to death.

He could barely see the end of the cabin where the steward sat. The steward's voice cracked as he barked into the com, "Yes, obviously the plane is filling with smoke! Stay calm!"

Oran glanced around. About half the seats in the Bombardier were still there, and soldiers filled about half those seats. They were hardened warriors returning from the front in Canada. Asians, whites, some Cheyenne, and even a Blood or two. Oran was the only South Piegan.

The ones wearing gas masks had already donned their gear, transforming their faces into something weirdly alien with giant eyes and canister mouths. Like Oran, their uniforms were as piecemeal as the army. Leather jackets, hunter's knives, any-ready-ammo feeders, and random camouflage. Ever since the wendigos appeared, the white man's world had been broken. There were no companies to make military clothes and no contractors to design weapons. There were only the people who fought the wendigo and the people who did not.

The soldier sitting in the aisle in front of Oran said, "I don't want to die."

"Calm down," Oran said. "Panicking serves nobody. Take deep breaths."

"I'm not panicking."

Oran would've rolled his eyes if he didn't think it would make the situation worse.

"Stay calm, like the steward said."

But the man was gasping for breath.

"Try taking off your parka. Sometimes that helps."

"Yeah, okay," he said. He pulled his parka off, took a deep breath, and coughed, shaking his head. His voice stammered as he said to Oran, "I know what you're thinking. Some pussy who can't take a little smoke. What's he doing in the army? But I'm not a coward. I've fought on the front. I just don't like the idea of dying before I get home."

The captain came on over the com. His voice was tinny, the radio connection poor. "So, here's the thing. There is a gasket seal in the back of the plane that keeps AC exhaust from entering the cabin. That seal sometimes breaks."

"So fix it, gawd-dammit!" one of the Cheyenne shouted.

The captain continued, not hearing anything from the cabin. "The good news is that the exhaust is nontoxic. This isn't smoke. We've been through this before, and we'll be okay. The bad news is that we won't make it to Browning. We're rerouting to Spokane. I know you all had other places to be. I'm sorry. I'm putting the Fasten Seat Belt on until we land, which will be in a few minutes."

The Fasten Seat Belt light flashed, then the bulb behind it fizzled and died. Oran flicked it. That didn't help.

"Spokane?" the man in front of Oran shouted. "But there's fighting there. Wendigos began raiding last week. We can't go there!"

"Well, the option is there or here," Oran said, thumbing to the window while trying to stay calm. He wasn't sure if he was saying this for the panicking man or for himself. The cabin was really thick with smoke.

Oran opened the window blind. The modified Bombardier was still above the cloud line, so the sun loomed large overhead. The sun was bright yellow, with giant waves of light fluttering in the sky. Because of all the smoke in the cabin, the sun appeared milky white.

The wing of the plane was a dirty, gray knife cutting through the blue sky, an offense to the sun.

Oran said a prayer and thought of his home, his wife and his son in Browning. The war with the wendigos had been long on him. He'd fought many battles, orchestrated many victories, and now it was finally time to rest. He'd handed over his war to other people, and now he needed to cleanse himself and live a life away from war.

The smoke tickled Oran's throat. He coughed a little.

From below the clouds, smoke rose up to meet them. Half the world was on fire. A faint burnt smell lingered in the air even at 30,000 feet. At least, he assumed it was the world below burning and not something in the plane. If something was on fire, would there be any benefit for the pilot to tell them? Oran figured not, which discomforted him.

The soldiers onboard had melanoma scars on top of their battle scars, and where there were no scars, they had robotic prosthetics.

Somebody else coughed. To Oran the cabin seemed smudged, like his eyes were bleary after waking from a long dream.

Many of the other soldiers stuck their heads down the aisle, questioningly. They had all been to war for a long time. They knew when to look for an answer and when to duck.

"I didn't go to war for three years only to die in a fucking plane," a man across the aisle said.

"I do not think we have a choice," Oran said. He pulled a bandana over his mouth.

The smoke was getting thicker. More soldiers were coughing.

Oran was coming to the conclusion that he was truly trapped, and that unlike the rest of his life, he had absolutely zero control over what happened between here and Spokane. Biology, physics, and the competency of the pilot would determine whether he lived or died. For him, that lack of control was hard to accept. He had guided troops into battle and steered them into victory or defeat, but he was the one determining where to go and how to win. Now, he was forced to sit and let other people control his destiny.

The smoke thickened. He could no longer see the steward at all. Oran began to doubt the captain's words about the cause of the leak because the smoke was not only coming from the back of the cabin, but it was rising from beneath the seats.

"I don't want to die," the soldier in front of him repeated. His face, like Oran's, was dirty from combat missions. They hadn't had a chance to stop and shower. When the plane arrived, they'd dropped everything and ran for their transport. Oran barely made it before the plane took off for the south.

"Be calm," Oran said. "Do not panic. That will do none of us any good."

"I hate planes. The tight spaces. I just need to move around. I need some fucking fresh air."

"Stop talking. Take longer breaths. We'll be fine."

But then there was a loud blare followed immediately by a large explosion in the cabin, like a high-caliber gunshot or a small detonating device. At the same instant, the oxygen masks deployed.

"Jesus!" the man in front of Oran shouted.

Oran grabbed his oxygen mask and pulled the yellow cup over his mouth. He pulled down his bandana, and then he tugged on the hose tightly. The oxygen bag didn't inflate. The man in front of him was having the same problem. On the other side of the plane, the bladders were thick and full of oxygen. Somehow the masks on their side had failed to inflate.

"Sorry about that," the captain said over the com. "Mask drop is standard operating procedure. I have no control over it. I want to assure you, though, that you've got the best damn pilot in Washington State sitting in your cockpit. I'm doing everything I can to get us out of the sky quickly."

"Will we make it that far without oxygen masks?" the soldier in front of him asked.

"Be calm," Oran said again, but he could feel that little rise of panic inside himself.

"Hey," the soldier said to some of the infantry nearest him. "You've got an infantry oxygen mask. Give me your gas mask."

The soldier wearing the gas mask gave him the one-finger salute.

The man in front of Oran suddenly unbuckled and stood.

"Please sit down," the steward said from his foggy position. Oran still couldn't see him.

"I need air!" The panicking man's voice was uncannily high pitched. Oran recognized the sound of overwhelming fear. It was the enemy to any good unit.

The panicking man grabbed an oxygen mask from the other side of the plane and put it over his face.

Oran crossed the plane and placed his hand on the man's shoulder, coolly pushing the man into his new seat. "Do not get up," Oran said. All the soldiers in the plane, about forty in all, were watching him to see what he would do next. Oran pulled his bandana over his nose and sat back down in his seat.

The captain said over the speakers, "We've been cleared for prioritized emergency landing. I promise we'll be on the ground in a few minutes."

Oran was glad. He couldn't see more than four rows ahead or behind his seat. Many of the soldiers on his side of the plane were coughing, including him. He reached for the window shade again. As he did so, he felt the rush of the plane descending rapidly. He reached for his seat belt, then remembered that his seat didn't have one. Back when there was a world with governing bodies, this never would have happened. No plane would've been allowed to fly without seat belts, but that was back before the wendigos went to war. Back then, there were regulators. In the first years of the war, soldiers flew in military aircraft, but then the wendigos destroyed most of the stockpiles and the vehicles. Now, the military were scavengers searching for any working vehicle to support their war. Sometimes that meant taking the bad with the good. At 30,000 feet, the bad looked really bad to Oran, though.

He opened the window shade, but no sun streamed through. They had descended below the clouds, which were as dense out there as the smoke in the cabin. It was like descending through a dream into a nightmare, and the bottom was falling out of the world.

The coup lance was in the storage above him. The parfleche his wife made was there, too. He closed his eyes and breathed deeply and suppressed his cough and thought of his wife and child. Jodi was a beautiful woman and quick to laugh with or, if needed, at him. She was clever, like him. His son, Daniel, was always exploring and getting into something. Oran had been a little scared for his son when he left because Daniel was the type of kid who frequented ERs, whether it was because he had bounced off the trampoline or, after the trampoline had been thrown out, he jumped off the house. His wife and his son filled him with happiness.

Then the plane began to rip itself apart. That's what the scared soldier said. When the wheel housing opened, it made another big bang, like a piece of the fuselage had split apart. This meant they were getting close to ground. Oran was glad for it. He was having a hard time catching his breath.

"I don't wanta die," the scared man said. He pulled off his oxygen mask. The man was hyperventilating. Oran reached over to strap the mask back on, but the soldier swatted his hand. The soldier rocked back and forth as he heaved, his lungs gasping for clean air that wasn't there any longer. Oran took the opportunity to squeeze into the seat in front of the hyperventilating soldier and pulled the mask over his mouth. He breathed in the fresh oxygen and immediately felt better.

The scared man stood up "We're going to die!"

"Sit down!" the steward squawked from somewhere in the front. He was losing his cool, too. How he saw the soldier in the aisle, Oran didn't know.

"Sit yo ass down now!" another soldier commanded.

Panic hears nothing. "I've got to get out of here." Desperate, he reached upward and unclipped his storage bin. The plane banked, spilling the storage bin's contents everywhere. This included Oran's coup lance.

The scared man puzzled over the coup lance, then reached for it. Oran grabbed the lance first. When the other soldier tried to grab it back, Oran punched him in the jaw, knocking him back. The man watched Oran for a moment, dazed. He laid down back against the seat, his breathing deeper, yet quieter.

A loud groaning from the airplane told Oran that the wings were preparing to land. His body sensed the descent ending and the plane leveling off to land. He would be glad to be on the ground.

As the plane continued its landing, the steward yelled, "Prepare for emergency landing! When this plane stops, exit the doors and emergency doors. Leave in an orderly fashion, but when you're on the ground, run for the terminal. There are barricades there. The soldiers there will evacuate you."

"Oh my God! Look over there!" one of the soldiers shouted from farther up the aisle.

"What could make this worse?" another soldier grumbled, but Oran suspected he knew. He leaned over and looked out the far window. Beams of sunlight penetrated the cloud cover. Between the beams, a monster walked. The soldiers onboard gasped.

Wendigos. Wendys or Wendy, they were called by the soldiers who fought them. A lifetime ago, monsters like the Wendys began appearing all over the globe. They emerged from the mountains, from bogs, and sometimes even the oceans. They were tall, powerful, and immune to all modern weapons. That didn't stop armies the world over from fighting back. But how do you win a war against something that wants to eat you? Evil, sentient, and ravenous, there was no bartering with them and no stopping them. Countries dissolved. Governments collapsed. Humans scurried away like rats hiding underground in basements or subway tunnels, or they fled to the plains where the Wendys never went.

This Wendy stood seventy feet tall, easily the biggest thing at the airport. It even dwarfed the airplane tower. The creature was powerfully built, with giant claws and hooves. Blood and gore dripped from its skull mouth. Velvet hung from its antlers like thick blobs of mucus. The wendigo backhanded the soldiers defending the airport. Eight went flying across the runway where they had staged their operation. The others kept firing on the wendigo, which had little effect on the monster. The bullets glanced off its exposed rib bones.

The wendigo ran at the landing plane, roaring its unholy anger. Oran didn't know that the plane would make it to the ground. All it would take was a little push to send them spiraling to their deaths.

"We're not going to make it," one soldier said, while another cursed.

Rather than respond, Oran tightened his grip on his lance. If they could land, he could change everything. He prayed to the sun for his safe return. "Natosi, watch over me. I will do everything I can to get to my beloved Jodi and Daniel. I swear I will return to them, just get my boots on the ground."

At that moment, it seemed to Oran that the wendigo saw him, looked him in the eye, and hated him. The monster pushed harder and closed the distance in half the time. As the ground came up to meet the plane, the wendigo reached with its outspread fingers for the Bombardier. Its fingers barely touched the plane's wing, but that was enough. The plane's back end swung wide. The first wheel touched the ground, then the other one slammed into the tarmac. A giant rush of wind and sound of rubber against asphalt erupted around them. The soldiers screamed, but their screams were drowned out by the giant cacophony. The plane spun one way, then the other as it careened recklessly off and then back onto the runway, crossing back into the grass.

The plane shook violently, and then the back began to rise. The plane was slowing down, but it was flipping. One wing went up, and the other crumpled into the ground, gouging a scar in the earth. All soldiers not buckled into their seat belts smashed into the overhead storage bins. At the last second, gravity won, and the plane slammed into the ground, snapping the landing gear's struts.

The plane shuddered to a sudden stop. Oran was on the ground. He had a gash in his cheek from hitting the storage bin, but he was finally safely on the ground. He ripped off his oxygen mask. While the other soldiers burst out of the exits, smoke billowing out of the cabin, Oran checked on the soldier who'd panicked. He was face down in a different row. The plane had tossed the soldier like a ragdoll. Oran felt guilty for his part in the man's story. He flipped the soldier over. Blood drained freely from his nose, so Oran guessed it was broken from where he hit the storage bin. His cheek was smashed, too. It was nothing the medical team couldn't fix with metal and pins, if the man was alive.

Oran placed his hand close over the man's nose and felt air. The man was breathing, so Oran flung him over his shoulder and carried him off the plane. He yelled at two soldiers from the airport who'd come over to help.

"This man is injured," Oran said.

As the two soldiers got under each armpit, Oran began to cough. The soldiers carried the panicked soldier away. Oran went back into the fuselage and helped more soldiers out. None of them were injured, but they were all coughing like Oran. Oran hadn't realized how much his lungs were beginning to burn from the cabin smoke.

Most of the soldiers who were out of the plane were fleeing for the terminals, where a barricade of spikes defended the airport terminals. An Abrams tank was charging across the runway at them. *No, not at us*, Oran realized. Behind the plane, the wendigo was running toward the airport. Its footfalls shook the ground as it ran.

Oran's eyebrows tightened in frustration as he watched the tank go charging into battle. Wendy rarely lost a fight in the open battlefield.

Charging head-on was suicide. The soldiers inside the tank were either new, or incapable of learning.

The Abrams tank's treads churned the soft ground as it jumped into the grass, then came to a sudden stop on the other side of the plane. The wendigo kept coming. The tank fired its cannon, throwing up dirt and debris all around it. The round knocked the wendigo to the ground, but did almost no damage. The wendigo got right back on its feet, then rammed the tank from its side. The Abrams tank may have weighed sixty tons, but this was an old wendigo. It got low on the tank and lifted. The tank jerked up sixty degrees in the air. The wendigo snorted, then heaved upward, flipping the massive tank on its back.

Oran grimaced. There was a better way. He ran to the front of the Bombardier. He crept along the fuselage, keeping close to the ground. The wendigo had a hard time catching small movements.

Oran listened to the weight of the wendigo's hooves thumping on the far side of the plane, where he'd been only moments ago. The steps were slower and more deliberate. The creature was searching for survivors. Their hunger was never over.

A great searing, groaning sound told him that the wendigo was pulling apart the fuselage. He hopped onto the plane's wing, then steadied himself. The plane angled to the sky, then dipped back down. Some poor soldier screamed.

Using the rising smoke to hide himself, Oran pulled his bandana back over his mouth and nose, then crawled on top of the plane. Through the smoke, he witnessed the wendigo's feast. It held a man in full winter camo in both hands, then ripped him apart. The wendigo held the soldier's open torso to its mouth and sucked the man's insides out, then began to lick the blood out of the man's rib cage.

Oran scowled. On the front, he'd seen this scenario played out again and again, with the wendigos almost always triumphing. He hoped that in leaving the front he'd leave this kind of insane image behind him. *No more*, he thought. *Not here*. Oran ran along the fuselage and leaped at the hunched over wendigo, yelling "Ki-yi!" Oran flung his lance.

The feathered lance plunged through the monster's exposed rib cage and into its heart. The creature bellowed. The sound was something like a cross between a dying elk and a screaming vampire. The monster heaved, puking out the soldier's insides that it had been so enthusiastically enjoying, and then it slumped dead into the fallen plane.

# CHAPTER TWO

Oran reached between the wendigo's ribs and pulled out his lance. Blood splashed on the ground. Oran cleaned off the lance with a cloth he kept explicitly for cleaning it. He said a prayer of thanks to the four winds and the Sun, then he took his bag from inside the plane and tied his parfleche to the back of his belt.

Stepping outside, the airport's defenders had rushed out to meet him.

The man who greeted him was a shirtless white man. His skin was as dark and leathery as jerky. Giant melanoma scars and burns punctuated his body. He had a captain's tattoo inked on his right pec.

"I'm Captain Barrett Matthews," the man said. He had a firm, yet soft voice. "I'm sure glad you came here." The men shook hands.

"Who are you?" Barrett asked.

To answer, Oran pulled a paper out of his parfleche and handed it to the captain. Barrett read it while a small group gathered around Oran, admiring the great warrior who'd brought down the giant wendigo. Many of the men and women shook Oran's hand and thanked him. Oran nodded his appreciation. They were an ugly lot, soldiers of metal and machine. They may not have been to the front, but they'd seen their share of calamity.

"I'm going home," Oran said to Barrett.

"You're Oran Old Chief," Barrett said, trying to hide the awe in his voice. He saluted Oran, and the other soldiers followed their captain. "I've heard of you."

"I can assure you, the stories are exaggerated."

A man next to Oran clapped him on the shoulder with his metal hand and pointed to the dead wendigo. "I can assure you, they aren't."

"Stand down, Riddarck," the captain said angrily. "You don't have the rank to even breathe this man's air. Do you understand? This soldier is going home."

"No disrespect, captain, but you've got to be joking," Riddarck said. "Did you see what he just did? He's a wendigo slayer." To Oran, he said, "Come on, man. We're desperate here. We could really use you."

Oran said, "I'm sorry, but I cannot. I am needed at home."

Before Riddarck could prod him more, the captain interrupted him. "This man has earned his rest." Barrett handed Oran his papers. "Come talk to me in my quarters."

While some had pulled on their hoods and gone on to rescue the tank operators, the rest returned to the barracks set up under the airport's terminal. Oran followed Barrett to his personal quarters up in the airport's offices.

The captain offered him a chair and a cup of coffee, both of which he accepted. Barrett winced as he walked to the coffee pot.

"I can do that. Why don't you sit down?"

"Okay." The captain leaned back into his chair and groaned.

"How are you doing, Captain?"

The captain did not respond. He fidgeted in his chair till he found the right spot, then he drank from the cup that Oran had given him. The moisture strengthened the captain's voice.

Barrett said, "I wanted to say what an honor it is to meet you. That paper says you are Oran Old Chief. And by the way you handled that Wendy, I'd wager you're the same man from the Battle of Mt. Tecumseh. I don't have much to offer, but what I can is yours, name it."

"All I want is to return home."

"I've heard stories of how bad it is up north. But you'll find since you left, it isn't exactly rosy down here either. All throughout the northwest we're dealing with starvation, disease, and of course wendigos and wildfires. It's like the Earth is trying to swallow us. And if that isn't bad enough, we're losing doctors and technicians. Every day we lose skills that I fear we'll never get back. It's like the new dark ages out there."

Oran sipped his coffee.

Barrett said, "That paper says you're out in Browning. That's the other side of the Rockies. I can't fly you out today. Pilots are rare. That's one of those precious skills we're losing. Soon the only creatures in the sky will be the birds and the wraiths. The flights we do have are usually going to Alberta. But if you can wait, I might be able to get you another flight in the next week or two."

"With all respect, I'd rather get going. I know the mountains well, and I've waited long enough." He put his coffee down.

"Hold on. Before you go, I have to make sure you know what you're getting into." He pointed to an old Montana map on the wall behind him. "You've got a couple hundred miles of mountain ranges that the military considers wendigo territory. There are rumors of even worse monsters living in there, and then there's the wildfires. Nobody goes in there deliberately. I can arrange a convoy that will go around the mountains. It'll take longer, but it'll be much safer."

"I'm South Piegan Blackfeet, Captain. My people were created in those mountains, and before the wendigo and the white man, it was where we hunted and lodged. I will not go around them."

The captain breathed a sigh of exasperation. "I understand. I don't want to be the reason you kill yourself."

"You won't be." After a brief pause, Oran asked, "How long do you have, if I can ask?"

"We're at war against the most invulnerable power the world has ever encountered. I don't have time to worry about dying."

"You are at war against the sun."

Barrett held out his burned arms. "I stopped wearing a shirt 'cause I stopped caring. I told the doctors to stop treating me. They've talked about sending me home, but I don't want to die there. I want to die in battle, serving humanity. I think I've earned that end as much as you've earned yours."

They shook, and the captain led him out of his office and back into the main terminal and the barracks. Far to the west, the wildfires reached up to the setting sun, and the sun shrieked back at them his war cry.

In the garage, Captain Barrett pointed to his vehicles. They were mostly fortified pickups and Jeeps covered in concrete blocks, metal spikes, and water jugs.

"Take your pick," the captain said. "But if I was you, I'd take the Chevy. She has good tires, strong horsepower, four wheel drive, and shouldn't break down on you between here and Browning. I can't say the same for the rest of my so-called armored division."

Oran chose the Silverado. The captain ordered food and water for Oran, but only if it had been thoroughly checked for radiation poisoning.

While the water was being triple-checked, six soldiers approached the captain and Oran.

Captain Barrett raised his eyebrow at their appearance. The team was suited for action. They saluted the captain, and he saluted back. "Recon Team?" Captain Barrett said. "This is a surprise."

A man with three metal fingers stepped forward. He wore a beat up cowboy hat as part of his uniform.

"We'd like to escort Oran to his home, Captain."

"But you have duties here."

"With all due respect, Recon Team hasn't been used once to any advantage over the past six weeks. Our advantage is on the front."

"This is an act of pure honor and nobility?" Barrett asked. "Or do you have family back east?"

The leader of Recon Team motioned to his team. "Yes, sir, we do. And some of us haven't heard from them in a while. But we're only doing this to help the Devil of Tecumseh. He is a legend, and it'd be an honor to escort him home."

"That sounded positively genteel. Did you rehearse that, Teller?"

To Oran, Teller said, "Family is the most important thing in a soldier's life. Your work family and your family at home. It's more important than any training or ammunition, and we'd like to honor that importance in your service."

"You definitely rehearsed that," Barrett said, catching Teller's eye.

"No disrespect, Captain Barrett, but this ain't the twentieth century. War is different. Military is different. We've loved working under your command and will gladly return here after delivering this hero to his home."

"You won't go anywhere unless I say so, Sergeant." Barrett said flatly. He waited until he had all their attention, then surveyed the seven members of Recon Team, careful to look them each in the eye. "You all feel the same way? That this is some call to arms?" The rag-tag warriors of Recon Team nodded their heads in support. Captain Barrett thought about their request for a moment.

"I'm low on resources, firepower, and even moreso, skilled soldiers. I cannot just let any unit go on walkabout whenever they decide they're bored. But, there have been more incursions from Wendy out of the Rocky Mountains to the east, and you are my recon team. You are to recon wendigo country and report back to me once you have delivered this man to Browning."

The soldiers breathed a sigh of relief. They began climbing into two sedans with concrete buffs over the windshields. Captain Barrett stopped Teller on his way to the Chevy. "But you get back here, Teller. We can't win this thing without bodies in boots, you understand?"

"Yes, sir."

As the geared-up cars started their engines and drove slowly out from under the airport terminal, the captain waved. Oran hoped the man would be able to die in battle like the captain wanted, and he hoped that the battle would come soon because there was no way that man outlived Oran's journey to Browning.

# CHAPTER THREE

Oran led them out, but they didn't get far. Wendigos appeared with nightfall, so Recon Team made camp outside of Spokane and waited for the dawn to drive into the Rockies.

"Driving during the day means driving while radiation's high," Teller said. He handed Oran a small black bottle and said, "We need to make sure we're taking iodine to keep us safe."

At the campfire while everyone was eating MREs, Teller said, "I'd like to introduce you to your escorts. As you know, my name's Teller. I'm up from Texas, *if'n y'all* didn't guess already." He made sure to lay the drawl on thick.

"This metal head is Troy." Long cords of metal fanned out from the back of Troy's head like steel tentacles. "He's our communications expert. Those attachments help him collect noise from all over."

"Pikani?" Oran asked.

"Masikota Cheyenne," Troy said. "Troy Hopkins." They shook hands.

"Welcome," Oran said.

"Dog soldier?" Troy asked. He raised his wrist to show the white and black bands tattooed on his arm.

"Crazy Dog," Oran said. "I fought with dog soldiers at Mt. Tecumseh. George St. Cloud and Billy Mendez."

Troy laughed. "I remember George! Best point guard under five feet five I ever met. I lost fifty bucks on a bet to him. How is he?"

"Keeping people like me poor with that trick shot of his. It is good to have you ,Troy."

Standing behind Troy was a tall, broad-shouldered man who'd clearly suffered a horrible injury. His right leg was completely replaced with metal, and the right side of his face was horribly scarred. The man's face was disfigured, like his left eye was sliding away from his face. Oran did his best not to stare at the man's injuries. Unfortunately, war had given him lots of practice.

Troy introduced him. "This is my man, Iain Phelps. He was born in Scotland, but came here to fight the Wendys after the Fall of Edinburgh. We joined together in Basic and we've been tied at the hip ever since."

"Everybody calls me Molotov," the big man said with a hefty laugh. He had a blustery Scottish accent from the Highlands. Smirking, he purred, "You ken prob'ly guess why."

Oran grinned. He'd get along with this man just fine.

13

"A sick twist of fate makes me really fockin' good with chemicals," Molotov said. He patted the implement connected to his backpack. "I'm a flamethrower kind of guy."

"I'm glad to have you with us. Thank you."

After shaking hands with Molotov, Teller took him to the other side of the campfire. There were two people there. One wore a helmet that covered his entire head. Another had spinal implants.

Teller said, "The guy in the helmet insists on being called 'Nobody.'"

"The helmet protects my noggin from the sun's rays," Nobody explained. He was dressed all in black.

"The bald woman with all the spikes is Ghost. She's the ultimate in recon technology. The whole team is built around her. You'll never hear her coming."

"I'll make sure we know where the monsters are," Ghost said. Ghost also had metal in her face and eye and nose implants.

"That last guy is some dude we picked up named Jack. I've thought about calling him Jack Off only 'cause I hate the name Jack so much. What kind of name is Jack when you can be a Ghost, Molotov, Troy, or Nobody?"

"Or Teller," Oran said. "Is that your real name or a call sign, too?"

"I was born Barabas Helmick Teller."

"So Teller it is."

Oran noticed Jack was sitting away from the others eating his eggs. Oran recognized him as the man in the parka from the plane.

"I know this man. He panicked when our plane filled with smoke."

"You know him?" Teller shrugged. "He told us he just wanted to get outta Spokane. Should we be concerned?"

Oran's eyes tightened. He felt a little pain growing in his temple. "No," he said.

"Well, that's us. Recon Team is Troy, me, Molotov, Nobody, and Ghost."

"Specialties?" Oran asked, his mind distracted from the man in the parka. "Besides the flamethrower, which I get. Fire is the one thing besides lances that have an effect on them."

"Our only specialty is kicking wendigo ass," Teller said. Oran scrunched up his face. With less joviality, Teller said, "No specialties here, sir. We're just grunts."

"Kill first and die last. It's a philosophy that has served me well."

"Pardon me, sir, but what's your rank? Are you a colonel, a corporal, how should we address you?"

He hesitated, then said, "Just call me Oran."

"Hoorah," Teller said.

The next morning, they broke camp early and drove north into Idaho. They had a long day ahead of them because driving was slow. Concrete added a ton to each vehicle, and while the vehicles' suspensions had been upgraded, the extra weight slowed them down. On open road, they only cleared a hundred or so miles, stopping frequently to move vehicles off the road and scout ahead. Wendigos preferred night, but they still came out at day sometimes, and it was better to avoid them.

They entered Idaho and drove by Lake Pend Oreille. From the road, Oran watched the Couer d'Alene forest burn. The fires had already swept to the giant lake. The trees on the opposite side of the lake were like black quills jutting from the body of a dead porcupine. He felt sad to see their loss and devastation.

The convoy stopped outside of Sandhill Point while Ghost reconned the small town of retailers and tourists. When she came back, she was distraught.

"There's nothing there but dead bodies. A Wendy came and finished off this town a few months ago, I guess."

Blood-drained bodies of men, women, and children lay thrown along the roads and beaches. Sometimes a head or arm was missing, but mostly the people had been ripped open so the wendigos could suck out their insides. Oran thought of the soldier back at the airport eaten in Spokane.

Some of the buildings were pushed over. Giant, bloody handprints adorned the other buildings. Wendigos liked to slap their bloody hands on the walls of tall buildings and water towers to mark the towns they'd destroyed.

Outside of Sandhill Point they came to their first problem. The long bridge had been damaged. A giant gash bifurcated the bridge, separating Oran and Recon Team from the other side.

Teller said, "Should we go back? There ain't too many roads going through this area. This could add a day or two."

"The wendigos are fond of destroying roads," Oran said. "It's one of their tricks. The less roads, the more traffic on the only open roads, which makes hunting humans much easier. Going south through the Bitterroot Mountains is a trap. No, we must cross here."

"But how?" Nobody asked from inside his black helmet. "That's at least fifteen feet across. There's no way we're getting our cars over that long ass gap."

"Maybe we could get a boat," Molotov suggested.

Troy punched him in the shoulder and held his hands up in a way that asked him if he was born stupid.

"This is a resort town, Molotov," Teller said. At 30, he was the oldest of the men deployed with Oran. "The only boats they have here will sink with one of our cars on it."

"We build a road," Oran said.

He led them back into town, scanning both sides of the road. Before long, Oran found what he was after in a car dealership. It was parked alongside the road.

"An auto transport?" Teller asked, his voice full of suspicion.

"Sure. We take it off the rig. It should be long enough to cross the gap."

"Pure barry," Molotov cursed. "How do we get it across the fockin' bridge?" Molotov asked.

"And after we've got it on the bridge, how do we make sure it doesn't slide the hell off?" Troy asked.

"I've got a couple ideas on that," Oran said. "Get the rig back to the bridge, and I'll find everything else we need." He walked off into town.

An hour later, Oran caught up to them, driving a giant mobile crane down the road. He pulled over next to the soldiers and the rig that they had driven to the gap.

As Oran rolled down the window, Teller said incredulously, "You're a crane operator, too?"

"No, but I figured it out."

"I've heard that about you. You figure shit out."

Oran smiled. He lowered the cable, which Ghost and Molotov tethered to the rig-side of the car transport. Oran slowly maneuvered the transport into place. It fit, angled from the near side because of the wheels.

The team walked the new bridge to test it. When Nobody started jumping up and down, Jack stopped him. "Are you crazy? Don't be a dumbass, man," he said.

A roar from somewhere in the depths of the Sandyhill Point downtown area warned the team it was time to get moving. First, Teller and Ghost crossed. Oran volunteered to be the first to cross, but they wouldn't let him go. "That's the reason we're here, right? To keep you safe?" Teller said.

Oran came second in the Chevy, followed by the last sedan with everybody else. They were glad to be across, too. A giant antlered figure had appeared in the downtown area.

They drove the rest of the afternoon down along state road 200. As they passed the "Welcome to Montana" road sign, Oran felt a little thrill inside. He was back in the same state as his wife and son. He wondered how they were doing back home. Was Jodi still keeping a garden, and was Daniel helping her keep it now? When Oran left for war, Daniel was 8. Now he was 12. How different would he be, and would he accept Oran as his father?

"Two states down, this is it," Troy said in his Midwesterner accent. He was speaking over the CB radios installed in the cars. Troy gave a high-pitched shout of joy that Oran appreciated.

But not long after, Oran's mood soured. The mountains on either side of the road were a patchwork of denuded trees and cinder. Sometimes he saw living deer or elk grazing on the new foliage, but mostly he saw grim death: charred bodies twisted and tortured. Smoke wavered in the breeze, and ash fluttered like butterflies from the underworld. What Oran felt was less sadness and anger and more regret and shame. But it was not a pressing shame. It was a shame that had been around so long he sometimes forgot it was there until moments like this when the mountains forced him to gaze upon their destruction and remind him of how little he had done in his lifetime to protect and save them. For centuries, the Blackfeet had staved off companies and governments that abused the land. The wendigos were a power altogether different. It was the difference between fighting against an army versus an assassin. The wendigo were hard to find except when they wanted to be found, and they attacked quickly and mercilessly, and their war brought down the destruction of the mountains.

The Bitterroot Mountains were bittersweet. The Cabinets on the northeastern side of the road were not much better.

The caravan stopped outside of an RV park surrounded by unburned black spruce and quaking aspen. The fire had stopped about fifty yards ahead of the RV park, leaving the campers completely unscathed. A mile up the road was the bend that would lead them to the Flathead Reservation. Rather than move on, the convoy stopped to rest for the night among the RV campers. They drew wires the way people used to draw straws to determine the order of camper picking. Oran refused first pick and drew second to last. He entered his camper to discover it full of white supremacist and Nazi flags. They made good kindling for the small campfire he built in the camper's kitchen sink.

Ghost opened the door and climbed the steps. She noted the flags being burned, then glanced around the trailer. There were still more flags, and posters of cars and beer models.

"It's a different world now," she said. "My mom used to tell me stories about how society used to be. People weren't treated as equals."

Oran nodded, but kept burning the flags.

"Not that they still are. I'm not blind. My eyes were just replaced."

Oran stirred the ashes. "What happened?"

"I was conducting recon on Sulphur Mountain. My target was an old weather observatory building high up on the mountain. We climbed all day to get to the top, and then used the observatory to watch wendigo routes. We weren't watching the area closest to us, though, and we were ambushed by three Wendys. Of the six of us, only two survived. One was the guy who ran five and a half miles down the trail to get help from our base in Bamf. The other was me. Wendy knocked me off the side of the mountain and forgot about me. My good luck, I guess. Search and rescue ops picked me up ten hours later. Most of my face and my back had been shattered, but you know the Wendigo Forces. They had a fix for that."

"They have a fix for anything except death," Oran said. He smiled while the last of the swastika burned. Ghost walked through his camper.

"I will always be grateful. The metal they put in me reinforced my back. I'm always stiff, but not much can take me down."

"Do the spikes bother you?"

"They used to. It's hard to find boob coverage when you've got spikes coming out of your backbone. The doctors wanted to snap off the spikes once I'd healed, but I told them 'no.' I liked it that way. My eyes, though, they are grade-A military goodness."

"What do you mean?"

"Oh, brother. I can see things most people only wished they could see. Did you know that Wendys show up in the UV spectrum? It's true. I'll never be ambushed by another Wendy as long as I live. And my nose is as good as most dogs. It makes me the perfect scout."

"This fire must smell awful to you. I'm sorry."

"Don't be. I'm leaving. But before I go, I want to warn you, you better sleep on the couch if you know what's best for you. That bed was a very lonely bed."

Oran looked up, but the lithe reconnaissance specialist was already out the door.

"What do you mean, *lonely*?" he shouted. She flashed him a peace sign as she walked back to her camper.

Oran had a pretty good idea what she meant. After he burned the flags and the sage, when he went to sleep, he took her advice and slept on the couch.

A pounding fist on his door woke him in the early hours after midnight. Oran grabbed his lance and went outside where the other seven were converging. Cold had settled into the mountains as it always did. Oran guessed it was in the mid 40s outside.

"What's going on?" Oran asked.

Troy said he didn't know. "It was Nobody's watch. Teller's been going around waking everyone. Maybe ask him."

Just as he said that, Teller motioned for everyone to circle around him. He pushed back his cowboy hat and briefed the team, "Nobody was on watch. When he discovered movement, he got Ghost, and she confirmed it: Wendys are nearby."

Oran thought of the woman's UV sight. He was glad she was with them.

"There's about ten of those sons of bitches, and they're attacking the town down the road. We're going to go around the town, try to cross using some dirt roads. We'll get out of here safely."

"What about the town?" Troy asked. "Are there people there?"

"I don't think so," Ghost said. "I might have seen somebody in a window, but at this distance, I can't be certain."

"I think we should check it out," Troy said. "Just to be sure."

"Are you crazy?" Jack said. "Teller said ten Wendys. Remember what happened at the airport? That was one."

"Maybe, but I bet they're smaller and younger, too," Troy said. "The young ones hunt in packs, the older ones alone."

Teller said, "Our mission is to recon the mountains and safely return Oran Old Chief to his family. I'm not risking y'all's lives on 'might be.'" To Oran, he said, "You're the ranking officer, what do you think?"

"Well, let's think about this for a moment," Oran said. "If we go around the town, what assurances do we have that the vehicles can survive the dirt roads? The cars are under significant weight as it is."

Teller loaded a map on his laptop. He had to bat the monitor a couple of times to get it to work. According to the map, the roads didn't hold much promise.

"That leaves us with two options," Oran said. "We could stay and wait and hope the wendigos don't come back this way. We could make preparations just in case."

"Or we could maybe save some people by running into town and taking out Wendy," Troy said.

"Even if we did do what you're saying, Troy, how do we stop ten Wendys?" Jack asked. "I don't suppose you brought seven more of those magic lances with you, Oran?"

Oran said, "First, it is sacred, not magical. And second, we do not need seven lances. We do not need one."

"You're saying you know of a way to kill those shit-bones without using a spear or lance?" Nobody interjected. "We already know that their skin and bones are stronger than Kevlar. They repel bullets."

"But they still burn," Oran said. He looked over at Molotov. As he did, everybody else in Recon Team looked, too.

Molotov grinned. "Never tired and full of fire, boss. Just show me the way."

Twenty minutes later, the group was maneuvering quietly through the underbrush and circling the town.

"You sure it wouldn't be better to go directly into town?" Troy asked. "This doesn't feel very heroic."

Oran said, "I've seen many good heroes killed that way. It's better to think and devise a plan of attack that keeps the enemy away from you. Avoid what is strong, and strike what is weak."

"Sun Tzu, Art of War," Teller said. Oran nodded.

Ghost led them to a wendigo that was farther away from the others.

Oran studied the wendigo. Like the elk fought in Spokane, the bull bison stood on two legs that ended in giant hooves the size of chairs. He couldn't be more than a year old because he was twenty feet tall and mostly skin and hide. His bones were not showing yet. His eyes burned blue and cold in the night sky.

"It is not enough to light him on fire," Oran said. "If we do that, he will charge us, and we don't want a flaming wendigo coming at us. We must strike him where it counts. Their internal organs are very sensitive."

The soldier named Nobody took the end of a rope and walked ten feet away. Troy held the other end of it.

To Troy, Oran said, "Remember, they are very strong. This only works if you are quick and take him by surprise."

Troy and Nobody quietly moved tree by tree until they were behind the wendigo. The monster was holding a woman upside down. He enjoyed biting off little pieces of her while she screamed and struggled.

Nobody and Troy ran at the wendigo, flipping the rope high. The rope caught the monster around his thick bison neck, and they kept running, making the wendigo fall on the ground. As it fell, Molotov ran and shoved his flamethrower down its flesh-filled mouth. "Burn in hell," Molotov said as he ignited the flamethrower. Flames flared out of the creature's mouth and nostrils.

Nobody went to check on the woman, but her skin had already turned white from blood loss.

"That's one down. Only nine more," Oran said.

They worked throughout the night, waiting for a wendigo to be alone, then pulling it down for the kill and taking them out of the town so that they would not be seen. One wendigo they pulled down from opposite sides of the street while it was tearing up a small house and gobbling the children inside.

The wendigo bellowed angrily at the soldiers.

"Quickly! Hide!" Oran instructed the team once Molotov had blasted the wendigo with fire. "The rest will be coming for us."

The last four wendigos came barreling around the corner. One of them still had an intestine dribbling from his mouth. The monsters gawked at their fallen wendigo comrade and roared.

"Go!" the largest bison yelled. "Find them! Gut them!"

The bison-headed wendigos began a Sherman's March To The Sea through the streets. They used their large bodies to throw around cars, crash through the abandoned store fronts, and generally level the town. While the Wendys obliterated the town, Oran circled around the buildings to flank them. He climbed a ladder up the back side of the closest building, the town's bank. He raced low along the rooftop. Seeing the fat hump of a bison-headed wendigo below him, he ran at the ledge. This was the biggest of the wendigos they were fighting. Oran estimated the monster was maybe 25 feet tall. He leapt off the roof and came down upon the wendigo from behind. His lance ripped into the wendigo's back. He drove it down, digging at the wendigo.

The monster roared and arched his back, but this only gave Oran a better purchase on the wendigo's back.

The bison reached behind him for Oran, but the Piegan warrior jumped off at the last second and fell down onto the ground. He rolled out of the way as the bison stomped his enormous hoof, trying to squash him.

From behind a dumpster, Nobody and Teller shot the bison. Its face lit up with gunfire.

"Target the belly, and you might pierce it," Oran shouted. This was the general tactic of every military defense. While bullets and explosives could not kill, they could frustrate and slow down the wendigo until it decided to leave the area. Sometimes, with enough force, a bullet might pierce the belly (if the wendigo had not gone all to bones). Piercing the belly, though rare, was painful enough for the wendigo that the monster would flee. Apparently gut shots are painful even in the world of the undead.

Oran didn't have time to fight back against the largest bison. Another was coming at him. He ran at it, then slid down and slipped underneath him. He stabbed his lance into the awful beast's heart as it reached low for him. He was so close to the beast, he could smell dead people on the wendigo's breath. Wendigos had an unmistakable smell, like an open grave. The bison-headed wendigo collapsed as its insides spilled out, and Oran had to leap out of the way to not be crushed under the great creature's weight.

Another bison's hide was on fire where Molotov had lit him up. The awful stench of burned hair joined the smell of dead people.

The soldiers fired their weapons, most of them AR-15s, at the wendigo. The head wendigo, wounded, yelled to the others, "Run! We will come back for them later."

As the wendigos retreated into the cinder trees, Oran's group cheered.

"Holy shit," Jack said. "I've never seen Wendys run so fast!"

Teller stood, stunned. "We've never taken out Wendy before. Not Recon Team. That was amazing."

"I can't wait to tell my family about this," Troy said. "They'll be telling this story for a long time."

"We should celebrate," Ghost said. "Maybe this town still has some alcohol left in it."

Unfortunately, the convenience store with alcohol was one of the stores that had been destroyed by the rampaging wendigos. There was little chance of anything surviving that attack. Ghost and Nobody wanted to try anyway. They stepped over the broken glass and pushed aside the busted door. They came out a minute later with five warm beers.

"Okay, at least one of these goes to Oran," Ghost said. "For orchestrating Recon Team's first official wendigo kill."

"No, thank you," Oran said. "Besides, we should be leaving. Those wendigos will not stay gone for long."

"We've got bigger problems," Teller said. He pointed back into town.

People emerged from out of the buildings. They pushed through broken windows and out from behind piles of bricks. Except for three elderlies, they were all children, twenty in all. Seeing the kids and fearing how they might react to their appearance, Ghost, Troy, and Molotov moved behind Teller, Jack, and Oran.

A man with ragged whiskers and an old Gus-style cowboy hat approached the soldiers. "Thank you," he said. "We've been trapped here for days."

"You live here with these children?" Teller asked. While he did, Oran pulled an old granola bar from his pocket and broke it into pieces, then handed the pieces to the kids nearest him. The children ate the granola greedily. Oran put his hand on the dirty face of a little girl. Her cheeks were sharp, the skin pulled tight over the bone. Her eyes were craters.

"These children are starving," Oran said.

The old man said, "We fled Sandyhill Point after a couple of tree-high wendigos invaded. It took us weeks to get this far. We've been living off the land ever since. We thought when we got here it would be our salvation, but then a wendigo came through and carried off most of the adults. We've been picked at for the past few months. Starvation and monsters have dropped us from sixty to twenty. Please help us. It's been months since we left Sandyhill Point. Surely the wendigos have left there. We can get these kids back to their families."

Teller's face darkened. "I'm sorry, sir."

Before he could say more, Oran tapped Teller on the shoulder and nodded to the children.

The old man understood. He started to tear up, but steadied himself. He wiped the tears and sniffed. "Guess I always hoped."

"Can we go home now?" one of the kids asked.

"Not yet," the old man's wife said. "We need more time."

"They could go with you," the third person said to Oran. By the similar shape of her face and body, Oran guessed she was sister to the wife.

"We are going east. You cannot come with us," Teller said.

"East has to be better than here," the old woman said.

"East is very dangerous," Oran said. "It is too treacherous for children."

"Then what should we do?" the old man asked. "We have no food and very little water, and the wendigos are always sneaking around."

"Go south to Missoula. That is your best chance," Oran said. Out of the corner of his eye, Ghost and Troy flinched. They all knew that going south was dangerous, too. But where wasn't dangerous?

"We can't make Missoula without help," the old man said. "There is no way to go that far through these mountains without an escort. Please, look around! These are children we're talking about."

Oran's heart ached, as did his escorts'. He could see in their eyes that they wanted to say yes to the old man, but they wouldn't say no to Oran. They had sworn to get him home, and they would, but they would do it with a heavy heart if they couldn't figure out a way to help the children.

"Give me time to think about this," Oran said.

"Yes, sir, but don't take too long. Like you said, those wendigos won't be gone forever."

After giving away most of the food they had on them, the soldiers went back to the convenience store. They stood around waiting while Oran thought about it.

"We trust you, sir," Teller said. "Whatever you decide, we're behind you."

"We don't have the resources to support those kids," Oran said to the rest of the soldiers when he told them he was ready to talk to them. "To take them anywhere is risking all their lives. They aren't soldiers, and we aren't babysitters. Taking them with us would be jeopardizing us."

Oran studied his seven escorts. In their forlorn faces, he recognized his own fractured convictions. They remained silent until finally Troy said in his Midwestern lilt, "I know this is a hard decision for you, Oran Old Chief. You're weighing the lives of people you don't know. This makes you a good leader of soldiers. But I think you've been away at war for too long cause there is something you're not seeing that I think would make the decision much easier for you. I could be wrong about what I'm about to say, but I don't think I am. The Cheyenne and the Pikani are alike in this regard. There is a truth about us, and that is that there are no orphans among the Cheyenne. We are all the Like-Minded People, and we take care of our own."

"I think that's what I've been waiting for," Oran said. "Yes, thank you." To the others, Oran said, "We need to make preparations for these children if we are to take them to Browning, too."

Oran told the old man that they would return later that day to pick up the children. Troy happily accepted the job of staying with the children and guarding them should the wendigos return before Recon Team. Troy could communicate to the team, and they would race back.

To the old man, Ghost added, "While we're gone, I need you to do something. As much as possible, remove all reflective clothing and anything white. These kids light up like Christmas trees in the UV spectrum. I think that's how the Wendys found you so easily."

At the RV campground, the soldiers scrounged for any working vehicle. They found an RV that, when Nobody turned it on, blew out a cloud of smoke and then chugged for a minute before roaring to life.

"It has no extra radiation protection," Teller said, "And half its circuits are fried."

"The wheels roll and the pistons fire," Oran said. "It's all we need."

Back with the children, Ghost was happy to see that the children had changed clothes. She smiled the best that her metal face would allow her. Her face looked petrifying when she smiled. The muscles didn't move correctly around her upper lip. Her grin was a skeleton smile on Halloween. One of the youngest children began to cry and had to be consoled.

"We have room for more," Oran said to the old man, his wife, and his sister-in-law.

"You've done enough by taking these children, and we'd only be more mouths to feed and more people to take care of."

"But we are a military unit," Oran conjectured. "These soldiers know nothing about taking care of children."

"That so? Your second in command seems to be fine with the kids." The old man pointed to Teller, who was twirling his cowboy hat in his metal fingers over a five year old's face while the child happily jumped up and down to grab it.

"And a man your age doesn't have kids, or at least nieces and nephews?"

"I have a son. His name is Daniel."

"That makes two of you, and that's almost as many as us, and you're young and have more energy. No, I think we'll stay here and make the best of what we can. There's nothing left for us in Sandyhill Point, so there's nothing left for us out there. I've got a rifle and a box of bullets. If wendigos come back, we'll show them what Montanans are made of. I'll fire a shot to let you know they're on the way. No, I think I'd rather leave this confident that you will deliver these children to a better place than we ever could."

Oran shook hands with the old man. Their handshake conveyed much more than either man could say in words, the transfer of the contract each had accepted to ensure the survival of the children.

"I never caught your name," Oran said.

"It's not important."

"The children will want to remember who took care of them before us."

The old man looked at his wife and her sister and said, "Our family name is Duncan."

Cramming seventeen kids into an RV was not an ideal situation, but if military training had taught Oran anything, it was how to stuff essentials into an impossibly small place. The children were all between the ages of five and twelve except for a few sixteen and seventeen year olds.

"Two Flathead twins, a Cheyenne girl, and seventeen white children," Oran said, "being driven in a dead man's RV across northern Montana while surrounded by wendigos and forest fires. If my grandfather was alive, he wouldn't believe it."

# CHAPTER FOUR

Recon Team decided to drive at night when the radiation levels remained low. During the day, they slept inside deserted buildings. Concrete buildings were best because they shielded everyone against solar radiation. Recon Team slept in shifts so that somebody was always on guard.

The cars switched around. Ghost found a dirt bike, which she appropriated for scouting ahead. Molotov and Nobody took the first car, then came Oran in the Chevy Silverado. Teller followed in the RV, and Troy and Jack anchored the convoy. Driving with the lights off was Recon Team policy. This way, they didn't attract any creatures, and it had the added benefit that Ghost saw better without the halogen glare from the headlights. Duct tape covered the tail lights.

Twenty children was way over the illegal limit for the number of people in the RV. Good thing there was no highway patrol in wendigo country. Kids sat on the queen-sized bed in the back or on the long couch behind the driver's seat. They crammed into the table seats, and anyone who couldn't find a proper seat had to sit on the floor, wherever they could find a spot. The kids on the floor got antsy quickly, and their backs would get tired and they would want to stand up and walk around. Between the children's need to go to the bathroom and move around, very little progress was made. This troubled Oran, who knew the wendigos they fought earlier in the abandoned town would be coming for them and would catch them quickly if they didn't make better progress.

"There is another complication," Ghost said when they stopped after their first night of driving. The children were finishing their Meals Ready to Eat. The soldiers had shared two MREs between the entire team and were now setting up camp. Ghost continued. "Children pee and poop and pick their noses, and all that shows in the UV spectrum."

Jack grumbled, "So we're practically leaving a runway strip at night pointing the Wendys where to go."

"Sounds like someone needs to go on latrine duty," Oran said. He leaned against a concrete column. Molotov lifted a crate on top of a stack of crates positioned against the windows to reduce the amount of sunlight that infiltrated their hideout. Oran disliked hiding from the sun, but he didn't see another option.

"Mother fucker!" Troy yelled.

He was working with some radio equipment they'd found in the building. He hoped to use the equipment to magnify his capabilities.

26

Getting a signal in the mountains was always difficult in the best of cases. Troy twisted another dial, then another. He wore a microphone headset. "Come on, work, you old piece of shit," Troy said.

Oran ran over to Troy, who had his back to the room. Troy began another torrent of profanity. "If I have to rewire this God-da..." he started to say when Oran popped his headphones off.

"Hey! Those are mine, assho..." and as Troy turned to Oran, he noticed the crowd of children all standing around, staring at him in shock. Some had covered their mouths as if to say "Oh, look what he said. I'm going to tell!" The youngest ones appeared genuinely curious as to what these new words meant.

"Ho, I'm glad to see you, Oran!" Troy said. Oran scowled. "I'm sorry." Troy lowered his head. Oran continued to scowl. He crossed his arms over his chest. Troy said, "Why don't I take this outside?"

"Good idea."

Teller and Ghost ushered the group of excited children to the far side of the room. They were practically giddy with excitement over the coarse language they'd just heard. A little boy wanted to know what "piece of shit" was and if he could play with it, too.

"What's the problem anyway?" Molotov asked Troy before he could escape outside.

Troy exhaled his frustration. "I don't know. I was trying to call in to Spokane to let them know how we're progressing, but the radio is working worse than a...broken radio," Troy said, eyeing the children and correcting his language.

"In the mountains, radios go down all the time," Oran said. "You cannot trust radio equipment up here. Keep at it, though."

Molotov said, "I ken help."

The same young 5-year old boy who wanted to know what a "piece of shit" was walked up behind Molotov and joyously announced, "I can help, too. I'm a mother fucker!" He smiled fiendishly as his voice crackled with his new favorite word. Oran shook his head and walked away. Molotov glowered, then immediately regretted it as the boy began to cry.

"No, wait," Molotov said, but the little boy ran off to Teller, bawling.

"I'm so, so bad at this," Molotov said, grimacing.

"What's wrong?" Teller asked the little boy who ran up to him, arms out wide to be lifted.

"He's...SCARY!" the kid sobbed.

As Molotov watched this, his heart sank. He felt badly about the effect of his face on the child. Surrounded by soldiers, he could always find a way to joke about it. His teammates would laugh, and then somebody else would tell another joke, and he wouldn't feel like such a monster. But there was no stopping the blunt-edged truth from a young child.

"From out of the mouths of babes," Molotov said.

"Don't let it bother you," Troy said. "He's just a kid. Why don't you walk outside with me? I can cuss your ear off, and you tell me about how much better life is in Scotland."

"Because it is!" Molotov roared and clapped Troy on the back. But as they walked out, he glanced back at the crying child. He wanted to approach the child, but he didn't want to scare him further.

After the children were put to sleep, Oran pulled out his lance and inspected it. He went over the feathers, the buck skin, and the smooth carbon rod. He said prayers to Natosi while he cleaned the lance with his cloth.

While he prayed, a little boy tugged on Oran's shirt sleeve. Oran finished his prayer before acknowledging the boy. "Yes, child?" Oran asked.

"I can't sleep," the little boy said, yawning. He rubbed his eye with his little fist.

"Did you try closing your eyes?"

"Uh-huh."

"Did you try taking deep breaths?"

The child took an exaggerated deep breath, then said, "Uh-huh. I can't sleep. I keep trying, but sleep is being mean to me and won't let me sleep."

Oran chuckled. He stood and led the child back to his blanket. Each child had a wool blanket to sleep on and a buffalo hide to sleep under. They also had a little flat pillow. Ghost found the gear in an abandoned souvenir shop.

He lay the boy back down on his wool blanket and pulled the buffalo hide to the child's chin.

"My name is Ben Pederson," the boy said. "What's yours?"

"Oran Old Chief."

"Are you a Native American?"

"I am Pikani."

"What's that?"

"Blackfeet."

Satisfied with that answer, the child pointed at Oran's parfleche. "What's that?"

"That is where I keep my things."

"What's that?" he pointed to Oran's beaded necklace.

"That's a medicine wheel. It is like a spiritual compass."

"And that?" Ben pointed at a small leather bag tucked into his shirt.

"Why don't we talk about something else?" Oran said. "Would you like me to tell you a story?"

"Yes, tell us a story," another child said. At least five sets of eyes were watching him from the dark.

"I will tell you a story, but after that, you must go to sleep."

"Okay," the children said.

"This is a story my grandmother used to tell me. It is how the world was created. The world was created by the sun, Natosi. Natosi was the light in the darkness, and in the beginning, everything was dark, and the Earth was covered in water. Natosi sat on his little raft with all the animals of the world."

"You mean his ark," Ben said. "I know this story."

Oran shushed the child. "If I am going to tell the story, you must listen. So Natosi wanted to create land. First, he needed a little mud, so he sent animals out to look for mud. He sent beaver and duck and loon and otter, but they came back empty. Finally, he sent muskrat, and muskrat was gone for a very long time, so long that Natosi feared muskrat was dead. But muskrat finally came back, and there was a little mud on his paws, and Natosi used the mud to make the world. Then he went throughout the world making rivers and trees and roots and cherries and huckleberries. Do you like huckleberries?"

The children nodded. "So do I," Oran said. "After he created all the trees and animals, he decided it felt right to make a woman and a child. He made them out of clay."

"No, Adam was made out of clay," Ben argued through a yawn, then rolled on his side.

"This is not that story," Oran said. Then he heard Ben snoring. He tucked him in.

"Please, don't stop. What happened next?" An eight-year old girl asked.

Oran nodded. "So Natosi created woman and child. He and the woman argued over where the parts should go on a child. The eyes here, the nose there. In most things, Natosi would suggest one thing, and the Old Woman would change it. She got her way. They gave birth to the first Piegans.

"Old Woman was very glad, but she wanted to know if people should die forever or only die for four days. Natosi said, 'Let them die for four days, then come back.' Old Woman disagreed. 'Let them die forever, because that will give them sympathy for each other.'"

"My parents are dead forever, aren't they?"

Oran wanted to tell her no. He wished he could tell her the story was wrong, that Old Man got his way and that people came back after four days. But he knew that was wrong. Life had an end, and sometimes that ending was robbed.

"They live through you and through your memories, and if you tell the stories, they will continue to live."

Bringing up her parents, Oran half-expected the child to cry, but she did not. She watched him, then nodded back. "That's okay. I think they would be happy knowing you were taking care of us."

The child flipped on her side, and Oran stood, a little wiser to the weight of the responsibility he'd accepted.

# CHAPTER FIVE

The next night they traveled no more than ten miles up the road.

"At this pace, we won't make Browning until winter, and by then, we'll all be frozen burritos for the Wendys to warm up whenever they get hungry," Teller said. The Texan was exaggerating, but there was some truth in what he was saying. If they didn't run into any encounters, at 10 miles a day, they were at least a month away from Browning, and they didn't have that kind of food, water, or fuel. The RV was already burning through gasoline at about five miles a gallon.

Nobody said, "What if one car runs ahead and gets help from Browning, and brings back more cars and more people to help us? A single car could travel quickly through the mountains. And because they're so small, they'd probably go unnoticed."

"They'd be easy to kill if a Wendigo detected them," Ghost said. "They see, hear, and smell things we don't."

Oran said, "And then they would have to find us back in the mountains. That's a lot of distance, and I don't plan on sitting around waiting for help that may never come."

Oran made a decision. The team would stay together, but he would make some modifications. First, he changed their driving to include mandatory restroom breaks, and instead of having Ghost recon for a mile before they drove out, they drove while she scouted out the road ahead of them. They drove so slow, and Oran was so suspicious of the Cabinet Mountains around them, that the soldiers took turns walking alongside the convoy. In this way, the team was able to double their mileage.

Still, Oran didn't like the mountains that hung over either side of them. It forced them to keep to the low ground, which made them susceptible to ambush. With Bull Lake still far away and the only town along the route, they slept in the shade of the mountains or down in river gullies. One time, they slept in the hoofprint of a gigantic wendigo. The hoofprint was in the blunt shape of a bison hoof, and it was so big, the entire team and all the children fit inside its indentation.

Nobody slept well in those conditions.

Molotov had found crayons and a stack of printer paper in an old vacated house. The paper and crayons did a lot to relieve the stress of the children. Sitting for hours on end in an old RV led to disruptive kids. The older ones had been assigned babysitting duty, but they were children watching children. They would tell stories until they got tired or bored. The colorful crayons and paper were a break in everybody's favor. The children loved coloring, and they drew all kinds of things.

Some things were images from their past: families and monsters and mountains. Others focused on the trip to Browning: the strange spiked cars, the soldiers looking like superheroes. By the night's end, the inside of the RV was canvassed in the drawings.

The two Flathead twins showed Molotov a picture they drew together of him. In the picture, a large man was smiling from atop a mountain that was maybe one-tenth the size of him. He had fat arms and tiny little legs, one of which was black.

"I dinnae look like that, do I?"

Troy took the sheet out of Molotov's hands and laughed. "Yeah, looks just like you."

"See?" the 9-year olds said. "We wanted to make him just like you, so that's why your face is Atomic Tangerine, and your shirt is Laser Lemon, and your flamethrower is Outer Space."

"Aw, kids. Ye warm my heart," Molotov said. He was happy that the Flatheads were not afraid of his ugly face. He gave them a big hug, one Flathead in the crux of each arm.

The next evening as they made their way down a dark and lonely stretch of mountain road, Ghost drove back to Recon Team. "There's something you all need to see."

Oran left Troy with the children, and the rest walked ahead. A few hundred yards down the road, they came to a bend. As they curved around the road, the wind suddenly picked up. Oran felt a shiver of something unnatural nearby.

Up ahead, in the darkness, the tree branches were knocking against each other. They sounded like bamboo wind chimes.

"I didn't want to talk about this in front of the children," Ghost said. "They go through enough already. I didn't know what to do. We can pass through here, but it doesn't seem right."

On either side of the road, hanging from the trees were hundreds of dead bodies. Some were from lower branches and some were strung up at higher limbs.

Troy covered his mouth. They were all hanged.

"That is unimaginable," Teller said. "What happened to these people that they would do this to themselves?"

"Everybody reacts differently to the end of the world," Jack said.

"But to do this? To give up? Why?"

"You can't conceive of it because it's not in you," Jack said. "I've had some dark nights where those kind of thoughts have entered my head."

"So have I," said Molotov. "Not long after mah surgeries. I saw a gruesome monster every time I looked in the mirror. I didn't know that I could go on like that."

"What do we do?" Troy asked. "Do we turn around? Maybe we go south after all."

"This could be another barricade," Oran said. "Psychological instead of physical."

"Or it could be a warning," Ghost suggested.

Oran watched the bodies swaying in the breeze. Maybe it was a warning.

"I know what we should do," Nobody said. He walked toward the trees. "We need to do the decent thing and bury these bodies."

"I don't think so," Oran said. He couldn't give a reason why they should back away, but in his gut, this felt wrong, and he wasn't a "by the gut" kind of person. He won his battles through reason and logic, and he'd been very successful using those assets. This felt...it was something different.

"We've done the honorable thing and adopted those kids," Nobody said from within his black helmet. "Now we need to do the honorable thing and not let these bodies be disgraced."

He approached the first body, hanging limp and naked above him.

"If they're all dead," Teller said, "then where are the vultures? The crows? There should be scavengers here."

Oran shouted "Wait! Come back, Nobody!" but it was too late by then.

The soldier pulled his knife, a thick and serrated monstrosity made to end people's lives.

Suddenly, the hanging man opened his red and yellow eyes. Nobody didn't have time to react. He stood there transposed, frozen in his tracks. A mouth full of needle-like fangs hissed at him. Leathery wings spread from behind the back of the head. The head flew down at him. He heard Oran shouting behind him, but the words didn't register. A large crunching sound filled his ears. He realized, too late, that sound he heard was the sound of the demon biting through the tendons in his neck.

Nobody screamed, and everybody opened fire. The bullets grazed off the thing that looked like a dead man's head but was now attached to Nobody's torso. He raised his arms and pushed against the head. Its leathery wings beat against his helmet. Pulling the monster away hurt, but it was worse to leave it attached to him, so he pulled the monster away with all his might. He felt his flesh ripping from his neck. The creature smiled hideously, a long trail of bloody sinew string dangling from its mouth.

He screamed again, but this time no sound came out, and his arms started to fall away from him. The world rolled drunkenly. He looked around at the rest of his team. The outlines of their bodies lit up among the staccato flashes of gunfire. Recon Team was falling lower and lower around him. Nobody thought, *This is what death must be like,* for he certainly didn't feel any pain anymore, and his body seemed to be flying away to heaven, which made him happy. But then he learned he was wrong. The rest of his body was firmly fixed on the ground. He realized it was just his head flying away.

"What the hell was that?" Ghost shouted.

Several of the men grimaced as Nobody's body fell from his head, and the demon head flew away with its prize, Nobody's head. Nobody's head, still covered in his black helmet, disappeared into the upper limbs of a tall tree.

A tree that was full of other hanging bodies.

"Kanontsistonties," Oran said, hope sinking as he stared up at the dead bodies. His mouth went dry.

"Kanon-what?" Molotov shouted back.

"Hold your fire!" Oran ordered among the staccato bursts of gunfire. "And step back. Bullets won't hurt these monsters."

As the team slowly took Oran's lead and began to fall back, the trees around them came to life. Bat wings flapped in the night sky.

"Are those things Blackfoot?" Teller asked.

"Black*feet*, and no. I think it is Iroquois or Mohawk. Legend has it that the tribe was being moved off their land. The elders wanted to leave, but the young warriors wanted to stay and fight. To get their way, they young warriors beheaded their tribal elders and buried the decapitated heads. But the heads sprouted wings and began to terrify the people, flying around and carrying off *their* heads."

Heads and skulls flew over the soldiers, laughing and screaming and shouting obscenities in languages they did not know.

"How did they stop them?" Teller asked, ducking as one of the demon heads flew at him.

"A woman scared them away by roasting acorns on an open fire."

"Fire?" Teller looked at Molotov. "Molotov, do your thing."

Molotov lit up the sky. The heads fled, shrieking.

"Careful!" Oran warned Molotov, who was fanning his flamethrower side to side. "This whole place is a tinder box. Forest fires have been started with much less."

"Gotcha, Oran," Molotov said. He raised the flame away from the trees. He kept the stream aimed above them, so if any kanontsistonties flew nearby, he could barbecue them.

The team backed away around the bend. As they did, the kanontsistonties returned to their bodies.

"They didn't luminesce," Ghost said. "I didn't know they were alive."

"We need to burn them to the ground for what they did to Nobody," Teller said.

Molotov agreed, "Let me at 'em, Oran. I'll make sure they pay for what they did to our brother in arms."

"And take half of Montana's forests with you? No, we need another way."

"We will honor him in their deaths," Molotov said.

Oran gathered some pine needles from the ground and let the wind catch them out of his hand. They blew into his chest.

He asked, "And what about the children? How will you honor them when the fire rages out of control and we can't escape?"

"We can go back the way we came."

"There are wendigos hunting us back that way."

"There's no way to know that. Those bison-headed cowards probably ran off to find an easier-to-kill food source."

"I've seen them," Ghost said. "I didn't want to say anything because I didn't want to alarm us. We're all pretty stressed as it is. But a couple days ago in the warehouse, I observed them from the rooftop. They were too far away to catch up to us, and there were more of them."

"How many?" Teller asked.

"I'd say six or eight. Getting numbers was hard. But they've definitely brought more wendigos."

"Hrmm," Oran said in thought.

"All the more reason to blaze through here," Teller said. "To hell with consequences." Molotov nodded.

"I have another way," Oran said. "But you're not going to like it."

Half an hour later, the convoy drove forward into the forest of flying heads. Oran had everybody who wasn't driving or walking outside hide in the cars out of sight. In the RV, all the blinds were shuttered and the curtains pulled. Plastic bags were stuffed and placed on the soldiers' shoulders, and the wool blankets were draped over the plastic bags like capes, with a little slit for the soldiers to see through.

"This better work," Molotov said, "or we're as exposed as a stripper's tits after midnight."

"Hey," Ghost growled.

"I'm just saying," Molotov started to say, but then Teller silenced them. "Be quiet, you two. We're about to enter the trees. I hope you're right, Oran. Molotov may have said it crudely, but I agree with him. There ain't no chance for us to change our tactic if we're wrong."

Oran said, "The kanontsistonties left Nobody's corpse alone. They were only interested in his head, which is consistent with the legends. If they don't see our heads, they will leave us alone. According to legend, the only way to kill kanontsistonties are to shove hot coals down their throat. So unless you have a collection of coals, I think this is our best shot."

The soldiers agreed reluctantly.

Despite Recon Team's protests, Oran demanded that he go first.

"We're here to protect you," Ghost said. "You should be in the pickup."

Oran thought of the soldiers he sent into battle to die, and shook his head. "This is my idea, and if it doesn't work, you can all backtrack. If one of you goes first, and I'm wrong, then I will have to live with that. No. I appreciate what you are doing, but I will be the first to enter the trees."

So he walked out front, his lance in both hands. In the trees ahead, the bodies began to sway from their nooses. His fingers tightened around the lance, and he took a deep breath. He hoped the disguise would work.

The headless body of Nobody lay fallen in the road, a black puddle of blood oozing with the slope of the incline.

As the cars approached the forest, Oran checked one last time to make sure that none of the children were staring through blinds or peeking through curtains. He was relieved to see nothing but covered windows. Teller had handled them well.

Another few steps, and suddenly the air filled with the sounds of flapping wings. Eyes rolled and heads lifted off their sockets to fly in the sky.

He held his hand out to warn the team to stay put, and then he walked into the trees alone. The chittering was like no bird he'd ever heard. He reached Nobody's corpse. It was a stain on the asphalt, but it was also more than that. Because the body lay in the middle of the road, it was a bump that each car would have to drive over. They could not go around it; the road was too narrow. He glanced back at the men, woman, and children in his caravan. They were watching him.

The heads flew at him like a pendulum, buzzing past his disguise, then arching back up into the trees, but they did not attack him. He breathed a sigh of relief. He set his lance on the road, then stooped down like a weight lifter doing squats and lifted Nobody's legs. Oran had to be careful. If he bent over too far, the bags on his shoulders would fall over or the cape would fall off. So he was very slow and deliberate in his actions. With heads screaming and fluttering above him, he dragged Nobody's corpse to the side of the road where it was out of the way. As he moved the body, he couldn't do anything for the blood pouring out of Nobody's neck.

When he finished, he walked back out onto the pavement. One of the heads had landed on his lance. Its teeth made an awful sound as the little monster gnawed on the shaft. Oran ran to it and kicked the head. Suddenly two other flying heads swooped at him. As he ducked out of the way, he fell down on the head.

He landed on his hands as the creature rolled toward him, growling.

The flying head locked eyes with him. It opened its mouth to scream, so Oran jumped quickly and stabbed it through the skull with his lance.

From behind, he heard the other kanontsistonties flying over to investigate. Oran maneuvered the bags back into place, then pushed the head off of his lance before standing up. He walked away as if nothing had happened. The heads flew first to the dead kanontsistontie, then dove at Oran, buzzing him like angry mockingbirds when somebody gets too close to their nest. Oran did not flinch when they flew at him. He walked their gauntlet. After a while, the monsters lost interest. Some of the flying heads had landed next to the fallen kanontsistontie but were not gnawing on it.

Oran waved back at the convoy, then pushed deeper into the trees. The knocking he heard earlier that he mistook for tree limbs was actually the bodies. They were mannequins strung up in the trees to look like hanged people. Their plastic corpses knocked hollow against each other and the tree limbs.

They walked the rest of the night through the forest of the kanontsistonties. By morning's gray light, the trees with the hanging bodies and flying heads were behind them. The soldiers and the children were all weary, though, and had traveled less than two miles. They found an abandoned ranch house and broke inside. The soldiers were all upset and in low morale because of the loss of life.

"They are gaining on us," Ghost reminded the morose band of soldiers. "The wendigos. We should not stay here long."

Despite her warning, the team slept in the house all day long. They were emotionally drained and didn't have the strength for travel.

They never found Nobody's head or his helmet.

# CHAPTER SIX

Although the wendigos did not catch up to them, they were much closer.

"We must travel faster, or turn and make a stand," Teller said.

The children were struggling to sleep. A few had apparently snuck views of the nightmare fuel that was the kanontsistonties and the mannequins hanging from the trees. They had told others, and now most of the younger children were being cuddled by soldiers wearing bullet slings and melee weapons. Two Browning Hi-Powers were holstered on Teller's waist while he cradled a 5-year old in his arms. Still wearing his flamethrower, Molotov slowly swayed with a Flathead twin resting on each of his shoulders. Even Ghost had a bigger boy's hands clasped behind her neck in the spaces between her spikes.

"We're not fit to make a stand," Jack said. Oran put his hand on Jack's shoulder.

"We're not," Oran agreed. "The mountains are spreading farther from the road. Tomorrow we will drive to Kalispell. Any wendigos we will see from a safe distance and be able to avoid them."

"Are you going to keep the monsters away?" Ben Pederson asked. The little boy was cuddled up next to Oran, eyes closed. The other girl who heard the Blackfeet creation story was asleep on Oran's other side.

"Go to sleep, Ben," Oran said. He rubbed his forehead deeper into Oran's chest. He was hot, like a coal. Daniel had been the same way when he used to sneak into bed with Oran and Jodi.

"You didn't answer the question," the girl at his side said. Her name, Oran learned, was Amy. She rubbed her nose.

"I will fight all the monsters for you," Oran said.

Ghost smiled at Oran in her way, which was more like an egg cracking open than a human smile. Then she shushed the adults. While Oran waited for Ben and Amy to sleep, he watched the other soldiers. They were all very happy and content, though none more so than Teller. He adored holding the little child in his arms. Oran waited to say something until the combat soldier had sauntered over while he rocked the five year old in his arms.

"You are very good with children," Oran said.

"I have three at home in San Antonio. When I left, my youngest was 2. I guess he'd be about this kiddo's age now."

"It's hard being away from family," Oran said, thinking of his wife and son.

"Yes, it is. But we are serving them by serving others. If we can stop the wendigos, we can find peace in this lifetime. Maybe rebuild this nation or create a new one."

The sadness on Oran's face made Teller say, "What? You don't think we can stop the Wendys?"

"I've been fighting them for a long time. Some would say I have a knack for it. Yet today there are more wendigos than when I started fighting them. All evidence to the contrary, we are losing this war."

"That's 'cause we haven't found where they're coming from yet," Troy said, coming over after putting a child down to sleep. "I hear there is a hole in the mountains way up north and that is where they come from."

"These aren't trolls," Teller said. "They didn't just sprout out of the ground. They're animals, beasts of the Earth. Beasts unlike any we've seen, but this is our world. God gave us dominion over the animals, and that won't change. Science will catch up, and then we will find a way."

"Science?" Troy said, his voice a little elevated. "What kind of science lets heads fly around on bat wings?"

"Shhh," Ghost reminded them.

Troy lowered his voice. "As much as I would like to believe these monsters are anything that we can figure out with science, I doubt it." He untied the combat boot from his left leg and pulled it off, showing a metal foot. He wiggled his mechanical toes and said, "Science explains this. It doesn't explain how a creature with almost no organs can live off eating people."

The child in Teller's arms yawned, so Teller stayed quiet. He took the baby and put him down on his blanket.

"You're the smart one," Molotov said to Oran after putting the twins to sleep. "What do you think it is?"

Oran shared a look with Troy.

Molotov glanced from Oran to Troy and back. "What?" Molotov said. "What are you two not telling?"

"Maybe another time," Oran said. "The children are sleeping."

"No, you can't get out that easily. What is it? What's yer idea?"

Oran gently removed himself from the two sleeping children and walked to the kitchen area. The soldiers not putting children to sleep went with him.

"So, come on. Spit it out. What's your theory?" Molotov asked.

"I believe that the Sun is angry with the world."

"The sun?" Molotov balked, shrugging his massive shoulders.

"Natosi is the Sun, and the creator of the Earth. I believe that he is displeased with the world of the humans, so he is bending his rays to burn us out and give us cancer, and he is infecting the world with wendigos to devour man as punishment."

"What's he got against us?"

"Tell me, Molotov, when's the last time you prayed?"

"I pray every day that I'll be delivered a skinny woman and a fat wad of cash."

"I'm not talking a list of demands, I'm talking about conversations. I pray to the dead, to the animals, and to Natosi. I ask for understanding and compassion, and he usually helps me find it. But to steal from your Christian God, mankind has forsaken Him. We stopped caring about doing what was right unless we could slap a brand on it and sell it. So Natosi turned the world upside down. Have you ever noticed you never see a wendigo with the head of a predatory animal? They are always elk, deer, goats, bison. Not wolves, eagles, or bears. I believe this is because Natosi has flipped the world over. He is shaking it and he is baking it to see what is left, and he will remake the world with whoever survives."

"That's the craziest idea I ever heard," Molotov said.

"Easy," Teller cautioned him.

"I am taking it easy, Teller," Molotov said. "I just can't believe what I've heard. The sun is mad at us? I thought you was smart, Oran. Ye're just another crackpot."

"I believe him," Troy said, coming over.

"Of course ya do! The brotherhood of Indians always sticks together. What about your brothers in battle, man?"

"Brotherhood of..? You don't get to call me that, you sorry-kilting son of a...!"

"Hey!" It was Teller. Like all good leaders, he was maneuvering between Troy and Molotov.

Suddenly, a knife flew across the threshold and shoomped into the wall behind them. Everybody looked in the direction of where the knife came from. Ghost stood with one hip popped out so that she could hold the boy better and one arm still outstretched from throwing the knife.

"No. More. Talking."

Silently, everyone agreed.

Eventually, the soldiers fell asleep, too. Oran struggled a bit with sleep. He dreamed of a mother beaver and a baby beaver living in their dam. But when the beaver walked outside on top of its dam, she discovered an eagle floating high in the clouds way above her, so she scurried down below and stayed there, frightened. The next day she went out, there were two eagles. Again, she retreated to the sanctity of her dam where she was safe. Every day she went out, she discovered more eagles, until finally there were 13 eagles circling above her. Seeing all those eagles filled Oran with dread, and he woke all of a sudden.

Oran leaned forward and wiped the sweat from his brow. He looked around the room. Jack was also suffering from nightmares while the others slept. Was he shivering? This was not the first time Jack had tossed and turned under his buffalo hide.

Oran watched and waited. Jack got up, like he always did, and he rubbed his eyes like he'd been crying. Then he got out of bed and walked outside. A minute later, Oran slid out from between Amy and Ben and went outside. He waited beneath the roof's overhang under the shade of a young oak. The oak's branches swayed in the breeze, allowing the sun to occasionally wink at him. When Jack came back from using the latrine they'd dug behind some dead rose bushes, Oran confronted him.

"I'm sorry," Oran said.

"Sorry? What do you have to be sorry for?"

Oran saw in Jack's eyes that he was blanking out on him. He was somewhere else, but where? "I wish we had time to sweat together. I think it would be good for you if we sweated."

"Sweated?"

"Sweat lodge. They are used for personal and spiritual purification. They have also been known to help soldiers living with PTSD. Have you been diagnosed?"

"It's why I was on that plane returning home."

"You don't have to tell me if you don't want, but can I ask what happened?"

Jack stared at the ground, then the blue sky. "There aren't many fires right here. I think the wind is blowing the smoke away from us."

Oran nodded and waited patiently.

"I was in British Columbia, somewhere in the arctic hell that was the Coast Mountains. It was nothing but snow and ice and Wendys everywhere. I never meant to be up there, but you know, when you decide to serve, you don't get to pick how or where. Every day we were running at Wendys. The idea was to load them full of bullets and chase them off a mountain. We were having a real hard time this one battle because we were up against this giant, white, mountain goat of a Wendy. His skull was almost all showing, and he was at least as big as that monster that nearly got us in Spokane. We would force him off the side of a mountain, but he'd dart over some rocks and come up the other side. The first night against the Wendy was a real bad night. We lost fifty two of eighty men that night trying to get one wendigo. If we had a slayer like you there, maybe things would've been different. I watched as Wendy killed, tore apart, and ate five real good friends of mine. Some were still alive—screaming, yelling for help, praying, and crying while we could do nothing.

"The wendigo left in the morning, and officers ordered us to recover the remains. We gathered what we found and built a bonfire to burn the remains because the ground was frozen so we couldn't bury them. The stink of our friends burning up was beyond horrible. It is a smell I will never forget. We assumed we would leave and go back to base to regroup and replenish, but new orders came in to stand our ground against this Wendy.

"The commander in charge thought maybe we could do something from the air. He sent me and my buddy, Tom, up on a plane. The pilot dived at the monster as we shot round after round into the Wendy. On each of the dives, the pilot brought the nose of the plane up just before the monster grabbed at it. When we ran out of bullets the pilot decided to commit Kamikaze by flying into the Wendy. Tom and I tried to stop him but we couldn't. I remember that final descent. The Wendy slapped us out of the sky like King Kong playing with toy airplanes. We spiraled into the side of the mountain. The pilot was killed instantly and Tom was injured, but not me.

"It was a weird part of the mountain, and a difficult spot for anybody to reach us. Not so for the Wendy, which watched the plane crash. All of a sudden we could hear the Wendy hunting for us. I helped Tom to get away from the wreckage and we found a place to hide. We watched in horror as the Wendy played with the wreckage and slowly gnawed on the pilot as if he were eating a carrot.

"At morning, the Wendy went away again, and I carried Tom further away from the wreckage. For three days without food we played hide and seek with that monster chasing us. At times I had to hold my hand over Tom's mouth as he screamed in pain from his wounds. In his delirium and fever he called for his mother and told her he was coming home. One morning I woke up and Tom, who I was laying on to help keep him warm, had died. One of his hands had frozen gripping my wrist and the other hand was at my head, his fingers wrapped in my hair. I had to break his fingers to loosen his grip on my wrist and one of his fingers broke off in my hand. I had to use my knife to cut my hair to free my head from his hand. I tried to close his eyes but they were frozen open staring at me. Accusing me of not saving him to see his mother. I cursed him and beat on his chest blaming him for leaving me alone. Then I cried like a child and held him in my arms."

Tears were running down Jack's face. "It took another three days for my unit to find me. Three days. I wouldn't let Tom out of my arms. They tell me I kept saying over and over that I had to help him get to his mother. For the next several days I was in the hospital. I lost several toes to frostbite, I was dehydrated, and starved. They tell me I was in and out of consciousness. When I was able to sit up and start recovering they had already buried Tom and I didn't even get to say goodbye.

"From that moment on I did not want to talk or become close to any other soldier. I refused to let myself become close to another individual. I could no longer function as a human. After weeks of talking to a psychologist it was agreed I should be discharged and returned home."

Oran nodded. "That was a very brave sacrifice."

Jack wiped the tears off his face. "That's what everybody says, but all I see is a wrecked plane when I fly, and every day we pass mountains that remind me of those three days, or we fight monsters that send me back to the Coastal Mountains. And when it's cold, which it is every damn night, a dead man holds onto me for warmth."

Oran put his hands on Jack's shoulders. Jack began gulping air as he tried harder to wipe his tears. "I'm sorry, man."

"You have nothing to be sorry about. Life is twisted that way, brother." Oran pulled off his necklace. "This is a medicine wheel. Do you see the four colors?"

Jack sniffed. "Yes, sir."

"They are autumn, winter, spring, and summer. Hot, warm summer that brings the animals and makes the plants blossom. It is also the four stages of life, meaning birth, child, adult, and death. I want you to keep it with you, close to your heart, and anytime you start going back to the Coastal Mountains, I want you to remember this wheel, and it will bring you back here."

Oran handed Jack the beaded necklace. Jack was shocked. "I can't. This thing has got to be worth a fortune. I couldn't possibly take it from you." Jack pushed it to Oran.

Oran held the medicine wheel necklace and said a prayer, then placed the necklace around Jack's neck. "You can return it to me in Browning, if you like. We can sweat then. Until Browning, it is yours."

Jack took the medallion in both hands and rubbed his fingers over the intricate beadwork.

"I'm a good person, you know," he said. "Just a little broken."

"All soldiers bring back some of the war they've fought."

"Listen, there's something I've been meaning to talk to you about. That time from when we were on the plane."

"Think nothing of it."

"I need to ask you for your forgiveness."

"Forgiven and forgotten."

"I have something to confess, though. When we were on the plane, I didn't know who you were. I thought you were just another grunt like me returning from the front. And then after everything that happened, I found out who you were, and I'm embarrassed to say that all I saw was a quicker way out of this war. See, I lost my paperwork in the crash, so I was going to have to wait for communications from the front to catch up with me, and that could take weeks. I needed out now. So when I overheard the Recon Team talking about what an honor it would be to escort you back to Browning, I jumped onboard the bandwagon. I told them I'd flown with you and how great I thought you were and that I just wanted an opportunity to help you out. Of course they bought it. They're all too good. But I knew I was lying. I saw an opportunity to get out of this war even quicker. I feel horrible for what I did. But now that I've gotten to know you, and everything that's happened to us with the kids, I want to get them somewhere safe, and I want you to get safe. I think I've still got some fight in me."

"We all have some fight left in us, brother."

They pressed their foreheads together, and then they went back indoors.

# CHAPTER SEVEN

They woke to the smell of charcoal. The two children Oran watched over, Amy and Ben, worried that the ranch house was on fire.

"That's the forests burning," Oran said grimly. He was already up. Before the children rose, he had been meditating and praying while he cleaned his lance.

"When will the fires stop?" Ben asked.

Amy said, "My mom used to say that the wildfires stop with the first snows in September."

"Your mother was a smart woman," Oran said. He put away his lance and gathered his shirt and boots.

"You have weird scars on your chest," Amy said.

There was a question behind her statement, so Oran said, "The peoples of the Blackfeet Confederacy have a ritual we call the Sun Dance. These scars are from my participation in that dance."

"That sounds like a dangerous dance. Did somebody stab you?"

"No," he said with a curl of his lips. "And yes. It is a sacred ceremony. But I'm not going to talk about it now."

"Why not?"

"Because we must leave very soon. I want to get a lot of road under us today."

The two children didn't ask him any more questions. They used the bathroom in the latrine, which was then covered by Molotov, who Teller had assigned latrine duty for yesterday's arguments. Then they ate their breakfast, half an MRE for each of them. While the children ate their half-MRE, the soldiers shared two MREs and coffee between themselves.

The two Flathead twins gave their finished MRE to Molotov. It was licked clean. "I'm hungry," one of the twins said. He wasn't trying to complain, but rather just stating a miserable fact in that way that young children do.

Molotov patted the boy on the head. "Maybe if we're lucky, we'll see some huckleberries. We ken pick them like we're bears. What do ya think?"

The boy held up his hands like claws and growled menacingly. Molotov imitated a bear the same way, and the boy squealed as he ran off in mock terror.

"We need to find some food soon," Molotov said to the other soldiers while he watched the twins playing. "Otherwise, we might as well have left them where we found them."

45

"Troy," Teller said, "How much more rations do we have?"

"At the current rate, I give us two days before we're eating pine needles and birch bark."

They drove from the Cabinet Mountains to the Salish Mountains. The sky above them was so thick with smoke from the wilderness fires that the moon was nothing more than a blur in the atmosphere. Each mountain chain was lined with a bright red glow.

"I don't like this," Ghost said to Oran. She was in the passenger seat of the Chevy while he drove. "The smell is sharp and stings my nose. I'm not sure we aren't headed straight into the fire."

"We cannot go back, and if we continue in this direction, perhaps the fire will create a barrier between us and our followers. How are they doing, by the way?"

She looked behind her out the back window of the pickup, her eyes able to see distances Oran could not fathom. "They are now five miles behind us. Before we started, they were within a mile. They were so close I could smell their bodies rotting."

Oran pitied her and envied her. He wished he could see the things she could, but at what cost? He knew she must have been injured horribly in the face, but he almost did not want to know the details. The trauma must have been unbelievable.

She must have sensed his thoughts because she said, "I fell off a mountain, landed on my head, crushed most of my vertebra and ripped off my face."

"How did you fall off the mountain?"

"That's not important."

"On the contrary, I would think it is very important."

"I had a brother and a sister and a mother and a father. They were all eaten by Wendys in Washington State. I was spared because I escaped in the truck and they did not. I watched a single wendigo devour my entire family, growing as it ate every last person I loved. I was sixteen and I joined the military the next day. That is why I fight, and that is what is important, not that I fell off a damn mountain."

"You're right," Oran said. "I am sorry." She was a dedicated warrior, and he should have left it at that.

"Can I ask you something, though? What rank are you? I mean, Teller's our Sergeant, and the rest of us are specialists. But you've never said what rank you wear. Molotov thinks you're a specialist, but Troy said he heard you are a general."

"That's not important."

"Touché."

Ghost leaned forward against the dashboard. She scanned the road ahead from side to side. She opened the window and leaned outside to inhale. A rush of dry heat entered the pickup.

She closed the window and said, "We need to hurry up."

"That fire is intensifying. I can smell it moving this way."

Oran didn't know it was possible to smell the direction a fire was moving, but he didn't question her either.

"We're going to speed up," he said over the radio, then accelerated to sixty. He didn't like this speed. Especially at night, it would be hard to see any debris or traps set by the wendigos. For safety, they always drove with the lights off. If they truly were close to forest fires and one or more of the cars broke down because they hit something, that might be the death of them.

He flexed his fingers and tightened his grip on the steering wheel.

They rounded a bend in the road, and suddenly a landscape right out of hell opened up to them. Rivers of red zig-zagged down the mountainside. Bursts of yellow and orange heat flared on either side of the pickup.

"This looks bad," Oran said into the CB, "but I think we'll be okay."

"The kids are getting scared," Teller said.

"Not to worry, kiddies," Molotov said into the CB. "Uncle Oran will get us out of here. We might want to speed up a bit, though," he added.

Oran pressed on the accelerator again. The Chevy was giving as good as it could, considering that it was covered in a line of concrete.

"Ah, hell," Ghost said while surveying the mountains on their left. Oran followed her eyes. Up on the side of the mountain, a great elk-headed wendigo was moving through the burned out forest. What little flesh remained was on fire.

"It must have gotten trapped," Oran said.

The monster was waving its arms in fear and frustration as it slowly burned to death. Its eyes were like something never seen. But then the giant somehow discovered the convoy, and it bellowed its rage at them. It jumped from ledge to ledge, descending the mountain.

"Guys!" Teller said.

Oran caught a glimpse of a road leading away from the highway and into the burned out woods. He turned sharply, the truck's wheels spinning in the side gravel.

"Where are we going?" Ghost said. "We could get trapped."

"Anywhere has got to be better than that wendigo. I don't think he'll come in here chasing us."

All three cars made the turn, though the RV made it only because of good fortune. The RV started to lift as it came around. The children screamed, and Teller worried what would happen to all those bodies not in seat belts. At the last second, the RV fell back down on all four wheels.

"Let's not do that again," Teller said into the CB.

They drove up the mountainside. "As long as we're in the black behind the fire line, we should be okay," Oran said into the CB.

Saying it didn't make him feel better. This was driving a dirt road along the fire line. Fires were erupting all along the side of the road. The heat was so intense there that the cars dragged embers along with them in their wake.

Oran stopped the Chevy. In front of him lay a downed line.

"Any ideas?" he asked Ghost.

"Side road about two twists back, but I've gotta warn you, it was taking us to the fire."

The RV was the hardest to reverse. Molotov and Troy got out of the back car and helped them maneuver the RV. As it swung back and forth like a pendulum in the road, its bumper smashed into a burning tree. The tree toppled over onto the RV and rolled onto the side of the road.

The children screamed, and Molotov thought that was it, they were done. Ironically, he would say they were "cooked."

But the RV received only minor damage from the burning tree, which Molotov kicked off the side of the mountain. Teller pulled the wheel as steeply as he could and got back on the road.

"We can't do that again," he told Oran. Oran saluted him to affirm that he'd heard Teller, then he drove back to the turn and inhaled sharply. Ghost had pulled a bandana over her face not because the smoke and ash was too thick for her but because the smell was overpowering.

Oran led the convoy straight into the fire. It was like a labyrinth, except instead of dead ends, the road ended in fiery blazes and toppled trees. As he came up to one fallen tree, the flames still licking, Ghost said, "Go over it. Go!"

The fiery log burst under the weight of the Chevy.

At this elevation, all the ash was rising to them. Oran switched on the windshield wipers to wipe off the ash.

"Did we do the right thing here?" Ghost asked. "I don't want to die in a fire."

"I do not think we have much choice now." Oran followed the dirt road around the mountain bend. The ash and smoke was so thick here that he wasn't sure if he was still going up the mountain or down it. All sense of direction and altitude was gone.

He was also having a hard time seeing five feet in front of his car. To his side, something exploded, and a great phoenix of orange and red fire reached for the sky. Several trees were thrown onto the road. The sedan hit the brakes, and the RV swerved. Again the RV nearly lost its footing.

Molotov and Troy were in the last car. They drove fast as they could through the thick log. It splintered against the power of the speeding sedan.

"Come on, come on," Ghost said aloud. A stand of thin aspens along the dirt road were engulfed in flames. Aspens were one organism sprouting shoots up from the roots, so seeing a whole copse of aspens burning was like seeing someone dancing while covered in fire. Their flaming limbs slapped against the Chevy as it maneuvered along the dirt road.

Molotov said, "We've got to get off this mountain. This is too close."

"We can't turn around," Teller reminded him.

"This is leading us to a fiery grave," Molotov countered. "If we don't go back, we'll die."

"Where will we put the kids?" Teller countered. Molotov didn't have an answer.

Oran checked to his right and his left. Molotov was right. The fire line, a bright streak of crimson against the blackened Earth, was edging back at them, getting closer and closer to the road the farther they went.

"Can't back out now," Oran said.

In his rearview mirror, a red and orange flow outlined the other cars.

Up ahead, the lines came closer and closer to the dirt road. These were the heads of the fire.

"What is the plan?" Ghost asked.

Oran said, "This is not a plan, Ghost. This is running wild and hoping to escape. It is not what I would do, but we don't have a choice. We can move or die."

A scream of flames erupted out of the ground ahead. The winds whipped them into an inferno that spiraled upward, a flaming tornado growing on the side of the road. The tornado whipped trees into its hot winds. As it grew, an awful roaring sound bellowed from inside. The cars veered to the other side of the road to avoid the tornado.

The tornado dumped embers and sparkling fire on top of the trucks as they darted away.

Along the side of the road, the mountain abruptly dropped off. Time slowed for Oran. On his left, he knew the mountain had a drop off because the red line had vanished. Also, the next mountainside over was a wall of flames. Below him, where the fire line had disappeared, he spotted a lake of fire. Embers and ash flew up at him.

The car hit the edge of the dirt road as they cornered around the tornado. Ahead of them, a giant pine snapped and growled as it dropped across the road. It was too big to charge through, but if that's what was needed to protect the children, Oran was willing to be a human battering ram.

"There! There! There!" Ghost shouted, pointing to the side of the road.

Oran barely caught a glimpse of the opening of the side road, but he took it. He turned and went down into the tunnel of fire, leaving the fire tornado and the hellscape behind them.

Oran pumped his brakes as they descended the mountain.

"Stop slowing down," Molotov urged them.

"This is a soft dirt road," Oran said. "We could spin out of control, and then where would we be?"

"Check yer rearview," is all Molotov said.

Oran and Ghost both looked in the mirror. Their eyes went wide. The top of the RV was on fire. About a third of the roof was fanning flames as they drove down the mountain.

Oran sped back up. Teller didn't ask. He could guess the problem was with the RV, but everybody knew the kids were listening.

The dirt road twisted and turned for what felt like hours, but the clock showed only ten minutes had past. But as they descended this side of the mountain, the orange glow faded and the fires disappeared.

Just as suddenly as the fire swept around them, they were back on asphalt at the bottom of the mountains. They pulled over and took care of the fire. They created a fire line from a mound of dirt. Using buckets, sheets, and pots, they scooped the dirt up, transferred it to the top of the RV, and doused the fire. Then Molotov and Teller went inside the RV and inspected the ceiling. Once they had the thumbs up, they finally felt able to lean back and take a breath. They were all sweating, though whether from heat or nerves, Oran couldn't tell.

"Do ya think we lost the Wendys in that inferno?" Molotov joked.

"It's supposed to get easy from here," Troy said. Molotov scoffed, but Troy shot back, "Hey, give me my delusions!"

They wiped the sweat from their brows and drank from their water bottles before getting back into the cars and heading out into the open valley.

# CHAPTER EIGHT

Smoke and ash wafted through the valley, shielding the convoy from the angry sun while stinking the world with the smell of burned trees and animals.

Ghost picked out two very large, very old wendigos prowling along the northern banks of Flathead Lake.

"You can see them all the way from here?" Oran was astounded. All his eyes gave him was orange and gray ash dotted with bright, floating embers.

"I see them in the mist. I see their shadows, and then the wind changes and I see all of them. They are each as wide as a two-lane highway, and they're almost a hundred feet tall from the tops of their antlers to the bottom of their hooves. The one must have a stitcher because it wears a hide of human skins over its bony chest. They are so heavy that when they walk, their hooves sink into the ground."

"Well, then we need to go south. I do not want this journey to be defined by their gluttony. What of our stalkers?"

"The bison Wendys?" She scanned the area. "I haven't seen them since we ran through the forest fire."

\#

As they descended toward the lake, inside the RV, the two twins walked to the front next to Teller. They had to maneuver between the other kids. Children sat or laid all over the floor.

While keeping his eyes on the road, Teller said, "We're not stopping for a bathroom break for at least another hour."

The two boys leaned over the front dash, which was very wide in the RV.

"Hey," Teller said, a little angrily. For this to work, he needed the kids to keep busy, but not too busy. That's why older kids like Janelle, who was sixteen, had a seat where she could watch over the little ones while he drove.

"Janelle," Teller said.

Janelle, who sat in the passenger seat, put her hand on the shoulder of the twin closest to her. His name was George. The boys were barely nine years old.

Teller and Janelle followed the gaze of the twins to a fallen sign on the side of the road. In faded yellow lettering, it read, "Entering Flathead Indian Reservation" and "Salish, Pend d'oreille and Kootenai Tribes." Underneath were more words in tribal language.

"This is where you're from," Teller said.

George's twin, Henry, just nodded.

"I'm sorry, George. Do you all want to stop?"

"My name's not George anymore," the boy said. "You all have cool names. We asked Molotov, and he gave us cool made-up names, too."

Janelle's eyes grew wide. A list of Scottish curse words flashed in her mind.

Teller didn't mind too much, though. "What names did he give you?"

"I'm William," George said. "And he's Wallace. I don't think it sounds very cool, but Molotov told us it was the coolest."

A smile tickled Teller's lips. He saw what the Scotsman did. "Those are great names."

"My grandmother lived in a town by the lake," William said. "But she died long ago. The wendigos got her. Mom and Dad moved to Sandhill Point and then had us. The wendigos would come out of the mountains to attack Sandhill Point. Usually it was only one or two, and soldiers had come in to protect us. They could usually steer the wendigos away from the town, get the monsters to follow them back out into the mountains until they forgot what they were doing in the first place. But then the soldiers had to leave, and one day a bunch of wendigos walked into town. All the children were sent away. While they were sleeping in the middle of the day, we crawled through the sewers and in the ditches to escape."

"You are a very brave boy, William. So are you, Wallace," Teller said. He adjusted his mirror to better view the rest of the kids. Some were standing to see the sign, but they had passed it by then. "You are all very brave. You will have to remain brave a little longer, but I promise you, as long as we are alive, we will protect you."

William said, "You don't have to protect me, Teller. Molotov is teaching us how to fight."

"What?" Teller wasn't against it, but he was a little shocked they'd convinced the soldier.

"Ai," Wallace said.

Teller didn't make them sit back down. He watched the road and thought about the powerful statement of two orphan Flathead twins adopted by a displaced Scotsman in the middle of the Rocky Mountains.

"I'd like a new name, too," one of the children in the back said.

#

Crisscrossing between abandoned cars, they drove 93 south around Flathead Lake.

They were forced to pause when the ground began to rumble. Some of the children cried out, but Teller silenced them by reminding them of the Quiet Game. The Quiet Game was for when absolute and total silence was necessary, like when a wendigo was close by. He had practiced the Quiet Game with the children several times on the road. The children were getting very good at it. He said, "Quiet Game!" and they all had to huddle somewhere out of sight within three seconds and remain completely silent until he gave the all clear.

The soldiers shouldered their rifles and scanned the area.

"What do you see, Ghost?"

"You're not going to believe me."

The rumbling grew louder and louder as whatever it was came nearer. All at once over a nearby hill, hundreds of American bison appeared. They were running toward Flathead Lake.

"They're coming straight at us!" Molotov shouted over the CB. "What do we do?"

"Stay calm, and stay inside your vehicles," Oran said. He grinned broadly. The herd was easily the largest herd of bison he'd ever seen in his life. *Countless bison. When has anyone been able to say that?* He thought. As the herd moved toward the caravan, he felt a great joy tempered with mild trepidation. His grandfather's grandfather had never seen such an image. Not since the time of the white man had so many bison run through Montana.

The herd swelled in size and swept around them. The animals were smart enough to avoid the convoy, blustering around the cars covered in spikes, sometimes bumping into the RV, but never striking them. Inside the cars, it was hard to tell the difference between the vibrations on the ground and being pummelled. It was like they were running a gauntlet made of bison. To Oran, it seemed the cars had fallen into a giant river of brown, curly-haired heads with black horns. The bison kicked up a great dust cloud around them.

"Kyo!" Oran shouted gleefully. He wanted to go outside and watch them from the back of the truck bed. Maybe he could squeeze through the opening in the back window, but he knew better. He wasn't so young anymore that he could cram through small windows. He'd have to content himself with watching the bison storm all around him.

The only thing that could make this better would be to have Jodi and Daniel with him. He wished they could see this, too. The fact that this moment was so important to him soured him even more that his family could not share the experience. He was sitting in a Chevy in the largest herd to grace North America in over a hundred and fifty years, and he was homesick.

He glanced to the rest of the convoy. Troy had climbed atop the RV and walked around its blackened roof. He was singing and dancing to see such a beautiful sight. His iron tentacles waved with his movements.

Then Troy suddenly stopped and fell to his belly.

Ghost cursed like no kids were listening.

Oran felt the shadows flowing over him, and then he beheld the monsters, three of them, running alongside the bison. Now Oran knew why the bison were running to Flathead Lake. They were fleeing ghoulish moose. The mother was as big as an elephant, and her skin was like cords of rope tied between her bones. Her two calves, each the size of a horse, tagged along at her side. They snarled and snapped as they drove at the bison.

Mama ghoul ran between the cars. Her giant mouth cocked sideways. The soldiers could see the long, serrated teeth hanging out of her mouth. She clamped down on a bison. The bison squealed and shook its legs. The moose shook the bison in her mouth, snapping its neck, and then she dragged it back out onto the boat ramp, where she and her calves began to devour the bison. The hundreds of bison not being eaten by carnivorous moose waited on a rocky bar not far off from the lake. They huddled close and bellowed at the moose, which ignored them. Dinner was ready. The calves came at her, and together they began to strip the flesh off the still-living bison. The poor bison screamed, yet its herd and the moose continued on.

The moose family ate. First, they devoured the bison's intestines, and then its kidneys and liver. By then, the bison had slipped into shock. It kicked one of its legs either reflexively or futilely against its killer. The mother finally got annoyed and kicked the leg hard enough to break the bones. The bison stared at the caravan, wide-eyed. It did not move (though, as Oran noticed, air continued to snort from its flaring nostrils).

A moose calf came around and put the bison out of its misery, biting its nose off, which it chewed back and forth between its gums like he was relishing a strange delicacy.

"We need to move on, but slowly," Oran cautioned the others. He shifted into Drive and slowly drove away. The mama moose took notice of the gasoline guzzlers moving but didn't care enough to investigate them. And why would she? She was queen and empress here. They weren't worth the time it took to look down the food chain at them.

#

They drove cautiously around the lake. Despite the grisly emergence of the giant bears, Oran was in a good mood. He'd seen a great heard of bison, something nobody in Browning could say they'd ever seen.

Despite the smoky air, the beautiful Flathead Lake did its best to tease her beauty, giving them glances of serene waterfronts framed by the majestic Mission mountains. They drove around the southern bend of the lake, and then veered north. The mountains rose up steeply on their right while the lake stood to their left, often almost right next to the roadside.

The road curved back and forth as it meandered along the lake's edge. Eventually the signs for cherry orchards stood next to actual cherry orchards. Most of the orchards were picked clean, but Oran did find an orchard that had yet to be harvested. He pulled over. Per the wooden sign outside, the owners had declared this the "Best Flathead Cherry Orchard."

Children all over Montana, Idaho, and Eastern Washington knew cherry-picking season. The kids poured out of the camper, giddy with delight and carrying porcelain bowls, Tupperware, and plastic colanders that they'd pillaged from the RV. They ran cheering into the orchard, plucking cherries off the trees and gobbling them instantly.

Molotov and Troy wandered into the orchard's store to scavenge. They returned an hour later triumphant, a bottle of cherry wine in one hand, and two jars of cherry jam in the other.

"Hey, I see something," Troy said.

"You always see something," Molotov said. "Remember Yellowstone? That was a geyser."

"No, really, shush," Troy said as he pushed back a cherry tree branch and pointed to the wild turkey who was sleeping in a nearby pine tree on a sturdy branch about ten feet off the ground. "Do you have something to shoot it?"

"I've got a flamethrower. I don't think that'll work. There's an AR-15 in the car."

"I want to kill it so that we can cook it and eat it. I don't want to eviscerate the bird. Get one of Teller's pistols."

Molotov came back ten minutes later with the pistol and gave it to Troy. "He said to be careful with it. He wants it back."

Troy sneered at Molotov and aimed the pistol at the turkey, careful to keep the turkey's heart in his sights.

"Are ya gonna shoot it or not?" Molotov goaded him.

"Shutup."

"It takes hours to roast a turkey. I'm just saying."

Troy growled and fired the pistol. The turkey screamed and flapped its wings as it fell to the ground.

"You got him!" Molotov cheered.

"Aa, I clipped him."

The turkey flapped its wings while running in circles and making a horrible gurgling sound that was the poor bird's distress call. Troy fired again, and this time he completely missed. But the flash from the gun was enough to tell the turkey where its predators were hiding. The turkey charged them. Anxious, Troy fired two more rounds. Both missed. The turkey jumped at Troy, feet first. The two soldiers ran out from behind the trees where they'd been hiding, the turkey chasing them.

"Somebody shoot it!" Troy shouted as they ran through the orchard, the rampaging gallopavo running after them.

Oran laughed at the sight of the two soldiers, one of them as big as a bear, being chased around the orchard by a turkey.

"You've got to show it dominance!" Teller shouted at the two failed hunters.

"Just shoot the blasted thing!" Molotov yelled as the turkey lighted into the air and swiped at his back.

"We can't shoot it. There are children near," Teller said. "You're just going to have to turn and fight the turkey."

Finally, Troy ducked behind a cherry tree and came up behind the turkey and kicked it. The turkey fell over and Troy shot it with Teller's gun. The turkey fell down. When he went to inspect it, the bird jerked its leg. Troy shot it again.

"About time ya killed that wee bird," Molotov said.

"Me? You're the one who's killed Wendys, remember? Why didn't you kill it?"

"Do you think either of us will ever live this down?"

"I have hopes for my afterlife."

They roasted the turkey all night in the orchard store, which had a kitchen and a small house attached. The house had no electricity, but it had a gas stove, and the gas still worked, so they lit the oven and cooked the turkey.

By morning, they were feasting on fresh turkey meat. As much hassle as everyone continued to give Molotov and Troy, everybody in the convoy was overjoyed eating real meat. The drumsticks were given one each to Molotov and Troy as a thank you for their "heroic" efforts killing the meal.

"I can't keep food from the bairns," Molotov said. He and Troy took a bite, but gave the rest to the children.

"So, about our names," Ben Pederson said.

Oran raised an eyebrow.

Between bites of food, Teller told the other soldiers about the conversation he had with the children in the RV. "So now they want code names."

"I want to be Big Gun!" Ben said enthusiastically.

Oran put down his plate. "These are nicknames that are earned in combat. By brothers who have trained and shed blood together. Don't you think giving you a name you haven't earned would disrespect other soldiers."

"Awww," the little boy said.

Ghost said, "These kids have seen as much horror and war as most people encounter in a lifetime. I think they've earned their names."

"Okay," Oran said after a moment's thought. "But there's always one rule of nicknames: you don't name yourself. That means no 'Big Gun.'"

"Awww," Ben said.

"I will name you instead Blood-Clot Boy. He was a Blackfeet who had many adventures slaying monsters. How does that sound to you?"

"Gross. I like it!"

The other children begged for new names, too. Oran named Amy, Old Woman, because she had stayed awake to listen to his entire tale so many days ago.

Recon Team helped name the other children. Eighteen names later, they were all sleepy from the turkey. It had been no Butterball. It was a small wild turkey consumed by 20 starving people. But the few mouthfuls were more than enough to fill their diminished stomachs with tryptophan and cherry wine. Everybody fell contentedly asleep.

#

The unmistakable sound of a shotgun pump sliding a shell into chamber woke Oran. He opened one eye. Standing in the open doorway were two boys not yet old enough to grow a beard, though they were trying. The boy on the left carried the shotgun. The boy on the right had two old Colts aimed at Oran's head. They both wore hoodies and blue jeans with holes in the knees.

"Those were our cherries," the boy with the shotgun said. "And that was our turkey."

Oran raised his hands. "We did not know whose property it was. We searched, but did not find a No Trespassing sign, or painted posts, or even a rope or stones or other demarcation. We would not have entered except that we were starving and desperate."

"That's not our problem," the boy with the shotgun said.

"I told you we should have left a pile of stones outside," the other boy said.

"Hey, not in front of them, okay?" the boy with the shotgun said in a hushed tone, but Oran and everyone else heard him.

Some of the children were rising from their sleep. Seeing Oran with his hands raised, a few of the younger children began to cry.

"Can you put your guns down? You're scaring the children," Teller said.

"That sounds like a 'you' problem," said the boy with the pistols. He raised his gun to Teller.

"Can we turn this into a situation where nobody gets shot?" Oran asked. "We do not want to get hurt."

"Good. Cause we will kill you if we have to," said the boy with the shotgun.

"I don't think we have enough bullets," the other boy whispered. Oran would have laughed if a sixteen year old kid with a chip on his shoulder and a shotgun in his hands wasn't standing in front of him.

"What do you want?" Oran said loud enough to drown out the boys' aside.

The two boys conferred, then they said, "We want all your food, water, and your cars."

"That's not going to happen. Come on, kid."

"Kid? Oh, is that how it is? Fine, let's dance," the boy with the shotgun said.

Oran cursed under his breath. He moved to jump between the shotgun and the children. The other soldiers were maneuvering kids out of the line of fire or shielding them from the weapon's discharge.

The rifle flipped out of Ryder's hands as Molotov grabbed the shotgun out of the boy's arms. The other boy raised his guns, but Troy pulled a knife to the kid's throat. "Don't do it, kid," Troy warned him. The boy sighed and dropped his Colts.

While Teller and Jack took the children away to the far side of the store, Molotov cuffed the two boys with plastic wire ties.

"Don't kill us, mister," the boy with the Colts said.

Unseen to the boys, Oran shared a smile with Ghost and Molotov.

"That depends on how you respond," Molotov growled. He stood up tall between the two boys, who were sitting on a concrete bench in the orchard's garden. Molotov was built like a wrestler. When he didn't want, he was impressive. When he wanted, he was a special kind of scary intimidation.

"I haven't killed a child in three weeks. It's a new record," he told the boys. "Whether or not I can extend that record is up to you."

Ghost watched the boys coldly, her mechanical face revealing even less than usual.

The second boy, his words coming out rapid as machine gun fire, shouted, "We didn't mean anything by it We were just protecting the orchards We haven't seen Mom and Dad in months and are scared PLEASE DON'T EAT US!" The first was shaking his head, embarrassed that his comrade had cracked so easily.

Oran noticed the boy shaking and stopped the intimidation factor. "I think that's enough, Molotov. Can you give us a minute?"

"Sure thing, Boss," Molotov said. He lifted their shotgun over his shoulder and walked away.

Oran pinched his nose, then sat down on the concrete bench across from the boys. The old garden was overpopulated by weeds and vines that had grown out of control without anyone to cultivate or remove them.

"First of all, nobody is going to harm you. My name is Oran Old Chief."

The first boy scoffed. "Battle of Tecumseh Oran Old Chief? No way. He's taller and meaner, with a giant scar down his face. He's a wendigo slayer."

Oran reached behind the concrete bench and casually pulled out his lance, decorated with eagle feathers. He placed it in his lap and said, "I assure you, my name is Oran Old Chief. I am returning to my home in Browning. These soldiers are doing the honor of escorting me."

"No way! My name is Coby. This is my brother, Ryder. We want to fight for you on the front!" the second boy said.

Oran had thought the boys looked too similar to not be related. He held up his hand. "I am not going to the front. Besides, I think the best thing you can do is wait for your parents to return."

"Our parents aren't coming back," Ryder glowered. "They left us before the first snowfall last year. That's a long time."

"Can we come with you?" Coby asked, his voice full of hope. "We could help you."

"Thank you, but for now, we need to know more about this land. Are there wendigos in the area?"

"Lots. The mountains between here and the plains are full of them," Coby said. "You shouldn't go there. Nobody returns."

"Is that where your parents went?" Oran asked. A dark cloud had settled over the brothers' faces.

"People say Browning is the place to go," Ryder said. He was no more than a year or two older than Coby, but his voice was more mature.

"What people?"

"Travelers, mostly. Then there are the Fergusons and the Bent-Nots up the road. We sometimes have dinner with them when the fires aren't fierce or there aren't too many monsters about."

"And you've just been surviving on your own since your parents left?" Ghost asked.

"Yes, ma'am," Ryder said.

Coby said, "Since most people have either been killed by the wendigos or moved on, we've taken over the properties of eight orchards in the area. We rotate between them for food and shelter."

Oran turned to Ghost. Her skull-like face still showed no signs of emotion. Since she had no eye-lids, she did not even blink.

"Can we go with you?" Coby asked.

Oran side-eyed them. "Be honest with me. Have you killed anyone?"

When the boys didn't answer, he said, "If I walk your properties, am I going to find bodies? Do you eat people? It's understandable. Some do."

Incredulous, Coby said, "Ugh, not us. No, sir. The orchards and game are enough for our bellies."

"And if you come with us, how are you going to help us out? We have almost twenty children in our care. We do not have room for freeloaders."

"We'll do whatever you want, won't we, Ryder?" Coby asked.

Ryder stared at the ground. "I don't want to leave," he said.

Oran's voice softened. "Why not, son?"

"What if Mom and Dad come back?"

Coby put his hand on Ryder's shoulder. "Ryder, Mom and Dad aren't coming back."

Ryder shrugged his hand off his shoulder. "How do you know?"

"He has a good point, Coby," Oran said. But Oran had already made up his mind how this was going to play out. "Ryder, I have an idea. We will leave them a message that only they will find. If they come back, the message will say to look for you in Browning. Will that work?"

Ryder nodded. "I guess."

"It is settled, then. You will come with us. In exchange for the drive to Browning, you will help us care for the children. Have either of you babysat before? No? You will learn quickly."

He pulled a knife out and cut the wire ties open. "I want you to go find some clothes, and then come back to us. We will stay here one more day to regroup and eat, then we will leave. Also, we are desperate for gasoline. Can you help us find some?"

Ryder said, "The Bent-Nots can help. Mr. Bent-Not makes his own gasoline. We can go there, and maybe you can trade for gasoline."

"Very good," Oran said. "Get your gear and come back to us."

"Thank you, Oran," the boys said.

Ghost put her hand out to shake. "Welcome to the tribe."

The boys smiled, but Oran shook his head.

# CHAPTER NINE

The children spent the rest of the night playing and picking cherries for the drive. They poured the cherries into large garbage bags, which were then placed in compartments under the RV. Jack found fishing equipment. He took them down to the banks of the Flathead Lake, keen to add fish to their diet. There were only so many wild turkeys in the forest, and unlike the first one they killed, the others proved harder to locate, nesting much higher in the pines.

"Trout tonight sounds delicious," he said to the others as he walked down to the lake.

"I would not do that," Oran said when he overheard Jack talking about fishing to the other soldiers.

"Why not?" Molotov asked. "You got something against fish?"

"Hrmm," Oran said, then added, "The fish here are poisonous. Radiation and mercury have made them unfit to eat."

"Well, it can still be fun to catch fish," Jack said. "I'll just throw them back."

Jack went down to the lake's edge and set down his tackle box and fishing rod. He sorted through the box. The owners of Best Flathead Cherry Orchard were stingy on their fishing supplies. Jack guessed they fished only for food. They had J-hooks, which had that tiny barb that made a nightmare of removing a hook from a fish that was meant to be returned to the lake. They also had spinners, worms, and lures. Most of what they had was trout fishing, which he couldn't do very well from the lake shore. Bass fishing, though. Well, there were trees along the edge of the lake and bushes, too.

He decided on a worm, which he weighted and attached to a J-hook. He casted in front of the bushes as dawn began to emerge from her slumber. The Missions were not on fire, and the wind was taking the Cabinet Mountain fires south, which gave him a good view of the past day's journey. He couldn't see any wendigo on the far side of the lake, but he could see the mountains clearly. They smoldered like logs long after the bonfire had ended, burning slowly and passionately, mostly black with tiny red lights glowing from within.

A couple of the kids came down to watch him fish. After a few minutes, they began a game of tag, and then a couple of little girls wandered down to the water's edge and sat on a log. Before long, most of the kids were either near the water or barefoot in the water.

Jack warned them to stay away from his fishing area. "You don't want to get hooked like a bass, do you?" he asked while pulling his cheek out with his crooked index finger. He crossed his eyes, and the kids laughed.

"Hey!" Ryder shouted from the back of the storefront. He was waving his hands.

"What?"

"Get away from the water!" Ryder shouted back.

"I'm watching the kids. They won't drown."

He growled under his breath, "Stop bothering me, kid, and give me some peace." Jack had his parka and his shirt off. He rubbed onto his back some sunscreen that he'd discovered in the back of the store, and if that wasn't enough, to hell with it. He was enjoying this moment and wanted to stay here as long as he could. It'd been a long time since he last felt this at peace. This was what he was fighting for.

Ryder came running down to the lake. "Hey! Didn't you hear me?"

"I heard you, and then I kept going on with my life. You don't know how long it's been since I've had something this peaceful."

"You don't understand. There's a monster in the water. Nobody is safe here. Haven't you heard of the Flathead Lake Monster?"

"Right. The Loch Ness Monster. That thing's just superstitious BS."

"Like wendigos and Bigfoot, right?" Ryder asked. "It's real, and it's killed. We fear the water here, not the mountains."

Standing there, Jack was overwhelmed by a growing sense of cold dread wrapping around him like dead arms. In the distance, a small curl, like a brightly colored eel, slithered out of the water toward one of the children.

"Shit!" Jack dropped his fishing rod and ran for the child.

"Run!" he shouted at the kids. They screamed, high pitched, and ran for the orchard.

The monster's eel-fin was too quick for the boy, and knocked him down in the water. The boy was stunned. He didn't see what had happened, and he began to panic.

Jack ran at him, waving at him to get out of the water.

As Jack raced along the shoreline, something big under the water rushed at the child. It was big enough to create waves. He thought of killer whales snatching up baby seals lost along rocky arctic shores.

What came out of the water was much scarier. It had the head of a dragon with horns and teeth and shiny scales that were red and yellow and green. The monster opened its mouth as it crashed into the child.

Jack couldn't beat the dragon to the child. The timing was off. If he'd just listened to Ryder and ordered the children away, or if he'd never gone down to the water's edge, maybe the little boy wouldn't die. He hated himself in that moment. At the same time, he realized he didn't hate himself for what happened up in the Coast Mountains. That was soldier's misfortune and the great suck at work. This was true hatred for himself. To let a child die while under his watch. Was there anything worse a man could do in his life?

Just then, when all was lost and teeth were snapping down on the boy, something happened that Jack would swear was impossible. He felt his war buddy Tom's cold arms tightening around him, and it was like he'd been zapped back to the Coast Mountains. Frozen fingers gripped the back of his head and his waist. Part of Jack wondered if he was having a heart attack. But then he felt his legs pumping faster and faster. He knew his body. Moving this fast was beyond his natural abilities. But Tom was there with him, telling him it was okay, pushing him forward, and suddenly Jack was in the dragon's mouth, and he shoved the scared little boy back on shore.

Tom smiled at him, and Jack felt right in the world, really right, for the first time since those three wretched days on the side of the mountain with Tom's dead body. Jack had added something good to the world, and the child would live.

When the teeth crushed into Jack, he didn't care. He was ready for death and welcomed it like an old friend.

# CHAPTER TEN

Recon Team ushered the children away from the shoreline. They dashed up to the orchard, where Teller gathered them in the old store and told them it was now time to play the Quiet Game. The children, as scared as they were, found a spot to hide and then silenced themselves.

"Stay here until one of us returns," Teller said. But he wasn't going far. He walked outside, closed the door behind him, and drew his two Browning Hi-Powers. He watched Oran and the rest of Recon Team from far away and hoped they could save everyone from the powerful creature rising out of the water.

#

Down at the shoreline, the giant serpent monster rose out of the Flathead Lake, blue water dripping off his magnificent horns. His scales shined like the beaded jewelry of plains tribes. Oran recognized some of the patterns in the monster's hide.

"Are you the headless warrior the kanontsistonties told me about?" the monster asked. "They complain all night from over the mountains."

In response, Oran asked, "You are Omahksoyisksiksina, the Great Water Serpent?"

The serpent bowed. As he did, he noticed the lance in Oran's hand and flicked his tongue. "You are Oran Old Chief. The wendigos curse your name, slayer."

"I am not here to slay, Great Water Serpent."

The serpent laughed. "You could try. Many have, yet here I am." The serpent rose up even higher above the lake's surface. "Do you not see my scales and horns? Do you know where I get these scales? What do they remind you of?"

"Beads."

"Yesss. I am the King of the Drowned, and all my victims must pay tribute to me. Gaze upon the many beads given to me by the young Flatheads and Blackfeet who have wandered too close to my waters."

"I only want to protect these children. You have my word that we will not stray close to your waters."

"Oh, but I want you to. You people are so tasty."

"You have taken one of my soldiers. You will not have another of us. Or is Great Water Serpent a glutton who throws off the balance of the world?"

"Mankind unbalanced the wheel, Oran Old Chief, not me." He showed a medicine wheel design in his side, not unlike the wheel Oran gave to Jack.

"Yeah, well, two wrongs do not make a right."

The serpent considered this for a moment. "I will make you an offer, something I do not give to many, Oran Old Chief, so think it over wisely."

"What kind of an offer?"

"Venom," the dragon said. The word dripped like acid from his mouth. "One bite in these teeth, and my venom will make your heart freeze up. But if you drink it, there is no danger to you. Consumed, my venom brings sublime peace and tranquility. What would your soldiers give for a moment of pure, unadulterated bliss?"

"You lie."

"Do not insult me, Old Chief. We have fought our battles against each other on either side of the Moon and the Sun. To honor this fight, and to bring peace between you and I, I make this offer. Lower your lance, and I will give you my treasure. Take it or leave it."

"He's scared," Troy whispered to Oran. "He says he isn't afraid of you, yet he's trying to escape."

"He killed Jack," Molotov growled. "I say we haul this worm out of the lake and bash his head in."

While the soldiers conferred, the Great Water Serpent lowered back into the water, but not before putting his tooth in the fisherman's cooler. Beautiful golden honey drained down the serpent's tooth and filled the cooler. Then the serpent sunk underwater and swam away. From far away, the soldiers could see his horns piercing the water, the only evidence that the monster existed.

"Should we try it?" Troy asked when they were alone. The soldiers surrounded the cooler. If the cooler had been dirty before, it looked perfectly clean now, like a brand new bottle full of syrupy liquid.

"How much would it take to work?" Ghost asked.

"I wouldn't try more than a thimble full," Molotov said. "We don't know what chemicals are in this. The best way to do this is to put a wee bit on our skin and see if there is a reaction. If not, then put on a bit more and see again if there is a reaction."

"That is, if we even want to drink it," Oran said.

"The serpent said he wouldn't lie, and I believe him," Troy said.

"You'd believe anything," Molotov said. "You and gift horses."

"So, should we try it?" Teller asked. He had told the children they no longer needed to stay quiet but had to remain in the store, then he walked over to the others.

"Fuck it," Ghost said. She dipped her hand in the venom and drank a swallow of the venom.

"Well?" Troy asked.

She lifted a finger of one hand to his lips while licking the venom off of the fingers of her other hand. "This feels good," she said. She slumped drunkenly against a tree and fell to her butt, giggling. They'd never heard her giggle before.

"Is she smiling?" Oran asked.

"That is Ghost's smile," Teller said.

"Is she sleeping?" Molotov asked.

"Ghost. Ghost!" Teller shouted. He kneeled down and put his hand close to her nasal cavity. "She's breathing, so she must be asleep." He shook her by the shoulder.

Ghost rolled her shoulders. "What?"

"You fell asleep. Are you okay?"

She nodded. "Have you ever been given a full body massage? That's what this is like. I feel real good."

Troy drank a handful.

"You cockmite," Molotov said, slapping the hand full of venom, but it was too late. Some of the yellow goodness got into Troy's mouth.

Troy put his hand on Molotov's shoulder and gave him a big ole Montana grin. "That. Feels. SO. Good." His knees nearly buckled from under him, and Troy, too, fell to the ground.

Teller said, "One of us should stay awake."

Molotov and Teller both said, "Not it," like little kids.

"I will stay awake," Oran said. Teller took a handful. Molotov took two. He set his flamethrower down and sat in the grass beside Teller. Before long, they were asleep.

Oran parked his butt down on a stump and watched the lake and the horns, which were now retreating to the far side of the Flathead Lake. He enjoyed watching the lapping of the waves against the timberline. Occasionally, birds would fly overhead.

Ten minutes later, Ghost walked up behind him. He didn't know she was with him until the last second. Ghost was very quiet. She carried a cup full of venom from the Great Horned Serpent.

"You have to try this," she said.

"No, thank you." He pushed the cup aside.

"You don't understand," Ghost said, "because you don't have implants. When they put metal in your body, as good as they are, there's always a pain there. My face always has this gentle stink, my spine feels like it could always stand for an adjustment. But ever since I took that first drink of the venom, the pain is gone. I feel like perfection. Come on. Try it."

"I have earned my pain. I would not want it to go away."

"You can see your wife and son again."

"What do you mean?"

"Drink this, and you can spend time with your wife and son. It isn't a dream. At least, it didn't feel like one. It felt as real as me talking to you."

Oran's eyes widened. He took the cup in his hand. "I said I would keep watch."

"Don't worry. I'll be here," Ghost said.

Oran drank the whole cup. A warmth oozed over his body, and as it moved, caressing him, his muscles unwounded. He felt happy and content, like every decision he'd ever made was the right one, or at least, the right one for him. He felt hands working over his back and his neck. He hadn't realized how tight his neck was, or how grateful he was for somebody to work it out. He exhaled ease and relaxation, and then he drifted to sleep.

#

Little Beaver, come home! Mother Beaver called out. She could not find him. She ran out over the tree trunks of her dam.

The creek was a happy place for the fish. It cut through the forest, smoothing rainbow-colored rocks as it moved along. Mother Beaver and her son were sad, but fortunate. Their home was strong and secure. The forest was well populated with aspen and birch trees, the beavers' favorite food.

Little Beaver! She called out again. A little head popped out from behind some rocks.

What were you doing?

I was pretending I was Dad. Do you think he will ever come back?

One day, child.

When the eagles' shadows appeared overhead, the beavers flinched. Mother Beaver and Little Beaver swam for their home on the river. The eagles dived at the beavers, their ugly talons opened wide.

The beavers were too quick for the birds of prey. Mother Beaver and her son escaped into their den where the eagles could not reach them. They huddled together, shivering, in their home while the eagles screamed outside.

The beavers in their home reminded him of a pattern from a bead necklace he bought Jodi when they were young. She kept it in her jewelry box, and she wore it to all the dances.

The Old Chief house was built above a fat creek-fed lake where Oran liked to take Daniel fishing. The house was a mansion by reservation comparisons. Almost three thousand square feet, upstairs and down, with a mud room for leaving boots after coming in from winter storms or fishing. A central fireplace supplied heat to all the rooms during the winter months.

Oran's beautiful wife stood in the kitchen. Jodi was making a large soup. Dan was helping her. Oran wondered why they were making so much food for only two people, or were they donating food to the homeless, as she was wont to do?

Is the food ready? somebody called from upstairs.

Jodi yelled, Almost!

Daniel took the silverware out to the dining table. He put out place settings for ten people. Jodi poured the soup from her pot into the serving bowl. Then she raised her face to the metal sun above the kitchen and said, Natosi, please, I beg you. Deliver my husband to me. She side-eyed the dining room and added, Tell him to pack vengeance and hate in his luggage.

Strangely, men who did not belong in Oran's home began to wander down the stairways. Oran recognized Sam Dawn Breaker, a mechanic, and Joe DesRosiers, a teacher. There was Greg Falcon Runs walking beside old Ernest Upham. What were they doing together? Greg was a thief and a troublemaker. Ernest Upham was a tribal elder. Why were they carrying on like the best of friends, and why was his wife making them supper?

They sat at the table that Daniel had prepared. Five more men from town joined them. Jodi lumbered into the dining room, struggling with the large bowl of soup that she'd been toiling over. None of the men jumped up to help her carry the heavy bowl to the table. Most sat and ogled her while she worked and slaved for them.

Oran felt a deep anger welling up inside him. He'd been away at war, and these men were dishonoring his wife. Why the hell were they even there? The men ate the food greedily while she brought them flatbread from the stove. They didn't even thank her. While they ate, she walked outside into the cool evening and wiped the sweat from her face and rubbed her feet.

Oran wished he could wipe the sweat from her brow or massage the aches out of her feet. Why would anyone treat her this way?

From out of the horizon, a dark shape appeared. Jodi waited and watched the shape slowly grow along the plains. It became a large brown boulder, but then as it got closer, Jodi recognized Betty Marrow Bones. Nobody called her Betty, though. She was known as Marrow Bones because she'd always been an exceptionally heavy woman. She was riding her electric scooter out to Jodi's home.

Marrow Bones was not a person Jodi wanted at her house. If it was up to Oran, he'd have thrown a rock at her or folded his arms and just glared at her for a while, but Jodi was a better person than him, even in her very tired state. It took a lot of effort to do all the chores and clean after ten men.

Hello, sister!

You've come a long way. What brought you out this far? It must be an emergency.

Do you have any water?

Jodi walked back inside.

Where you been? One of the men at the table said. I'm thirsty.

She didn't tell them about Marrow Bones. She wasn't sure why. But she kept it to herself. She went to the liquor cabinet to pour whiskey for the men. Daniel came to her and took over.

You okay, Mom?

Marrow Bones is outside.

What brought her all the way out here?

I don't know.

It can't be good. She never brings good news.

Where have you heard that? Finish the drinks, and then go upstairs. I will get rid of Marrow Bones, and I'll be back inside soon. I'll finish with the men.

Are you going to answer their question today?

No, Daniel. Not ever.

Jodi poured a bottle of well water, then went back out to Marrow Bones.

What took so long? Marrow Bones asked.

I have a full house, Marrow Bones, so I appreciate you coming out to visit, but I really must go back inside. What do you need?

I was sent here, Jodi Wilcox, to deliver a message to you.

My name is Old Chief. What is the message.

The obese woman drank long from her water bottle. She held out a dirty finger to pause the conversation until she finished. Then she said, The women want their husbands back.

They can have 'em. I don't want them here, either.

Really? Because this feels like you're holding hostage half the male population of Browning.

Hostage? Come inside. I didn't ask for any of these men to stay here. They are a burden on me. All day I work very hard to be a good host, and they're abusing that privilege. I want them out. I'm tired. I'm exhausted. I go to bed late, bones aching, and I wake up early to start their meals while they lounge around doing nothing except talking about who should marry me.

And you say 'no?' Marrow Bones sounded doubtful.

Are you kidding me? My husband is in Canada fighting wendigos. Until he returns, I have no husband on the res.

Dust rose up off the dirt road and swirled around the two women.

Well, that is what the women want. For you to finally pick one so that the others can have their husbands back. They think you are relishing in their attention.

Betty, I want to be very clear about this: Fuck them. You scoot on back to Browning, and you tell them to come get their husbands. I do NOT want them.

It's not like that, Jodi.

Marrow Bones' eyes began to redden. She said, My Harry is in there, too. I know he doesn't love 'this' any more. Why love me when there's you? You're beautiful and you're rich, but that doesn't mean you should get all the men. That's not fair.

Betty, come inside and get your man. Please. I cannot compel him to leave, and they are trying to force me to marry one of them, but just like you, I love Oran.

The tribe's spoken, Jodi. You must marry one of the men.

Marrow Bones drove her scooter around and began the long drive back to town.

Jodi shook with anger, then screamed the worst thing she could think of. When she walked back inside, she slapped Harry Marrow Bones on the side of his fat face and said, Your wife was just here. She wants you to come home.

She rode all the way up here?

What kind of batteries does it take to power a scooter all the way here? Joe Desrosiers asked.

I don't know. Maybe if I had some cake, it would jog my memory. Jodi!

Oran wanted nothing more than to punch Harry Marrow Bones in the face. That lazy dog was wasting his time living off of Jodi's work when he could be home supporting his wife and raising his two kids. He knew he could fix this, if he could just get home.

Ernest Upham walked into the kitchen where Jodi was washing the men's dishes. Jodi, why was Marrow Bones here?

She wanted to tell you all it is time to come home. There, now I've said it. You should go.

The old man put his hand on her shoulder, and she shirked. Beloved, now is the time to be honest.

Jodi shoved his shoulder away and said, I am not your beloved.

I am clearly the best of these men. I may be an old man, but I am wise, and I am tender. I will best be able to manage your dead husband's business and run his household.

My husband is not dead, and you haven't volunteered to review the accounts or help pay the suppliers. All you do is talk and eat and abuse my charity.

You could tell us to leave at any time.

You know I can't.

Because you love one of us.

No! Because it is not right to kick people out of your lodge. Did Natosi kick Morning Star out of his tipi? I cannot kick you out, and you all know that.

Ernest reached over her for a roll. He took a bite and chewed it pensively in his mouth. Well, he said, I guess we'll just have to keep playing this charade for a while longer. You sure Marrow Bones didn't say anything else? You wouldn't lie, would you?

She isn't lying, but she isn't telling the whole truth, are you, little mama? said Greg Falcon Runs as he walked into the kitchen.

I don't know what you're talking about, Jodi said.

Marrow Bones told her that the other wives in town demand that she choose a mister. The tribe speaks.

Funny, I wasn't there for the council meeting, Ernest Upham said.

So it isn't true! Jodi declared. She rinsed and dried the washed soup bowls.

Hold on there, beloved. You don't need the full council to make a decision such as this. Now, let me walk you into the other room and introduce you as Mrs. Jodi Upham.

No! Greg retorted. I will introduce her as Mrs. Falcon Runs. You won't live another five years. I am still young. I can keep her satisfied, and I have the energy required to run his business.

Stop it! Jodi said, pushing both men out of her way. She put the clean soup bowls back in the cabinets where they belonged. When she finished, she leaned against a cabinet and took in her kitchen. The room was full of her "suitors."

Jodi, it is time, Ernest Upham restated. We've held competitions and games, both mental and physical. We've argued to death which one of us should choose. Now the council is ordering you. You must pick a mate.

Tonight, she said.

Before sunset, Ernest added.

She nodded. The men left, cheerful. They walked out onto the grand back porch and continued enthusiastically debating each man's merits and who she should choose.

Jodi finished the rest of the dishes.

Is it true? her son asked, coming in. I overheard them.

Yes.

You can't, mom.

I don't have a choice. All I can do is hope and pray that your father returns before they do.

At that moment, somebody knocked at the door. Jodi and Daniel shared an expectant look. Daniel ran to the front door and pulled it wide open.

But his father was not there. Instead, it was just an old homeless man who smelled bad.

Is your mother home? the old man asked.

Mo-om! Daniel shouted in that two-tone announcement that she had a problem and he did not. There's an old white guy here for you!

Jodi appeared at the door. What can I do for you? she asked. The old man was hunched over. His clothes were rags, and his face was scarred. His hair was not braided. She thought he was an old war veteran.

I am an old man traveling through the reservation. The sun has been very hot on my head. I was wondering, could I stay here tonight?

Of course. I am all out of rooms, but I have a couch.

Thank you.

I just finished cleaning up from lunch, but I can cook you something, if you like.

I do not want to intrude, but I am very hungry.

Don't worry. Intrusion is the word of the day around here. Sit down and relax, and I will be right back with some food. The old man sat down and fell asleep. When he woke, Jodi had returned with a ham sandwich.

I hope this works. I am running low on meat.

The old man took a bite of the sandwich and grinned. He held the food in his mouth for a moment, savoring its taste.

There is more if you need it. I also have a shower, too, if you like.

Running water? But how?

My husband is always thinking up new things.

Where is he?

Sadly, at war.

I'm sorry.

Thank you. She patted him on the knee. I must be going. I have other things to do.

At that moment, the laughter from outside floated in.

What is that about? The old man asked.

It is a sad story.

I am a walking sad story. You do not have to tell me if you do not want, but I would like to offer my services. My ears have not gone deaf. Yet. So, I can still listen, if that helps.

Tonight I must pick a new husband, and I think it will be one of them.

They do not look like good men.

No, they aren't. After being here for a while, they decided to hold competitions to determine who was best suited to be my husband. I hated it because it disgraced my marriage, but after a while, I started to go along with it because they stopped asking for my hand when they were holding their "games." But I feel really guilty, like a little part of me was tearing down my husband for allowing this to happen.

Tell me, are you doing any more competitions to determine your new husband?

No, but I guess we could.

I would like one more, and if it is okay, I will participate.

Jodi stood back for a moment and thought about this. Then she said, What the hell? How much worse than these assholes can you be?

Later in the evening, Jodi gathered her suitors. They were all eyeballing the old man suspiciously. Anticipating a trick, Ernest said, Jodi, you remember you have to pick one of us now, right?

Jodi glared at the men and said, I have asked you over and over to leave, but you dead-beats have imposed on me and my family for months now. You've taken advantage of my husband being away at war. And now your wives have told me that I have to pick one so that the rest of you lazy asses can go back to your wives. I want to shoot you all. Well, congratulations. Tonight, I pick somebody. But I'm telling you, even then, I will not marry for one full year. I want a long-term engagement because I still believe Oran is out there and will be coming back.

She was scared and furious as she spoke to the men, and she began to shake again. She stopped and took a deep breath. Nobody reached out to reassure her or calm her.

This traveler is also a guest and wants to compete for my hand in marriage. So I am giving him the opportunity to compete. Whoever wins his competition wins my hand.

The old man stepped forward. He said, I've spoken to Jodi and her son Daniel. They've told me stories about Oran Old Chief. He was a loving and dutiful husband, and he was a pious man. All good things. But one quality sticks out more than the others. He was a very clever man. So I think it is best that the person who marries Jodi Old Chief should be able to prove that they are the cleverest.

The old man motioned for Daniel to step forward. The boy carried a very large, very heavy rifle. He strained to carry it. The rifle was covered in ornate and interconnected detailing.

The old man said, The first person in this room who can unlock this rifle gets her hand in marriage.

How long do we get to figure it out? Ernest asked.

Ten minutes sounds fair, the old man said.

The suitors agreed. They were excited to start, and each suitor wanted to be first, so they drew straws to see who would go first. Harry Marrowbones drew the lucky straw. He laid the rifle on its side on the iron table on the porch. He studied the symbols and the connecting parts. He made several changes to the rifle's configuration, but he never came close to unlocking the trigger. After ten minutes, the other men shouted and cheered, knowing that they still had a chance.

One by one the men tried to unlock the rifle. One by one the men failed. With each failed attempt, they grew more anxious.

What if nobody unlocks the rifle?

We will deal with that bridge when we cross it, the old man said. I am confident one of us will unlock it. Otherwise, we do not deserve her.

Greg Falcon Runs drew the second shortest straw. He had been watching the other suitors, and he thought he saw where they all went wrong. He took a different route, moving parts along the top of the stock. Most of the suitors went straight for the trigger. He decided to go for the sliding bolt action. He moved along the spine, and then down over to the bolt. He pulled, and the chamber slid open.

The men smiled. By this point, they were beyond anger at losing the opportunity to marry Jodi and get her land and wealth. They just wanted somebody to win.

As far as he went, Greg Falcon Runs could not unlock the trigger. He cussed and slammed the rifle down when his time was up.

Jodi exhaled sharply. Of all the men, Greg Falcon Runs she liked least of all.

Ernest was last. The old man first copied Greg's work and unlocked the sliding bolt action. He then spent the rest of his time figuring out the trigger. But as he was nearing what appeared to be the end, he pressed the wrong button, and suddenly every move cascaded backwards. By the end of his time, he was no closer to unlocking the rifle than anyone else. When he lost, the men gave out a communal groan of disgust.

Ernest said, You still have to pick one of us, Jodi.

The old man stopped Ernest, saying, Not everybody has tried the rifle yet.

Are you kidding? Greg asked, aghast. We all drew straws, old man!

Some of the men laughed. Others, catching on, grumbled.

I said, whoever in this room unlocks the rifle first. There are still three people in this room who haven't had their try at the rifle. That leaves me, the boy, and Jodi.

But the boy cannot win her hand in marriage. That would be unnatural, Ernest said.

You mean, like a bunch of men not staying home with their wives? Jodi said.

The men could not argue against her words, so they let Daniel try.

Don't worry, mom, Daniel said. I remember seeing Dad unlock the rifle all the time.

But as often as he had seen the rifle unlocked, Daniel could not get the trigger and the bolt action to work.

I'm sorry, Mom, Daniel said. Jodi patted her son on the head. Don't worry, she said. I'm proud of you for trying.

Jodi's fingers traced the outlines of the intricate detailing along the rifle's stock.

She will never unlock the rifle, Ernest said. She cooks and cleans for us. Her husband is the warrior. She doesn't know how to unlock the rifle.

Jodi exhaled, and her body crumpled. You're right, of course, she said. My husband is the warrior in the family. The clever one. The Devil of Tecumseh. As Jodi spoke, her fingers danced along the rifle's mechanical switches, moving quickly. She maneuvered each piece of the latticework. With each click, the men's hearts sank. In less than a minute, she'd unbolted the slide action.

The old man placed a box of bullets on the table. Jodi chose four and chambered them. While the men watched her regretfully, she continued unlocking the gun. Click after click, the rifle began to unlock.

The men shared nervous glances with each other. A few backed away from the table. Joe DesRosiers ran out of the back gate. As Jodi neared the trigger, three more suitors ran away.

Jodi said, The funny thing is, don't you think that a man as smart as he was, a man who was that good a soldier, don't you think he'd marry a woman just as smart and just as much the warrior? Like attracts like.

With the final click, the trigger guard popped away. Jodi raised the rifle sight to Ernest and Greg.

#

Oran woke, not sure if what he'd experienced was a dream or some version of reality untouchable by him. All around him, everyone was asleep, including the children. Red Solo cups lay tipped over next to some while coffee mugs lay beside others. A few of the kids used soldiers as pillows, but the soldiers didn't mind, they were sleeping too soundly. Twenty eight faces of contentment.

From the lake, he heard a sound. A fish catching bugs in the evening? And when did evening happen? The shadows were long in the twilight.

More noise. A rustling sound? Leaves, he heard. He was sure of that.

Oran stood groggily, then nearly tripped over his feet. He'd been really knocked out. He grabbed his lance and walked toward the sounds by the shore, shaking his head. Something, perhaps a pig, was pushing against the ground, probably rooting around the trees.

Oran pushed through the bushes.

It wasn't a pig rooting at the trees. It was Troy.

# CHAPTER ELEVEN

Literature was hard to come by after the wendigos appeared. The internet died, and with it went much of the world's knowledge. But some books remained. Oran's father had comic books, and Oran remembered reading some of his Swamp Thing comic books. Swamp Thing had a love/hate relationship on the reservations. Some liked how he was a sentient entity in tune with the natural world. Others hated him because liking him made them cliché Indians. Of course they would love the noble savage who protected the Earth. They hated it because of what it made them feel like.

Not Oran. He liked Swamp Thing. The girls were drawn very sexy, and Swamp Thing was a colossal monster, ugly and scarred. He was cool.

To Oran, Troy looked like the Swamp Thing. He was being dragged along the ground, so the metal plates hanging from his head were catching in the dirt, collecting black earth and pine. Vines and thorns trailed behind him like the train of a wedding dress.

Oran jumped out and grabbed Troy's hand. He pulled hard, but Oran was not an exceptionally strong man. After a few seconds, whatever it was that was pulling Troy won that battle. Troy's hand passed out of Oran's.

"Wake up!" Oran yelled. Troy didn't wake. He kept sliding along the ground toward the lakeshore.

A beaded tail was dragging him.

Oran ran back to where he'd been sleeping with his lance. To the soldiers he yelled, "Wake up! It's a trick!" But nobody woke. They rubbed their noses and shifted in their sleep. Oran, frantic, ran back into the woods after Troy.

Troy's sleeping body had gotten hung up by some rocks. This was the only reason he wasn't dead yet. His hips were lodged between two large white rocks. His body rocked back and forth.

The beaded tail wrapped around Troy's leg jerked hard, but Troy's body didn't budge. If it jerked much harder, Troy's hips would break. Oran ran alongside the tail and stabbed it with his lance.

"Abominations!" the Great Water Serpent hissed as it winced from the pain of Troy's attack. It drew back its long tail, curling into the water and alongside its giant head.

Oran noticed that he hadn't been able to pierce the serpent's tough scales. He'd just hit it hard enough to get the monster to let go.

The Great Water Serpent snapped its colorful tail at Oran, striking his chest and knocking him down to the ground.

He rolled with the lashing, but the tail thumped down on him twice. Both times he was able to dodge the tail, but he had to scramble back up and away from the lake shore. The Great Water Serpent took advantage of Oran's retreat and heaved Troy's body over the rocks by sliding him sideways. Troy was now being dragged through the grass at the water's edge. If he disappeared into the water, Troy was dead.

Oran refused to accept that fate. He searched the serpent's hide for any blemish, any spot of weakness. Nothing stood out. The creature's scales were perfectly interwoven. There was no answer.

Some people gave up. Some stopped fighting. They huddled in their homes and hoped the monsters would not see them. They believed that if they hid long enough and didn't fight, maybe they could outlast this nightmare that was the end of the world and the rise of the wendigos.

Oran had known many people who clung to this belief like it was the last ounce of medicine in existence. That was how they defined survival. They didn't look out for friends and neighbors. They didn't stick out their necks for anyone.

Well, for Oran survival was the fight. That's what he'd told his men in Alberta and Saskatchewan. When they were cold and starving and facing unbelievable odds against a horde of the undead, that's when he'd remind them that they were there to fight, and that in their fighting, they were making a choice to survive and not just letting the apocalypse carry them away.

Oran refused to give up the fight. Troy deserved better. The world deserved better. So he ran to the water's edge. The lake was the Great Water Serpent's territory. There, the monster would be king, fully uninhibited in its abilities. And if it got the best of him, would his wife and son know that their father had died protecting the people in his convoy? Yes, Oran decided. They would know. Maybe a messenger would make it to them, but even if not, they would know he died protecting the people he was with because that was him.

He leaped onto the Great Water Serpent's slippery back. His fingers dug into the monster's beaded folds.

The creature yelled expletives at him while swinging his neck from side to side. It was all Oran could do not to be thrown off.

He stabbed the creature with his lance, but the tip of his weapon just glanced off the beaded hide. With one last shake, soldier and weapon skipped across the waters and landed in the dirt.

Oran grabbed his lance and dug it into the sand. If he was going to go down this monster's gullet, so was the lance.

"Kiyaia!"

Oran allowed himself a half-second to figure out who was coming down to the lake. It sounded like a woman, but it wasn't like Ghost to cry out when she attacked. She was the silent killer.

What Oran saw completely shocked him, and already since he'd woken up, he'd seen Troy being dragged down to the lake looking like a bog monster, and he'd fought a beaded dragon.

The woman running down to the lake on her horse was glorious. A beautiful blond woman with sun-kissed skin, she was a woman at the pinnacle of human perfection, like a dancer or an Olympian.

And she wore clothes that barely qualified as swimwear.

"Ki-yai-yaia!" she shouted triumphantly. The thunder of hooves stormed past Oran, who was so dumb-struck, he could only watch her charge. She nocked an arrow against her long bow string, pulled back on the massive bow, and shot her arrow at the dragon. She did this all effortlessly while riding horseback.

The arrow soared like a meteorite blazing through the heavens, even if it wasn't on fire. It found its mark in a pattern of eight-sided sun dials. The arrow sunk deep into the Great Water Serpent's hide.

The monster screamed and shook its head.

No sooner had one arrow landed than she fired another off of her bowstring. This one landed in a pattern on the opposite side of the Great Water Serpent. The creature screamed furiously. It let go of Troy and slithered away.

The woman wasn't going to waste her shots. She and the horse jumped into the water. She yelled at the serpent as it swam away, slithering under the water.

"You come back and you will answer to me!" she shouted, holding the bow high in the air. Then she slipped a rope around Troy's feet. He was still asleep, his body up to his chest in the lake water. She pulled him back to dry land.

Oran didn't realize he was still stooped over, his lance gouged into the dirt and ready for a final attack from the Great Water Serpent.

"Are you alright?" the woman asked.

Oran didn't respond at first.

"Are you okay?" she asked again.

"Yes," he finally managed to say.

"Come with me, then. It's not safe this close to the water."

She finished dragging Troy out of the water, then jumped off her horse. She stooped down next to Troy and pinched his nose. After about fifteen seconds, Troy sat up, gasping.

"What the?" he said. He looked at the girl, then Oran, then did a double-take.

"Oran, I think something's happened to me. Do you see a blonde white girl next to me?"

"She saved you," Oran said. "She saved both of us."

"Come with me to the others. You are all in danger," she said.

She walked up the shoreline, the horse following behind her. Troy watched her go, then shot Oran a questioning look.

"I have no idea, either," Oran said. "She just appeared."

The woman woke Molotov the same way she did Troy. Molotov needed more time to wake than Troy. He stared at her in disbelief, then studied his empty cup of venom.

Troy laughed. "She's real."

"Are ye sure? I didn't even think real women could look like that. Where's your scars, lass?"

"I have no scars."

If the young woman noticed her effect on the soldiers, she didn't mention it. She laid down beside Teller and pinched his nose gently. His eyes fluttered open, and she let go.

"Hi," he said groggily.

"Hi," she smiled back. The wind blew her hair into his face. She pushed it away, then wiped some grime stuck to his forehead. Finished, she got to her feet and sidestepped over to Ghost.

Teller looked from her to the other soldiers, who were following her. Then Teller put his hands behind his head, doing his best impersonation of Luke Skywalker in the Empire Strikes Back, just after Leia kissed him in front of Han Solo.

"Calm down, lad," Molotov said. "She's waking everybody up the same way."

"I think I could be woken up like that every damn day of my life, and I'd never miss it."

Ghost, unlike the others, didn't have nostrils. She didn't have much of a face, either, but this didn't bother the young stranger. She lay down next to Ghost, but since Ghost always slept on her side, the young woman crawled up right next to her. She caressed Ghost's metal cheeks. Ghost's ocular implants clicked open. She stared at this new young woman with her same mask-like demeanor.

"Time to get up," the young woman said. "I hope you slept well."

"Better than I've ever slept in my life." The words rattled out of Ghost's mouth slowly and suspiciously. Her metal eyes searched for her fellow soldiers. "Who is this?"

The young blond woman hopped back to her feet. Now that all the soldiers were awake, she started waking the children.

"No!" several of the soldiers shouted all at once.

"But they need to wake quickly. You are all in danger."

Oran took his bison robe and wrapped it around the young woman's body. "They're just children," he said.

She puzzled over the bison skin wrapped around her chest. Her nose scrunched up. "I don't like this. It itches," she said, and pulled the hide off.

Oran was about to stop her, but Molotov stuck his arm out, "Brother, you don't stop a beautiful woman who wants to stay in her bikini. You just don't."

"What about the kids?" Teller asked. To the woman, he said, "Ma'am? I appreciate what you've done for us, but these kids ain't used to seeing somebody without five layers of clothes. You might scare them."

The young woman put her hand to her lips, saying "Oh, dear." Then she said, "But this is how all people look. They shouldn't be afraid of the human body."

"It ain't fear, girl. It's decency," Teller said, and he handed the hide back to her.

Despite the bewilderment on her face, she wrapped the hide around her body like a towel. She reached out to one of the children, ready to pinch the little boy's nose.

"Actually, why don't you let us wake them," Teller said. "We don't want to startle the kids after all they've been through."

"What happened?" Oran asked. "Did the kids drink the venom, too?"

"I'm sorry," Ghost interjected. "It's all my fault. I was supposed to stay up while you were down, Oran, but I just wanted to be back in my dreams, or wherever I was. So I took another drink after you fell asleep."

"No, that's not true," Troy said. "I woke, and you both were sleeping, and I decided to take another drink."

"Same here," Molotov said. "I couldn't resist."

"Did anyone not wake up and take another drink?" Oran asked.

"I had three," Teller said.

"Jesus," Molotov said. "We were so fockin' concerned with our wee piece of heaven we forgot about the bairns. They must've come down to here and seen us all snoozling. They would've seen the cups and figured out the drink put us asleep, then decided to do the same. What if we'd been killed? What kind of parental guardians are we?"

"We aren't," Troy said. "We're soldiers, not a bunch of fucking babysitters. I'm regretting ever suggesting we take them in."

"The Great Water Serpent tricked us," Oran said. "I cannot believe I allowed myself to be tricked like that. It pretended to make peace with us so that it could give us its venom. It knew we would fall asleep, and then it would come back to eat us all when there was nothing we could do to stop it."

"You stopped it," Teller said. "You woke up."

"I didn't stop it. She did." Oran gestured to the young woman walking lithely among the children like a farmer checking her crops, careful not to step on any of them.

"Why did you come here, and where are you from?" Ghost asked the woman.

She said, "My name is Kai, and my family comes from the top of the mountains. I came down off the mountains when I learned that Oran Old Chief was in your company. We have heard tales of him. Where I come from, we call him, 'Mountain King.'"

"Can you take us to your home, Kai?" Oran asked.

Kai's eyebrows pinched together in thought. "I don't think you can make it there. My home is much higher in the mountains than you can imagine. Besides, my people do not want to be involved. They prefer to watch, and that is where I disagree with them. We owe it to take part in this world, every one of us. So when I saw you here, Mountain King, I snuck away from home and rode down to fight with you."

"Thank you," Oran said. "You honor us with your service."

"Oran," Ghost said. The concern in her voice caught Oran's attention. She was staring off at the lake. "We've gotta run."

Oran did not need Ghost's supersensory vision to know what she saw. A mist had gathered around the far shores of the Flathead Lake. From behind the shores, large shapes appeared.

The bison-headed wendigos had caught up to them, tromping along the shores on two legs. They were like giant, decaying zombies with the head and hooves of bison and the claws and teeth of a flesh-eater.

"I will stay and fight by your side," Kai said with joyous rapture. She patted her steed on the rump, and the horse took off, returning to his stable in the mountains.

"We will run," Oran said.

"But, what about the wendigos?" Kai asked. She sounded disappointed. Clearly, her people were warriors.

"The children are our first concern. If you want to stay here and fight, you can, but we are escorting these children to my hometown so that they may be cared for." He remembered his dream, and he wondered if what he dreamed had really happened.

Teller and Molotov were already waking the children. Many got up groggily. Some were crying.

"I didn't know if you were ever going to wake up!" one of the kids wailed at Ghost. Her lips trembled when the child began to cry.

"I'm so sorry!" she said, hugging the girl.

Troy, too, held two crying children in his arms. He felt lowly and awful and was ashamed of his behavior.

Some of the younger kids had wet themselves in their deep sleep. As they awoke, they were sent to go to the bathroom and wash, then get in the RV. "We're leaving in a hurry," Teller told them, "So be quick."

Ghost and Oran watched the wendigos trudging closer to them. They passed around the curve of the lake, their bodies moving in and out of the mist. They had not yet detected the soldiers, but they did stop to study their tracks. One of the bison monsters kneeled down and put his fingers on the ground. He licked the dirt he pulled up, then sniffed about the edges of the lake.

"We've got to hurry," Oran said. The children were already loading into the RV, but they were moving slowly. They had been asleep for hours, and they were grumpy. Many of them wanted answers for what had happened or what they saw.

"Not now," the soldiers told them. "Maybe later."

From behind a tree, Oran watched the bison-headed wendigos. The leader was sniffing the air. Oran was sure the monster raising his snout was their leader. He remembered him from their fight in the streets. He had grown in the short time since he saw him last, and he was uglier, too. His body had decayed, too. Now his one arm was almost stripped of flesh. But still, he knew this was the same wendigo that they had found hunting the children.

The wendigo's head rose up, then he pointed at Oran. Oran felt like the monster had singled him out. There was no way that could be true, though. A bison, even an undead one, could not triangulate his position based on scent alone. And yet, the creature's bony claw was pointed right at Oran.

"Go. Now!" Oran shouted.

Ryder said, "But my message to my parents. I can't leave without stowing a message somewhere."

"If you are not quick, there'll be nothing to write about."

"Please. You promised."

Oran looked over his shoulder at the lake shore and the wendigos that were too close for his comfort.

"Let's hurry. Do you have pen or paper?"

"Back at the store."

To Teller, he said, "You all go ahead. We'll catch up."

Teller nodded and turned the engine over. A few days ago, he would have fought Oran on this point, but the stakes had changed for everyone. Twenty two children made the difference.

Kai climbed reluctantly into the Chevy pickup alongside Ghost. Oran and Ryder did not wait for the trucks to drive away. They were already running toward the store.

They ran down the dirt driveway, past a few cherry trees, and opened the store's front door.

Ryder went to the register and pulled out a pen and pad.

"Dad," Ryder scrawled onto his pad of paper, "Gone to Browning. Will wait for you there. – Ryder and Coby. Where do I put it?"

"Put it somewhere you know absolutely they will find it."

"The door?"

"You don't want it to fly off."

Ryder searched the room for the perfect place.

"Hurry," Oran said. "The wendigos were close."

"Think, think," Ryder said, squinting his eyes. He snapped his fingers. "Got it."

He ran over to the stacks where wine would be kept and placed the paper in a cubby. "Dad loves wine, and Mom loves him. Either he comes in here looking for the wine, or she looks at the wine cause she's thinking of Dad." He didn't say why his mother would be alone, but Oran could guess. It was the bad thought everyone had, the results of wendigos rampaging over the land.

"What if the building catches fire?" Ryder asked.

"You'll have to hope for the best."

Behind them, a shadow passed over the window. Neither saw it.

"We have to go now."

"I know," Ryder said.

They went to the front door, and Oran was about to open the door, when Ryder stopped him. "Wait." He ran back to the wine rack. He rolled up the paper and stuffed it into a wine bottle, then flipped the bottle around so that it faced the opposite direction of the other wine bottles.

A wendigo sniffed very loudly at the front door.

Oran and Ryder froze.

More shadows passed the windows. To their luck, the windows were too dirty to see in or out.

A gruff voice said, "Humans been here."

"Ours?" Another wendigo asked.

"I think so."

Oran waved Ryder away from the front door. They creeped slowly away from the front door, praying that none of the floorboards creaked.

"Fan out," the wendigo said to the rest of his party. "Search the area. This scent is very fresh. They must still be here."

Oran went first, opening the door just wide enough to peek out of. He didn't see any wendigos, so he knew they must be on the front side of the house. He stepped through. Ryder came behind him. As he exited the back door, the front door opened. Oran gasped, shutting the door as quickly as he could without making any sound.

The expected bellow alerting the other wendigos never came, so the pair slid along the edge of the one-story house, staying low next to an overgrown hedge. Above them, bison heads loomed over the roof, searching for them.

Oran whispered to Ryder, "If they see either one of us, just run away as fast as you can. I will draw them from you."

Oran ran from the cover of the house to the first tree and spun around the narrow trunk. He hoped the foliage would conceal him. The three heads of the wendigos moved from side to side along the edge of the house. One stopped and sniffed around the side of the house.

"Hurry," Oran mouthed to Ryder, not daring to make a sound.

Ryder's legs didn't want to obey him. He shook his head at Oran.

A giant arm reached around the house. Claws scratched at the hedges.

Oran silently mouthed with as much authority as he could muster, "NOW!" He struck his fist down in the air for more impact.

Claws stretched out from behind for the boy.

Ryder dashed at Oran's side just as claws snatched at him, catching nothing but air.

The wendigo made a strange, disappointed face. He walked around the house.

Like rabbits, Oran and Ryder bolted from tree to tree through the orchard. Oran would run first, and then Ryder second.

A giant crash caught their attention. Two of the wendigos smashed down on the roof of the store front, pulverizing the old house.

"They were here just now," the leader said. "Their smell is all over my nose. They can't be far. Search everywhere."

Ryder reacted painfully. His message was now buried in the debris.

"I'm sorry," Oran said.

Oran ducked behind another cherry tree just as a wendigo was coming around. It stood in the middle of the orchard, towering over the trees. Then the creature grabbed the short tree by the trunk and popped the top off as easily as it was breaking off a head of broccoli. A turkey cried out in alarm and started to run, but a giant hoof came down, squashing it.

Oran pointed to the lake front, away from the wendigos. Ryder nodded. Oran zigzagged to another tree. After a moment's pause to verify that the wendigos hadn't heard him, Ryder ran to the same tree.

CRUNCH

Another cherry tree was destroyed. This one was lifted completely out of the ground. It was much closer.

Oran started to run for the next tree when a load of branches fell on the ground in front of him. He ducked back to the tree he and Ryder were hiding under.

Heavy steps told him the wendigo had caught up to them, but had not seen them yet. Giant hooves stepped next to the small tree they were ducked underneath. Oran positioned his lance for attack.

Two giant, clawed hands reached down and gripped the cherry tree's trunk.

"Over here!" one of the other wendigos shouted. "I've found something."

The hands disappeared, and then the monster walked away.

"Go!" Oran whispered, and he and Ryder dashed down to the lake front while the wendigos' attention was diverted.

Far behind him, Oran heard another turkey gobble, then the turkey's call died abruptly. The wendigos yelled at each other.

From the lake front, Oran and Ryder moved into the northern orchard. By this route, they escaped unnoticed to the highway.

"That was intense," Ryder said when they were far enough away.

At the road, Oran kneeled down in the ditch. He grabbed a handful of dirt and slathered it on the kid's face.

"You need this," he said. "You are too white. They'll see you for sure along the highway."

Ryder didn't argue with the South Piegan.

"Now, keep the tree line between you and the highway. That will add an extra layer of camouflage. Follow me."

They made their way along the roadside, keeping low to the ground for about fifty yards. They moved slowly, careful not to make much noise. Once they came to a bend, Oran wandered out into the road. Ryder followed him, and they began to jog.

As they came around the bend, Oran found the rest of the caravan waiting along the side of the road. Kai stood on top of the Chevy, an arrow aimed at Ryder.

"He makes a lot of noise," she said grimly.

Ryder stood as if struck by lightning. His jaw dropped.

"She's naked," Ryder said.

"She is not naked," Oran corrected him. "She's just wearing very little clothes."

"The hide chafes. It distracts my aim," Kai said.

They climbed into the cars, Ryder suggesting he could ride with Kai to free up room in the RV. He got put in the RV with the other kids. Then they drove away before the wendigos could reach them.

# CHAPTER TWELVE

Highway 35 meandered along the edge of Flathead Lake. Every curve provided another breathtaking vista of the giant lake crowned by mountainous peaks. The smoke from the fires had dissipated. Winds were traveling down onto the lake and pushing smoke back over the Cabinet Mountains. A single small chimney stack billowed from the Mission Mountains. The caravan drove within a hundred yards of that forest fire, and then passed it completely.

"Seems a waste," Ghost said over the CB. "All that water to our right. It wouldn't be too much trouble to put out the fire."

"It takes a lot of coordination and work to handle a fire," Teller said into his CB. "Before I joined up, I was a Hot Shot. Put out fires all over the Rockies. It's a lot like you're chasing a ghost you can never catch. Or running from a ghost you can't hide from, depending on which side of the fire you're on. Trust me, you don't want any part of that. It's best to move on and let Mother Nature work its course, if there is a Mother Nature to do that sort of thing anymore."

They drove past orchards and through map dot towns with names like Bear Dance and Hunger Creek. Eventually they came to a small resort town curled around a narrow bay. Long ago, Bigfork was a tourist destination, with a downtown that conjured up fantasies of a mountain cabin wonderland. Angler fly shops, galleries, warm inns, and quaint cafes serving huckleberry pie lined the streets.

The old roofs had sunken in from years of neglect, and a mudslide had destroyed much of the town's charming buildings. The caravan trudged on. They were anxious to get to the turn toward Swan Lake. Although the road would take them deeper into the mountains than they'd ever been, it would also empty them out onto the Blackfeet Reservation, and Browning.

Then there were the Bent-nots. They lived outside Bigfork on the far side of town, at the end of a rural road.

"You're going to like Mr. Bent-not, Teller," Coby said. He sat in the passenger seat, and Ryder sat on the couch directly behind Teller. Coby said, "He's a real cool guy. Not only does he make his own gasoline, but he has solar powers and generators hooked up. He has full electric capability, and air conditioning."

"Air conditioning?" Teller had to admit, he was wowed. Outside of a few buildings in some of the major towns of the northwest, air conditioning was a luxury few could afford. Electricity was a luxury few could master.

"How did you two get all the way up here, by the way? It must be a day by foot."

"Well, only if you're old or slow," Ryder said matter-of-factly. "We run a lot. Most of the wendigos keep to the mountains, so we don't worry much about monsters on the road. We can get here in two hours from the northern orchards."

"Yeah. We come here when we get tired of eating cherries. Mrs. Bent-not makes a mean huckleberry pie."

"What's a huckleberry pie?" one of the kids sitting on the floor asked. They had been listening to Teller and the two older boys intently.

"Hasn't nobody baked you a huckleberry pie?" Coby asked.

"No."

"Well, then. We'll just have to change that when we get to the Bent-nots. Huckleberry pie is like the best thing you can eat. It's sugary sweet and fruity and delicious, kind of a cross between a blueberry and a blackberry. Not like eating turkey or elk or grass. It's not rough in your mouth or lean in your gut."

"It makes you warm all over," Ryder added.

"What's that?" One of the boys pointed to a strange pile-up in front of them. Teller, who'd been giving the children too much of his attention, almost didn't see in time that the two forward cars had come to a complete stop. A couple of the kids shrieked as he hit the brakes. Kids toppled over each other.

After the RV came to a complete stop, Teller quickly turned to the children and demanded they tell him if they weren't alright. They were. Over the CB, he heard Ghost say, "Oran, you better take a look at this."

#

Oran and Kai walked behind the forward car, keeping low and weapons drawn. Ghost met them there. She was already scanning the area around them for signs of attack. The street ahead had been torn out of the ground and razed down to the dirt. In place of the missing road sat a five foot tall debris pile ripped out of the resort town: boat hulls, shattered windows, storefront facades, and signposts.

The stripped skulls of horses, elk, and dogs had been placed around the pile. Human heads had been impaled on large sticks as a further warning.

Oran heard the door of the RV open and wailing.

Ryder and Coby ran toward the pile, tears in their eyes. Oran grabbed both boys and tossed them back behind the car. Teller came running after them. "I told them it wasn't safe to come out here."

The two boys fell down on their knees, crying and holding each other. The soldiers, assuming an ambush, checked line of sights from house to house, anticipating the attack.

"Keep down!" Oran hissed. The boys did their best to stay quiet, but the tears continued to run down their cheeks. "I'm sorry," Oran said, "But this is dangerous. Tell me as calmly as you can what is going on."

"I can answer that," Teller said. He pointed to the heads. "That's the Bent-Nots there. And that's Ryder and Coby's parents over there. They must've been trying to make their way down to the boys when the Wendys got them."

Oran's spirit sank. His heart broke for the boys. He kneeled down with them. Ryder grabbed onto Oran and hugged him as he cried deep from his belly.

Coby reached for Ghost, which startled her, but she quickly accepted his sorrow into her arms, even while continuing to keep a defensive position with an AR-15 drawn.

The boys wanted to collect the heads and bury them, but Recon Team wouldn't let them. It felt too much like a trap. They were more concerned with finding who had set up the roadblock. They spent the rest of the day and well into the night scouting the area. On the bridge-side of the roadblock, they discovered giant hoofprints.

"Like the devil himself is wandering Bigfork," Molotov said.

"The tracks are old," Teller said. "There's a lot of debris in them."

They concluded that this was a roadblock similar to the broken bridge in Sandyhill Point, meant to funnel travelers along the road rather than ambush them at this spot.

Not far from the roadblock was erected a beautiful mansion with condos and houses surrounding it. Somehow, the mansion had escaped the mudslides.

Before the end, the buildings on the mansion's grounds were meant to be a kind of subdivision for the super wealthy. Bronze statues of bears and elks posed majestically inside the gated community. But once the wendigos came, many people had used the small luxury subdivision as a compound to protect them. Their false security was never rewarded. The punched-in holes in the stone walls told the story of many raids. Human remains and random, bloody articles of clothing were strewn across the grass lawns and stone sidewalks.

The biggest appeal was the main building, which had a large arching tunnel for cars to drive through. The tunnel was a great escape from the sun's deadly rays, but also defensible with clear lines of sight on either end of the tunnel.

That night, the soldiers held a small ceremony for Coby and Ryder. They stood along the walls of the tunnel while Oran spoke.

"I've seen many men and women die," Oran said, "but this never gets easy. You are all young, and I want to tell you that death is something you won't have to deal with for a long time, but we know that isn't true. You have all experienced the death of family. Now Coby and Ryder have, too. Let us welcome them into our circle of friendship. May they find comfort in knowing that they are not alone with this burden."

The soldiers first, and then the children, each approached the two young men. They hugged and they cried, then they went back to the camp they had set up.

The children quietly ate their cherries and went to sleep. Ryder and Coby went out walking along the compound. The soldiers watched them from a distance. The boys needed to be alone together.

Kai volunteered to take first watch. She went to the front of the compound and found a high perch on top of a roof where she could see all the nearby roads as well as the bay.

The soldiers sat by an unused, makeshift firepit that had been built outside the tunnel. They were quiet and pensive as they watched the children sleep. The only sounds were the singing of owls and the breeze in the pines.

"We need to talk," Oran said. "I need you all to understand the situation, what we're up against."

"I don't think there's anything to talk about," Molotov said.

"Fine, but I need the words to come out of my mouth. With the roadblock, our only option is to cross the mountains here on foot and make our way to Highway 2, which winds through and out the mountains. To get there, we'll be hiking across the Swan and Flathead Mountain Ranges. These are some of the wildest, most untamed lands in Montana, and they are fully the territory belonging to the wendigos. We will have no aid. We will be far from any signs of civilization, so ther'll be no mansions or orchard stores to hole up in while the wendigos are about. We won't have cars, so we won't be able to outrun or outmaneuver them. I don't expect many, much less all of us to escape the mountains alive. The sun exposure alone may kill you. This is probably a suicide mission at best. At worst, we're marching twenty children to their deaths."

He looked the soldiers in the eye and begged them to back down. "You are a highly skilled Recon Team, and some of the best combat fighters I've served alongside. The war still needs you. If you go back to Spokane, you'll continue the fight against the wendigos."

Ghost stood. "Oran, I hear your concerns. I want to turn it on you, though. This is not the fight you signed up for. None of us would blame you for wanting to leave us and taking the straightest path home as fast as you can. But something's come over me since we picked up those kids. A week ago, I was just a soldier, but now…." She sighed, then said, "No, that's not it. I've been with Recon Team for almost a year now. Our relationships have been forged in steel and blood. There's nothing I won't do for my guys." Her voice cracked a little, despite the blank face she wore. "I've been a mother to them."

"Hoorah," the team echoed.

She put a hand on Troy's shoulder because he was closest to her. "We've been down in the shit many times, with the only reason we got out being that we had each other's backs."

She paused for a moment, then shook her head. "I'm having a hard time saying this. What I mean is, I was never the girl who wanted to have kids and raise a big family. But since joining, I've found my family. And now it feels like my family has grown by about twenty two kids, and that makes me happy in a way that I've never felt before. I know we could drop them and that would make a lot of sense. Like you said, we don't have a road, we won't have vehicles, we'll exposed, and it feels like we're pretty much asking for a suicide mission. No way we march through hell completely unharmed. I'm not naïve that way. But there's no place for the kids here in these mountains. We need to get them to Browning. To someplace safe."

Troy put his hand over Ghost's. "These kids have made me a better person than I was ever meant to be. I was just a piece of…man, you see how it is. Now I can't cuss cause I'm afraid one of the kids might hear me. I used to live day-to-day, not caring much whether I lived or died. That was the kind of attitude that won me this pretty metal war bonnet on my head. But these kids make me want to be something better, and like I told you when we began, in my People's way, you don't leave behind kids. If we die delivering them through the mountains, fine. But we won't fare any better here. The water's poisoned and there are Wendys behind us and Wendys ahead of us. I'm in."

Teller said, "We all feel the same way, Oran." To Recon Team, he added, "I don't have to ask. I know because I've grown close to you all through dozens of missions and ops. Y'all are the best people I know. No matter what these demon monsters throw at us, you've always behaved in the best interest of others." He held up his own metal fingers and said, "There's nothing any of us won't do for our team, or our country, or our people. If we get cut, we plug it up and keep firing. If we get blasted into a hundred pieces, we get hammered back together and we fight on. We were born to take the fight to the monsters. Huh. We were made to be the monsters the monsters hate. We recon the Wendys, the slayers come in and destroy them. If we get caught in between, it'd be up to us to find our way out. This new op with the kids ain't nothing different. Just another version of the fight. These kids we'll lay down for."

Oran approached the fire. His body blazed red and yellow in the firelight. He reached into his pocket and pulled out an old printed photo of a young woman and a young boy. His wife and son were laughing at some joke he'd told to get them to smile. Oran said, "This was taken years ago. I paid good money for this photo. This is my wife and my little boy. He's older now, but he's not yet a man. I want you to see them so that you know they are real. Also, so that you understand my words when I say I want to get home to my wife and my son more than anything else in the world. My dreams haunt me. I have terrible visions, and I do not know what I will find there when I get home. I don't know if they are still alive, or if they're in danger. Every day I am not there I risk their lives. But I do know this: if I abandon these children, I will not be able to go home to my wife and son and look them in the face and tell them what I have done. Jodi and Daniel would not want a husband and father who abandons children in the middle of hell. We'll deliver these kids to Browning, no matter the cost."

There was no rousing cheer or ovation from the soldiers. They knew what they were all volunteering for. The passes through the deepest, wildest mountain sections was to ask for death's calling card. So nobody cheered. They watched Oran solemnly, with resolution in their eyes and love in their hearts.

"Alright, then."

Oran walked away from the group. It would be good to give the team time to talk without him there, but he also needed to go pray and clean his lance. He was almost finished, and the full moon was high above the dark timberline, when Molotov appeared out of the trees.

"I hope I'm not disturbing you," he said.

"No. It's fine, Molotov. What's on your mind?"

"Did I ever tell you about Edinburgh? We didn't call them wendigos there, but they were undying monsters, just different. Am Fear Liath Mòr, we called them. The grey men from the Cairngorms. They were so tall, you couldn't see the top of them unless ye were about a kilometer away. They had human skulls, and they destroyed everything. I was a grunt in the Queen's service when the Five Ghouls tore through auld reekie. Nothing we did could stop those bastards. They ate everyone and kicked over everything. I lost mah da and maw. Mah brothers, mah friends. I had nothing. Then Uncle Sam came calling. The chance to kill monsters was all I wanted in the world, so I signed up, crossed the Atlantic, and came here to fight. It's what I'm good at, and God willing, I'll die with my flamethrower down the throat of one of them Wendys. I took an oath to fight the wendigos at all costs, and I'm wanting to take an oath now to protect these bairns, especially William and Wallace."

"I have heard the twins really like you."

"By God, I think I love them. I didn't think I would at first. I thought of it as just the right thing to do, but I've gone and kind of adopted them now, haven't I? If I die, make sure they have a good home, will ye?"

Oran nodded. Molotov breathed a sigh of relief.

"God, I'm glad I got that out. I felt like a stuffed up air beige, you know?"

"No, I do not."

"An air beige." To translate, he lifted one leg as if to fart, then he laughed.

"Molotov, you're named for your personality more than anything else, I think."

"Ha! Ya got that right, mukker!"

He sat back down. "As long as we're squaring away with each other, I've got a question for ya. That lady, Kai, what's she about? I was thinking she was some kind of mutant cause it ain't natural for anyone to go around in next to nothing with no skin cancer or anything. What do you make of her?"

"I can't be certain, but I have an idea."

"What is it?"

"Not yet. Soon, I will tell you, but I need more time with her."

"As a man with mah face lookin like an overripe avocado infected with herpes, I'll say we all need more time with somebody that close to human perfection."

# CHAPTER THIRTEEN

Finding more backpacks was easy in the resort town. Troy and Ghost came back with dozens of packs. Deciding what to carry was different. Of course, all the kids wanted to carry their own pack. The soldiers decided that was a bad idea, though. The kids would tire of their packs quickly, and then they would be forced to discard the packs in the wilderness, which would be the equivalent of leaving a bread crumb trail for the wendigos to find them. All of Recon Team, plus Oran, Kai, and the five kids over fifteen would carry packs. The packs would be full almost entirely of cherries and water, though other high-value items such as tarps and knives would be taken as well.

"It's gonna take more than cherries to get us across those mountains," Teller said to Oran when they had some privacy.

"You are all soldiers, are you not? Part of 'Recon Team?' I assume you had to live off the land for days at a time."

"Sure, seven of us, but not with twenty kids in tow. Kids eat a lot, if you haven't noticed."

"The Blackfeet have hunted here for hundreds of years. I am not worried. Monsters aren't the only creatures here. There are squirrels, turkeys, deer, and elk in these woods, and trout in the lakes and rivers. Each night, two of us will go out to hunt, and we will leave traps."

The first day on foot, they made good time. The children were excited and happy to camp under the stars. All morning they walked through rolling plains of high grass. When a wendigo appeared on the edge of the mountains south of them, the caravan squatted low in the grass so as not to be seen.

The wendigo was taller than the trees, and he had a gigantic crown of horns on his gray skull. The giant weaved back and forth at the edge of the mountain for over an hour before returning back to the Mission Mountains.

They stopped outside of the small town of Ferndale while Troy and Molotov cleared it. When the two gave the all clear, the soldiers scavenged the grocery store for supplies, but almost everything had been pillaged years ago. Only ash and leaves were left on the grocery store shelves. Along the side of a garage, somebody had long ago put up the black relief of a walking bear. For Oran, it was a subtle reminder that they were entering bear country, and that meant something totally different than it did when people still lived in Ferndale. There was no such thing as encroachment anymore. The land had returned to the animals. They were in the bear's territory, not the other way around, and they should be mindful of that.

Kai shot and killed a black-and-tan cat. Her arrow impaled the feline through the heart, killing it instantly. Oran showed the two children, Blood-Clot Boy and Old Woman, how to respectfully gut and clean the cat's body for consumption, thanking the cat for its nourishment. Neither of the kids felt any hesitation to eating the cat. They were hungry. Oran cooked the cat over a small fire, then sliced her meat into tiny pieces too small for a sample of sushi. The children ate their lunch eagerly, then the caravan set out again.

Something felt off to Oran. The town was like any other ghost town he'd visited. Vegetation overgrowth covering the buildings, small animals making nests in cars and on top of store fronts, and a weaker building caved in. But he couldn't shake the feeling they were all being watched.

He approached Ghost. "I have this weird feeling," he said. "Could you double check and look for people in these buildings?"

"You mean, can I see through walls? No, I can't."

"But does anything come up on your UV spectrum to imply that people live here?"

"I've had the same weird feeling, too," Teller said. He was walking a few feet in front of them.

A couple of the kids glanced back at Teller. "Never mind, Rambo. We're just talking. Eyes forward." The kid named Rambo gave Teller a look way more serious than his ten years could imply, then redirected his concentration on the path ahead. Oran wondered if the soldiers were rubbing off on the children as much as they were on the soldiers.

A soldier's lifestyle was so distant from "civilization," even what remained of it in Montana. Soldiers conducted acts that were inconceivable and immoral, things that would horrify their family members. Adjusting to a life outside of the horrors was hard enough. Children living alongside it, and even within that lifestyle felt unethical to Oran, but he knew the reality was he had no choice. The only way to get these kids someplace safe was to run through this hellish landscape with the soldiers. As a result of that, Recon Team would soften; the children would harden.

Another fear drifted into his head: what kind of person (or monster) would he be when he returned to his son? Would he be able to adjust back to that "civilized" life?

Ghost motioned, so Oran followed her and Teller off the path and out of earshot of the children.

Ghost said, "I don't see anything on the UV spectrum. Little splotches here and there, but that could be any animal." She added, "But I get you. I feel like we're being watched."

The soldiers quickened the pace, but that paranoid sensation stayed with them until they left the town. At only one point did Oran think he saw something, but he didn't want to stop the caravan. They kept marching through town and on toward the northern end of the Swan Mountain Range.

At the base of the mountains, the caravan stopped. The soldiers and Kai stood in front of the children. They had them form into lines behind one of the teens. Oran addressed the children, saying, "We are about to enter the most dangerous path of our journey. It is not something six soldiers alone can overcome. This is a task that requires twenty eight soldiers."

The younger children began grinning once they realized what this meant. Oran summoned from within him the sincere power he'd earned from years of fighting at the front and said, "With the full powers invested in me as General of the Timber Armies, I authorize the indoctrination of the twenty two brave soldiers I see before me. Do I have a second?"

"Hoorah!" The other soldiers yelled. Their chorus was loud and powerful enough to make half the kids jump. These kids had been living with the soldiers for so long and gotten so comfortable with them, they'd almost forgotten they were soldiers.

"Congratulations, each and every one of you. You are now soldiers of the Timber Army, Crazy Dog Company, rank Private. You will be expected to conduct yourself in the manner according the greatest fighting machine in the world. That means respect and loyalty. You will obey your superiors.

"Men and women of Crazy Dog Company, I have a difficult assignment for you, but one that I believe together we can overcome. We must cross the Eastern Rocky Mountains. This encompasses the Swan, Flathead, Lewis, and Sawtooth Mountain Ranges. This is something we can all survive if you as soldiers follow three simple rules. First, if you see anything unsafe, or a situation where you may be in danger, say something, immediately. Second, chain of command. This is sacred. The teenagers standing at the front of the line are Privates First Class. You communicate to them, and they communicate to us. Third, you do not realize it, but we have been slowly teaching you in the ways of the mountain warrior, and a mountain warrior is first and foremost a quiet warrior. He can count coupe on many enemies and take their power away just by touching them. For the past week, you have been trained in the quiet game. From this point forward, we are full 24-7 in the quiet game. That means no more than a whisper from you. The monsters in these mountains can hear the wings of a bumblebee from a mile away, and they will attack if they hear twenty eight people talking and making loud noises as they traipse through the forests. So right now, I order you to yell as loud as you can. Get it out now, because until we are arrive into the plains, you must remain quiet at all costs."

The children glanced around at each other like they didn't know what to do. Was Oran really serious?

Troy was the first to begin howling. The children watched timidly. Oran joined Troy, and then the other soldiers began howling, too. Soon after, everybody was howling. Some of the kids started yipping like pups. Others laughed with pure joy at hearing everyone howl.

Oran held his left fist high in the air. The soldiers stopped howling and followed suit. At first, the children didn't understand. This was their first lesson in how to communicate. The teens caught on, lifting their fists, and soon after, the children stopped howling. They realized, though, that being quiet wasn't the only expectation. They raised their fists, too.

Oran spent the rest of the morning showing the children how to communicate with signals. He showed them how to count to ten, then showed them Hurry Up, Crouch Down, Move Right, Move Left, Stop. Within thirty minutes, Teller was leading the children in soundless drills, moving in different direction, crouching, crawling, and hiding. Always, they were pressured to move more quietly and without a sound.

Eventually, a child would start talking. If this was a regular army with adults, Oran would have chewed them up for disobeying an order. He knew he could not do that with children. So instead, he raised his fist for quiet and waited. Recon Team would stop the drill and raise their fists, and so on until the child realized what they were doing and self-corrected.

After the drills, he fed the children cherries. Each child received three cherries. With drills and lunch complete, Oran surveyed Crazy Dog Company. He grinned broadly and held his arms out so that they could see his happiness with them, but he did not speak a word. Then he entered the Swan Mountains. Quietly, the children followed him.

# CHAPTER FOURTEEN

Oran found a trail leading up the mountainside. The trail weaved under a sparse forest of spruce and fir trees. Pine needles crunched underfoot. As they gained elevation, the world changed around them. The wind chilled them in the summer heat. The fires hadn't reached the Swans yet. The rocks grew sharper and harsher. Spikes of granite jutted along the trail. As they climbed, the trail increased in difficulty. At times, it was like stair-stepping from one jagged rock to another. The soldiers would have to stop and help lift the younger children from one step to another.

Oran took them to a tree line between Big Hawk and Three Eagles Mountains. The sun rotated in the sky above them and began to set quickly, but they had not yet gained the mountains. Oran took them off the trail. He found a rocky gorge with lots of moss-covered fallen trees. There they made camp for the night. The children were exhausted. They had climbed nearly two thousand feet over five miles. They mewled and whined as little as possible. The soldiers gave them gentle reminders of the need for quiet. They did not like that they only had three cherries each to eat at dinner. Oran didn't need the alarmed glances of the soldiers and Kai to remind him how dire their food supply was.

Kai whispered to the soldiers, "There are lakes throughout this area. The fish there should not be poisonous."

"But how do we catch them?" Molotov asked. "We ain't got any fishing rods."

"We do what we always do, Molotov. We improvise, and when that doesn't work, we make it work," Teller said.

"Hoorah," Troy said.

"Hoorah? Don't hoorah that," Molotov hissed. "It makes no fockin' sense."

"We'll figure something out," Oran said. "Right now, I need eyes to the east and the west."

Ghost and Troy volunteered to take point lookouts until the early morning. After the backpacks were hoisted high into the tree branches where bears couldn't get to them, the others crawled under the tarps with the children. Each tarp had many punctures to allowing for breathing and humidity to escape. Small poles were erected to keep the tarps off the children, and rocks were placed on the edges to keep the tarps from blowing away. Ghost and Troy spread leaves over the tarps to provide even further camouflage.

Oran had trouble sleeping. Owls kept him up at night, hooting at mice. (He hoped that the traps they set would catch some of the mice, or even better, squirrels.) But owls were a harbinger of evil. He'd heard a few when they entered the tough wilderness, but now they were everywhere, flapping their wings and watching him with their strange eyes.

Somewhere out there were the monsters. He could feel their presence. How close they were, he did not know, but every once in a while he would hear the baleful roar of a wendigo. Sometimes the sound was far off. Sometimes it was much closer.

There was no mistaking a wendigo's roar. It wasn't like a grizzly or a mountain lion. Mountain lions sound like screaming women. Bears sound low and guttural. Wendigos sound like no natural born animal. Their sound is said to remind people of a hundred elephants dying all at once. The grim reaper's vengeance song. A percussion-and-brass band made entirely of ghosts. That was what the wendigo sounded like. Oran thanked Natosi for placing sleep in the children's eyes. He wished that sleep would come to him, too. And then it did.

#

Oran, it is time, his father said.

Oran was a boy not yet a man. His face and chest were painted. He had with him a blanket his mother made for him, and his lance.

His father watched him running, his eyes a fountain of kindness.

Did you remember your parfleche?

Yes, Dad. Oran showed his father the parfleche, which hung from his back beneath the blanket.

Come inside, then. It is time to dance.

Oran was excited, even though he knew this was just a dream. Or maybe more accurately, it was a dream memory. He sometimes had these dreams, which reminded him of things that happened to him when he was younger.

His father put both hands on his shoulders and led him into the large tipi. There, other boys were already gathered inside.

Who is this boy? the old man asked from the far side of the large tipi.

This is my son, Oran Old Chief.

And who sponsors him?

His father, Lochlan Old Chief.

The old man nodded, almost feverishly, and considered these words as if he was Anubis, and the weight of a man's soul depended on it.

While the old man muttered to himself, Oran took in the tipi. He'd participated in many aspects of the Sun Dance, but never this. Even though he knew what to expect, he was still scared.

About thirty people stood in the tipi. It was so hot, it was practically a sweat lodge. A drum and a drummer sat at one side, across from Oran. Already, two boys stood patiently waiting, their pierced flesh tied to the main lodge pole like some sick, perverted version of tether ball. Hanging from the top of the lodge pole was a holy medicine bundle, and four lines. Three were already tethered to nails driven in the boys' bodies. One line was free.

Step forward, boy, the old man said, and stood. As Oran approached, the old man pulled a stone dagger from his sheath. He cut the boy's chest.

Oran flinched. The pain was not as bad as he expected, more like when he was a young teen and his cousin decided to pierce Oran's ears. He'd gotten an infection later that week, and he nearly lost his ears. He hoped this didn't end up as badly.

The old man prayed over Oran and gave supplications to Natosi, begging him to accept the boy and give them back a man.

Oran, the old man said, you have been purified in the sweat lodge, and you have fasted this week. Now, the end of your spiritual journey is near. Remember that the journey of the Blackfeet endures throughout his life, and is not just a moment as he awaits adulthood. Your vision quest, you will see it tonight. This is the vision that will guide you into adulthood as a warrior or a healer.

The old man took a wooden nail and pierced it through Oran's flesh. Then he did the same again to the other side of his chest. After that, Oran's father brought the tethers that were hanging from the lodge pole. The ropes were tied to the wooden nails in Oran's skin.

The old man shuffled his feet as he exited the dance circle, saying, Let the dance begin!

The drum started off slow, and a high-pitched chorus of Blackfeet joined in. As the drum pounded, Oran and the three others began to sway to the rhythm. After gently rocking back and forth, testing the rope and its tether, they began to fan out, dancing around the lodge pole. This was the start of a very long and enduring dance. It went on for hours. The boys dipped, jumped, and at times hung against the rope, letting the tether nail hold them up. While the boys danced, their sponsors walked around the outer edge of the circle of singers. Lochlan gave his son encouragement to stay strong, not fall to the ground, and really earn his vision quest. Oran supposed the other boys' fathers were saying something similar, but he was in too much pain to really hear them.

The longer he danced, the more tired he became. It was hot inside the tipi, and he began to sweat. His vision got blurry, but still he danced on. The beat of the drum was everything. It was inside him, pushing him on, to keep dancing.

He lost his footing and slipped, but then recovered. The pain in his chest kept him from completely falling. The pain throbbed violently to the drum beat. But still he danced on.

At one point he woke from a blank stupor and noticed that the other three ropes ended in blood. Little scraps of bloody flesh lay at the base of the pole. He was the only dancer left. Still, the men sang, and the beat went on, rising and lowering like birds singing in the morning.

Finally, the boy saw something. Oran had his vision. The beating of the drum stopped. All the men were dead. They were covered in their own blood. The boy walked among the dead, neither scared nor angered. He shook a few of the men to make sure they were dead. They did not move.

Then the drum began to beat again. The drums were everything. All consuming. But it wasn't the drum in the tipi that was being played, so he walked outside. There, he discovered many wendigo dancing. The drums were the feet of the giants stomping on the ground. They sang in that discordant way the undead sang.

The wendigos frightened the boy. He had never seen one before. Now there were twenty. Or perhaps thirty. He couldn't be sure.

The ground shook as they danced. The beat was everything.

And then he woke from his vision. Lochlan was there, pouring water into his mouth. Oran didn't realize how dry his throat was until he drank. He nearly spit out the water because it was so hard on his esophagus.

Later, after he had rested, he told his father about his vision. His father was disturbed by what Oran saw. The other boys had seen mountains and buffalo and thunderbirds. Why was Oran seeing wendigos?

He took his son to the Tribal elders to discuss his vision. The boy stood there in the old brick building, feeling the pain in his chest where the wooden nails had been yanked out during the Sun Dance.

Once he told them his vision, they, too, were perturbed.

This is the problem with the world today. Our children only like violence, one elder said. Violence guides them through life. Not family or the tribe. Violence.

Hold on, Ernest, another elder said. I would like to offer a different opinion. Some men are healers, and some are warriors. But Oran, (he now was speaking directly to the boy) most men are a little both. Some heal through the act of war, and some wage war through the act of healing. An artist paints a vivid picture so beautiful that it brings both joy and sadness to the people. He is both warrior and healer, and neither. I think your vision of the demon dance means something significant. I have a task for you.

That was how the fifteen year old boy came to be wandering the foothills before the Sawtooth Mountains. He was alone except for his lance and a blanket. The lance in his hand felt warm. His face was flush. He had been praying all morning for the Sun to guide him. Now the sun was dipping into the Sawtooth Mountains.

He sat in the middle of a stone medicine wheel. The sun blazed hot, and a chinook wind blew off the mountains.

He held up his hand to shield his eyes from the sunlight streaming all around him. From out of the sunlight, a shape appeared. Large and skeletal, with antlers like bony vipers slithering to the sky.

The boy waited patiently. He needed the monster to come close.

The boy slumped backward, as if stricken by disease or starvation. He did this on purpose, to draw the wendigo near.

The giant raced to the dying boy, weaving back and forth across the hills.

The boy tightened his grip on the lance. He felt the wind blowing the little hawk feather in his hair. The cool ground softly embraced him. He closed his eyes and felt the warm sun on his eyelids, red and pure.

He waited.

Set the trap.

Spring the trap.

The Sun blinked and vanished. Everything was pitch black. Not even the stars winked in the darkness.

Oran could smell the wendigo's foul breath and hear its hooves pounding on the caliche, but he could not see him. By the sound of the creature's hoof-falls, it was moving around the Medicine Wheel but not crossing the circle. Could it not see him, too? The wendigo sucked in air, sniffing loudly for the boy. Oran squatted in a crouch holding his lance ready to spring from the ground and attack. His bare feet moved silently as his body followed the sound of air being sucked in and out of the monster's nostrils. Suddenly, first light appeared from the sun. Immediately, the wendigo swung a giant arm at the boy, expecting him to be standing. The force of air from the swinging arm almost knocked Oran off his feet. With a cry, Oran sprang in the air plunging his lance with all his might deep into the monster's soft heart. The monster flopped down in the middle of the medicine wheel, but the boy warrior refused to let go of his lance. The creature fell dead, and Oran, still gripping his lance, landed on top of the monster's bony ribs. The sun burst forth around him in all its glory. Oran withdrew the lance and raised it to the sun in salute and cried out his love for land and sky while wendigo blood streamed down the lance covering his arm.

Wham!

Wham!

Wham!

#

The sound whamming in his head was like a door slamming, or a gun cracking through the forest. The sound woke Oran in the middle of the night. His watch told him it was 3 am. His eyes told him a wendigo was out there. Giant eyes blazed blue in the night, staring at him.

He reached for his lance. It felt warm to his touch.

He would need the monster closer. Set the trap, spring the trap.

A hand pressed his shoulder. It belonged to Blood Clot Boy. His fingers clawed into Oran's shoulder. The boy watched the wendigo, terrified, but he did not move. Little eyes in the dark told Oran all the other children were awake, too. Good soldiers, they did not move or scream. They remained hidden and watched.

The blue orbs intensified.

Oran realized there was no sound in the forest. No owls, no birds, no bugs of any kind. And of course the children were all perfectly quiet, as he trained them to be. Oran was shocked. He'd never heard the mountains so still, and that scared him.

From too close, a tree trunk lifted its roots. It crashed down into the ground with the impact of a large bomb or small missile. The earth shook. What Oran thought was a tree trunk was really the leg of a wendigo. The large skeletal hoof landed on the edge of the tarp, not five feet from Oran. The hoof sunk deep into the soft earth.

A boy whimpered.

Oran glanced over at him. His first instinct was to shush the boy. Tears streamed down the child's face as he tried not to cry out. The boy kicked his leg. Oran's eyes followed the boy's leg up to his torso and to where his arm should be. It ended under the hoof of the colossal wendigo.

Oran's heart broke for the brave boy. He knew instantly that the boy's arm had been crushed, yet the boy did not cry. He endured the pain and agony soundlessly so that the others could live.

Above him, the wendigo stood still as the mountains. Bony arms hung like upside down ponderosas in the sky. Minutes that felt like hours passed. Still, the boy suffered in silence.

The boy was on the verge of crying, though. He was taking deep breaths to control the pain.

This was only going to get worse if Oran did not do something. He reached for his lance. Slowly, he shifted to his belly and crawled to the edge of the tarp. Suddenly, a large tree branch, perhaps even a dead tree by the sound of it, crashed in the dark.

The giant moved. The tarp flew away from them, like bat wings. It was stuck in the wendigo's hoof. All around them, two giant legs moved. The ground thundered as a hoof stepped over the small crowd of children and soldiers and slammed into the ground.

Paralyzed with fear, the children did not move. They did not scream, either. They had been trained not to. Two more giants walked over them, shaking the ground. A hand touched Oran's shoulder. It was one of the Flathead twins, William. Wallace touched William's shoulder, and a girl touched his shoulder, and so on. The line of arms was like an arrow pointing back to the boy with the crushed arm. Oran nodded.

The wendigos pursued the sound of the fallen tree, drawing farther and farther into the mountains. Still, Oran waited until the trees stopped swaying before he moved. Then he was like lightning to the boy with the crushed arm. His name had been Brad Miller, but they had renamed him Private Revere because he was supposed to be a good horseback rider.

Although all the children wanted to cry or talk about what had just happened, Oran raised his fist in the air. The little soldiers quietened.

Private Revere gulped air. He was covered in sweat.

"Was I good?" He managed to whisper between gulps.

Oran could cry. "You've been the best," he whispered back while wiping away the boy's tears. He kissed Private Revere on the forehead. While he did, Troy came behind the boy and pushed an ancient morphine auto injector in his arm. The poor kid was in so much pain, he didn't notice the prick of the needle. Within moments, Private Revere's eyes rolled back and he fell asleep.

"Count his breaths," Oran said as quietly as possible. "If he breathes less than 10 times in a minute, hit him with the Narcan."

Oran tied a tourniquet around Revere's arm. He tied it as tightly as he could, leaving just a finger's width between the wrapping and the boy's skin. Then he checked the arm. His heart filled with pain as his fingers counted the breaks. It was like a bag of flesh filled with pebbles.

"There's no way this is going to be fixed. We risk more injury leaving his arm alone. We have to cut it off."

To Ghost and Teller, he whispered, "Take the children ahead to the pass. We will catch up." The soldiers nodded grimly, then, using hand signals, commanded the rest of Crazy Dog Company to follow them.

When they were alone, Oran pulled his hunting knife. Molotov lit the flamethrower.

# CHAPTER FIFTEEN

Oran and Troy caught up with the rest of the group. The boy, still passed out, was being carried on an impromptu travois Oran and Troy made from birch. A bloody stump ended where Private Revere's arm should be.

As the day pushed out, children would come over just to touch the boy on the shoulder. They felt badly for him because he was a living example of the worst that could happen to them. Some of the kids began signing to each other the question, *would they scream?*

They hoped to never find out.

By noon they had crossed the Swan's ridge line. It was all rocky bluffs and peaks and especially difficult to cross with a travois.

Oran didn't like being exposed that long. As they reached the sparse bluffs of gray and black rock, the clouds parted. The sun glared down on them harshly. Oran had made sure that everybody was covered head to toe in spare clothes from soldier's packs. Even if it was just a bandana or a sock, the soldiers found a way to improvise it into a head garment.

The children did their best to stay low and move quietly, but they weren't soldiers trained in camouflage and stealth like Recon Team. Ghost kept a watchful eye on the tree line, though. At the first sign of trouble, they would create a defensible position and gladly die fighting for the children.

As luck would have it, a wendigo appeared on the near-side tree line. The children bunched together in a circle, and the soldiers took positions around the children. They were a herd of elephants or water buffalo circling to protect the young. Oran flexed his fingers around the lance's grip and prepared to die. If it charged, they had little in the way to defend themselves. He knew it'd be brute against brute and strength against strength, with the wendigos having the obvious advantage. But Oran had one thing they did not: the will to defend the children with his last breath.

Kai stood to Oran's right, her bow drawn and an arrow ready to loosen on the wendigo. Oran felt strengthened by her presence. There was a steeliness to her he could not explain.

At first, the kids were uncomfortable around Kai. They were accustomed to adults wearing leggings under pants, and a jacket over a shirt at all times, and usually some kind of head gear, whether it was something as simple as a cap or as extravagant as a head wrap under a helmet. The boys, not used to seeing cleavage, would sneak glances at her. That wore off quickly, though, as everyone got used to her presence.

Perhaps it was the way she treated her clothing, as if it was the most natural thing in the world to be wearing so little clothes while most people walked around hiding from the sun, covered in melanoma scars. Perhaps it was her confidence. Kai was more sure of herself and her effect on the world than anyone else, soldier or child. To her, it was obvious they would leave the mountains unscathed. Whether it was her natural demeanor or her confidence, the rest of the group accepted her as one of their own. Oran was surprised at how accustomed to her they could become.

To his right stood Teller. He knew that Teller, like him, would die before he allowed harm to befall any of the children. He was armed with two small Browning Hi-Powers and more grit than all of Texas could muster.

The wendigo shook its mountain goat skull at them, as if deciding if they were worth pursuing. This one was nowhere near as tall as the behemoths they'd encountered last night. It was as tall as the Spokane wendigo. An eagle flying overhead close by caught the monster's attention. It reached up and nearly plucked the eagle out of the sky, but the eagle dove down the mountainside. The giant goat-skulled monster chased after it.

Quickly, the children were ushered over the bluffs and back into the forest below. Once inside the trees, Kai led them to an opening with a small lake. The spring-fed lake lay like a bowl on the edge of the mountainside. The lake was full of cutthroat trout.

The children were allowed to roam around the lake's edge while the soldiers figured out the quickest way to catch the fish. Molotov found an old broken fishing rod. Troy, an avid fisherman, fixed the rod. He put an old spinner and weight on the line and dropped it in the lake. In no time, he was pulling trout.

Farther down the shoreline, Molotov found a spot to teach hand-to-hand combat to the Flathead twins, William and Wallace. He'd been giving them a good army education, teaching them how to fight every day. The boys took to the training and were eager for the opportunity. It was a way for them to get out pent-up energy from all the time having to stay quiet. Once they'd learned basic hand-to-hand, he worked in knife-fighting techniques. The boys began carrying sticks in lieu of actual knives for sparring.

Teller and Kai consoled Private Revere, who'd woken from his stupor to the tragic shock of losing his arm. The boy wailed, and Teller and Kai knew better than to tell him he had to be quiet. Teller pushed the boy's face into his chest to muffle the sound as much as he could. The boy cried and cried.

Private Revere's wailing got the attention of the children. They then came over to console him. They brought him flowers they'd picked and made a stick figure of him minus one arm. Private Revere kicked the flowers away angrily.

This made the children sad, so Oran explained to them that Private Revere was not mad at them but mad at the world, and he had a right to be. He told them to give the boy time and space. The children did, retreating to the lake.

When the pain began to rise back up for the little soldier, Molotov gave him another shot of morphine. Within minutes, the boy was asleep again. Teller stayed with him, shushing him quietly while he pushed the boy's hair around.

"Nothing like this should happen to a ten year old kid," he whispered. "He should be able to grow up playing football with his old man. Instead, he's marching around this No Man's Land losing his arm to monsters that shouldn't ever have been here. I mean, why are they here?"

"To punish humans," Kai whispered. "Humans became like wendigos, devouring everything. They drained the rivers of water, cannibalized the land for their raw materials, and began killing each other senselessly. So the wendigos were sent to show humans what real carnage looked like. When the countries of the world discovered they could not prevent this punishment, that they could not out-wendigo the wendigo, the world evolved. Humans became more focused. Instead of fighting with each other, they fought alongside each other against a common enemy. And instead of building walls, they fixed the bridges the monsters tore down. They reduced what they took from the ground, and the rivers returned. The world is a horrible, terrible place, but it's better balanced than any other time in the history of humankind. One day, these monsters will be killed off. If we strike a balance."

Kai soothed the boy's cheek. "This boy will tell many people about striking the balance, and they will believe him."

"I don't know. His greatest asset is that he is quiet when it counts."

"That will be his name," Oran whispered. "Quiet Child."

"That's a good name," Teller said. He coughed up the last word he said, "name," because a spear burst through his abdomen, missing Quiet Child by less than an inch.

# CHAPTER SIXTEEN

All he knew was hunger. His past was an endless frustration of missed opportunities. His present was the pursuit of a kill that would satiate his needs temporarily at best. His future he knew would be a long uphill road through hell, always searching for an end to the hunger.

The pit in his stomach would lead him to his prey. It always served him, just as it pushed him forward. Hunger brought him into the paths of others like him. Tall and bison-headed creatures with the same ravenous desires staining their souls. This was no small concession, grouping with other wendigos. As a general truth, wendigos were wary of others like themselves. Sometimes the hunger demanded a sacrifice. Something to assuage the eternal ache. There was always the chance an older and stronger wendigo would turn on a lesser monster and eat him. This was why they only packed together when they were young and about the same size and strength.

Or, as in Anuk's case, not so young.

He could remember the last three years, and the driving hunger. His first memories were as a darkness in the mud. He remembered pushing through mud and feeling cold moonlight on his head as he broke through the earth. He was small, not even four feet tall when he erupted from the ground like a broken cyst. His body ached. The very air hurt him. Above all that pain was the throbbing need surging through his body, a need he knew but did not understand because he was too young. He only understood it when he smelled them. People. The smell was the most beautiful thing in a world of pain and misery.

Their indescribable scent led him to a nearby cabin, not 50 yards from his birthplace. To him it was not a cabin. He had no inkling of what a cabin was. To him, it was an object with people scent on it. Faint people scent, true, but he was young and his nose was very powerful.

He made a terrifying sight shuffling onto the porch and standing in the moon beams, his hands dragging on the ground behind him. Mud dripped from his body onto the wooden floorboards beneath him. He sniffed at the door, inhaling deeply at the spot where the most human scent wafted through. It was a tiny gap between the door and its frame, a little lower than the keyhole. The scent was coming from *inside* the object.

He felt the push of the bullet before he heard the sound, and then he was falling backwards off the porch. He screamed. The pain was a dull flash against his shoulder. He was new to this kind of pain. As he rolled off the porch and ran around the cabin, though, he knew this was a lesser pain. Instinct told him this new pain came with the pursuit and the hunt. It would not kill him, not like ignoring the hunger. So he climbed on top of the house, hunting for another way in. He found a small opening and climbed down the hole and into the cabin. Anuk had to wiggle to force his small frame down the hole, but he managed because the hunger commanded him, and the first rule of life was to always obey the hunger.

His hand dangled down into the open air of the fireplace. As he searched for a grip, he could smell them in the room below. He recognized a different smell, too. Fear. This was the smell of prey. In this way, he learned the second rule of life: things that fear you are things that can be killed.

He wondered what they thought of his bony hand flapping in their fireplace. Would they shoot it? Would they try some other way to keep him out?

They shot it. His hand blew backwards, and fresh stinging blindsided him. He pulled back a stump where no hand existed anymore. Blood dribbled from his wound. Ugly, disgusting blood. His blood.

Anuk learned the third lesson of life: be careful of what you hunt.

He pulled back up into the fireplace hole and stayed there, thinking how best to get into the cabin. He climbed back out the chimney and dropped clumsily to the ground. He tapped his bloody stump against the wall. Nothing. He found a different piece of wall, a thinner piece. He tapped it. It sounded breakable. Using his stump as a club, he bashed into the window.

Another loud sound blasted through the window. This time it missed him. He was learning about guns.

He tried the other windows. Each window he broke, another gun blast burst through the window, shattering the pane completely. Its sound ricocheted off the mountains. But the last window, there was no gun blast, only a clicking sound. So Anuk jumped into the house. He did not know what a living room was, or furniture, but he saw the family of four and knew they were prey. He slammed the object that reeked of gunpowder. Then he bit the tallest member of the family. The first taste of human flesh was divine, as sacred as the first drink of mother's milk. Anuk laughed. The prey screamed. He killed them all. And when his body was full of their bodies, he slept. When he woke, covered in their blood, he was still hungry, though not as hungry as before. He was also too tall to fit through their door without ducking. He shoved the front door off its hinges. His heavy hooves clopped on the porch. His face itched and began to peel, so he dug at it with his remaining hand until the itching went away. When he finished, a glint of his cheekbone was sticking through his flesh.

For three years he roamed the wild searching for this greatest of treats. He'd consumed bears and wolves and eagles, but nothing compared to the taste of young humans. And as he hunted the humans, he learned the land, and he learned their tricks. He learned to sneak up on them and to overwhelm them. He learned to pick them off if possible. He learned that most of their weapons had no effect on him.

He had accumulated a team of other wendigos, too. All bison. They were close enough to his size, a little smaller and not as strong. When the pack wasn't sleeping in the day, they were hunting humans. The finding of Twenty Children in between the mountains was their greatest discovery. Twenty Children was a small human town nestled between the Baby Head Mountains and the Broken Back Peaks.

"Meat," Apraxis said while they were running over the Broken Backs. He picked up the scent first.

"Human meat," Jatunei said.

They both looked to Anuk, who took a deep whiff of the wind. He smelled the same tender meat he'd enjoyed on his first night of life. There were other, older meats in the air, but nothing like the flesh of the young. Anuk picked at his head, which was mostly cleaned of his flesh. He nodded agreement.

"Tender meat. Dinner is waiting," he said. The ten wendigos ran to the town. On the first night, they devoured old people, which did almost nothing to slacken their hunger.

Night after night, they returned to Twenty Children, which they named for the twenty children they killed and devoured. They found them like little ticks hiding on a dog's back. The only way to get them was to search every inch of the town. The children would hide under rocks, in the ground, or snuggled tightly into buildings. When the wendigos found them, they scattered into deeper crevices where their large claws couldn't reach. And the more they lived, the fainter their smell grew. They were beginning to smell like the town.

Some in the pack wanted to leave and go hunting for other humans. This felt like the logical thing to do when the prey can't be captured, but the hunger commanded them otherwise. The hunger dictated that they would keep searching for all the children. Maybe this place would be known as Thirty or Forty or Eighty Children.

But then the soldiers came. The pack believed humans were as dumb as cows, and they paid for their arrogance. Only Anuk and two others survived the battle of Twenty Children. They fled into the safety of the pines, and there they stayed for several days, regrouping and rehabilitating. Anuk thought of revenge. Jatunei and Apraxis thought of other prey. The hunger was strong, and growing stronger.

"Leaving for food," Apraxis finally said.

"No. We must avenge our fallen." Anuk was observing the empty space where his hand should be.

"Vengeance belongs to the sun. We consume and we eat. Obey the hunger."

Anuk growled low in his belly. He sounded like a faraway thunderhead booming.

"We forgot the third rule. We weren't careful of what we hunted. And now we must kill them before they lose fear of us. If they are not afraid of us, they are not prey, and then we will all die."

Jatunei and Apraxis agreed. The pack started running. They chased the runaways through the Baby Head Mountains. They nearly took them, too. In the Baby Head Mountains, they were very close, but the runaways fled into a forest fire. The wendigos feared the fire. But the hunger commanded them to enter, so they obeyed. They charged into the flames, searching for the runaways. They found them on the far side of a mountain. They charged through the ash line and singed their curly hairs. But the runaways found a way out and escaped.

At the Fatty Liver Lake, Anuk picked up the smell of the wendigo slayer again. By then, he'd grown his pack three-fold. Other wendigos had heard of the runaways fleeing the mountains.

"It's an insult to every wendigo," a newer member named Setli told Anuk. "No human should be able to move freely through the Shadow Mountains."

"Especially a slayer," Jatunei grumbled. "He doesn't fear us. If he's left to live, his strength will grow, and all humans will become wendigo-slaying monsters."

"But that doesn't mean we should be the ones to find them," another said.

"They stole my meat," Anuk growled. "They will steal more meat."

"Be careful your hunger for flesh is not transformed into a hunger for vengeance, Anuk," Setli warned him.

Anuk punched Setli in the head. Setli toppled into a creek, splashing boulders and dirt and water everywhere.

The other wendigo bit Anuk. Anuk pushed his head off, then reached into his bone throat and pulled out his tongue. The monster wailed. Anuk pulled harder, and the tongue popped out of the monster's mouth, bursting in a torrent of blood. The tongue didn't come easily, but it tasted so sweet, the meat of a predator changed into prey, which was the best kind of taste in the world. Anuk took note of that. While the wendigo's tongue dribbled like a spaghetti noodle being sucked into his mouth, the other wendigos took advantage of the moment and jumped on the fallen wendigo.

Weakness wasn't tolerated.

Prey was prey, and hunger needed to be satiated.

The wendigo squealed as his comrades ate him. They didn't wait for him to die. They pulled out his organs and fought over them. The last thing the poor beast saw was Apraxis and Jatunei pulling one of his kidneys back and forth between them.

The next morning, they found the human encampment. They had stayed close to the Fatty Liver Lake where the Great Horned Serpent lived. By the smell, Anuk determined that the Great Horned Serpent had eaten at least one of the adults.

Anuk was close. Very close. The scent was thick in the air. Little footprints dug in the ground where they'd been running. "Fan out," Anuk ordered the others. "Search the area. This scent is very fresh. They may still be here."

But they were too late for the runaways and the slayer. They lost them along the Fatty Liver Lake, but under the shadow of the Great Severed Mountains, they finally picked them up.

Anuk discovered their smell while the others were playing one of their favorite games. They rolled a human head between them, while saying out loud the body part they thought was the tastiest. The wendigo who won the game won the head. In this case, it belonged to a child they'd discovered in some ruins not far from the Fatty Liver Lake.

"Old man's fingers," said one. "They snap and crunch."

"Heart. Younger the better," said another. Many agreed that this was a very tasty treat. He rolled the head between the wendigos. The head landed in front of a brown-coated bison. The wendigo said, "Brain, cracked from a skull shell."

"No," said another. "Brain sucked from the neck."

"Oh, yes," said others. "That is best."

The game went on like this until Anuk stopped them. He lifted the tiny head in his one hand and held up his stump. He raised his skull to sniff the wind. The others did, too.

"I smell the wendigo-eater," he said.

"I smell tasty children," Apraxis added. The pack prepared to chase.

Anuk held them back. "He is smart, this one. We must be smarter than him."

So Anuk ordered them to carve spears out of tall pine trees. "We will sneak up on him with these," Anuk said. "We will impale him like he impales us."

"Eat his liver," Apraxis said.

"Suck his brains through his neck," said the one who'd won the game.

They ran long and hard up the Great Severed Mountains. The smell of the giant slayer and of the children grew stronger in their skull nostrils and tasted better in his teeth. By now, most of his skull had lost all its flesh. Only Anuk's tongue remained, and a few patches of fur around his big bison horns.

They stopped in a patch of woods. Many older ones were near, and they could be dangerous. Anuk thought of the weak wendigo killed two days prior at the Fatty Liver Lake. He didn't want to fall to the same fate.

Still, the hunger drove him on. Anuk stalked through the forest, following the human tracks. He found blood on the ground. He licked the blood. The taste was almost overwhelming to him. He was dizzy with hunger and the allure of the child's blood.

"What did you find?" Apraxis asked from farther away. The ugly wendigo monsters watched Anuk with ravenous eyes. Anuk tossed a dead child's arm at him. The arm was devoured gleefully, though not all the wendigos got to eat. A child's arm is a tiny morsel.

Excited by the lust for tender meat, they tore down the lodge pole pines, so named because the tribes used them to build their tipis. The wendigos stripped down the bark and sharpened the ends into spear tips. "We may have to defend our meal against other wendigos," Anuk growled.

Once they had their weapons, the pack ran faster up the side of the mountain, following the trail of the runaways.

They came to the edge of a clearing, and Anuk stopped them all. His pack was enraged. The hunger told them prey was very close. Now was the time to kill and eat and satiate the pain for just a little while.

Anuk pointed to the edge of the clearing. A large wendigo stood there, staring at the other end of the clearing. This wendigo had mountain goat horns.

"You cannot have my meal," Anuk whispered. He tightened his grip on his spear-tree and raised it to strike.

An eagle cried out. The pack looked up as the eagle soared overhead. So, too, did the wendigo with the mountain goat skull. He chased after the eagle, down the mountainside.

"Should we leave him?" Apraxis asked.

"He will hear our carnage," Anuk said. "Do you want to share?"

They descended on the unlucky monster as he came through the trees, an eagle screeching in his mouth. The smaller wendigos stuck him like a boar with their spears. Then they jumped on his body and ate him entirely. When they were finished, only blood stains and eagle feathers remained.

Anuk rose up, his rotten face covered in blood, and said, "Leave some room in your bellies, boys. There's a fresher, juicier meat still to kill."

# CHAPTER SEVENTEEN

*Thank God for Kai*, Oran thought. If not for her, they would've been wiped out and turned into the wendigo's feast within seconds.

Before Teller collapsed on the wendigo's spear, she was flinging arrows at the wendigos charging from out of the trees. Four more giant spears landed more or less instantly on top of the soldiers. They were crudely built spears, so most of the spears bounced off the ground. Ghost and Molotov dodged giant ponderosas, but Oran was knocked twenty feet down the mountainside.

By some miracle, he survived. There was tremendous pressure in his non-throwing arm, and a spiking pain in his leg where he'd landed on a stick and stabbed himself in the leg. He was lucky, though. Not only did he survive being throttled by a tree, the branch only grazed him, cutting a nasty gash along his leg.

He thought of his auto injector for only a second. Now was not the time to lose his wits. He'd have to deal with the pain.

He pushed off of the rocks. New pain along his arms told him he'd probably have bruises and micro-lacerations all up and down his arm.

Up on the mountainside, Kai was keeping four wendigos at bay with her arrows. One already laid dead, an arrow through his ugly heart.

The other soldiers had fallen back to the lake and circled around the children defensively. They were doing their best to establish a perimeter between the children and the other half of the wendigos. Without arrows or lances, though, they were seriously outnumbered.

Molotov laid down a blazing line of fire, but it was a poorly burning one. The few plants at this altitude were not catching well. Ghost and Troy were firing their ARs at any skull-headed monstrosity that dared approach.

Oran retrieved his lance, which lay farther down the mountainside. He ran to it, exposing himself and separating from Recon Team. Oran grabbed the lance. He felt its cool power in his fingertips. He raced back up the hill, his legs pumping like pistons, and pain shooting upward, reminding him that he was not in a good place functionally. An hour ago, he would've run up and down that mountain in half the time it took him to run up it.

In the short time that Oran was gone, Troy had maneuvered the children so that the lake was behind them. This made flanking Recon Team and the children more difficult, though the monsters were still trying.

Ahead of Oran stood the wendigos. They were now between him and the rest of Recon Team. That meant they could be forced into a two-fronts battle. The problem was, Oran would have the low ground, and that was never good. He quickly noted some reconvening safety zones: a thick bluff of pines, several large boulders he could hide behind.

Any battle was a numbers game. This one was currently 9-on-5. Those would be pretty decent odds if Recon Team wasn't out massed and outgunned. But if Oran could take down one or two, and if Kai could kill one more, Oran thought the odds might shift in their favor.

Oran stealthily ran behind the line of wendigos, raising the tip of his lance over his head. There were three ways he knew to kill a wendigo. Stabbing their hearts with a holy weapon was one. Burning them from the inside out was another. This was more applicable to younger wendigos. The more skeletal, the less effect flames had on the body. The third was decapitation. He'd seen it happen only once before, and that involved a flying wing from an A-10 Warthog that had been swiped out of the air like King Kong had just swatted it, which was close to what actually happened, but with a world ender, not a movie monster.

None of these options were really available to him, but if he was strong, and if his aim was well timed, maybe he could still stab the heart from the back side of the wendigo.

Silent as a chinook wind, he leaped at the closest giant monster. He pulled back his throwing arm and did his best impersonation of Joe Montana going for Dwight Clark in the end zone. The lance twirled in the air, the tip of the lance seesawing up and down. It found its flesh and dug deep into the back, popping the wendigo's lung sack. The creature gurgled and gasped at the same time as all air whooshed out of its lungs. The monster's eyes bulged, and it fell forward into the line of fire.

Before the other wendigos could react, Oran had already landed on top of the dead wendigo and pulled his lance out of the burning corpse. He rolled out of the way as a wendigo swung at him with its giant tree-spear.

The wendigos were not used to carrying spears, making them slow. He easily dodged their thrusts.

"Gore him," Anuk grunted.

Four giant wendigos charged Oran. He and everyone else scattered out of their way. The bison-headed monsters trampled into the lake. They rounded and came at the humans again.

"Run!" Ghost yelled. They ran down the mountainside.

Oran needed some protection. Right now, they were out in the open. Just rocks and trees below them. Well, that would have to do.

"Make for the trees!" Oran cried out.

The children ran as fast as they could. A few had to be picked up by Oran and Troy. They were simply too small to keep up. Molotov would have grabbed more, but he was dragging Quiet One in the travois.

Once inside the trees, Oran yelled, "Keep running!" He didn't have much of a plan at this point. They were being routed. He was looking for anywhere they could regroup and make a stand. They didn't have much more juice in their gears, and the wendigos were gaining on them. They were much taller and faster than the humans.

"Where are we going?" Ghost yelled as she shot at one of the bulls behind her.

"I don't know. Wait. I have an idea. The Hungry Horse reservoir is this way."

He did not point out that it was several miles away.

The wendigos were almost on top of them. The group separated, about half going down one side of the mountain at a lower cut, and his half taking a higher cut. With Oran were Molotov, Troy, and about half of the kids. Two wendigos chose to pursue them with the others chasing Ghost and the other children. Oran cursed their bad luck. If Ghost was caught, she had no backup. They'd be obliterated.

As they crisscrossed down the mountain, one of the wendigos, a stout thirty-footer, reached out and swiped at Molotov's leg. He fell down, rolling, and lost his flame thrower. He put all his effort into keeping Quiet One from being thrown from his travois. He did nothing to protect himself. The big guy tumbled through thorns and rocks.

When he came up, the wendigo pounced on him. He didn't have time to dodge or fight. His mind was still doing somersaults. But before the monster could rip him apart, Molotov's kids started throwing rocks at them. Troy, too, unleashed a flurry of rocks, but his were lead. Molotov and the kids had gone back up the side of the mountain with Troy and found a small rise above the wendigos. William hopped down and gathered as much of the flamethrower as a 10-year old could. He didn't know the intricacies of operating a flamethrower, but he knew enough to point the barrel at the monster and pull the trigger. The creature recoiled at the blast of fire.

The second wendigo roared and swiped at them with its long arms. Usually, this would have been enough to kill all the children, but not these kids. These were Molotov's kids, and he'd trained them tough. He'd spent several hours grilling them on basic wendigo maneuvers, including the standard duck and roll protocol. His kids knew how to move out of the path of the swinging arm and when to expect it.

The added firepower meant that Molotov wouldn't be instantly killed. He had enough time to push back on his feet and run. But then the bison-headed monster slammed his elongated arm down. While Molotov could jump aside easily, William was putting all his concentration into holding the flamethrower. He had no way of avoiding what was coming. He was going to become mush. Molotov didn't think twice. He shoved William down the mountainside and was throttled.

His body collapsed and crumpled. One leg stuck out at an unbelievable angle.

The boys screamed, and the wendigo smiled grimly at them from the side of his mouth that still had flesh. He scooped Molotov in both hands. Molotov's legs hung limply below him. Blood drained from a gash in his side. The monster greedily lapped up his spilled juices like it was the first water the wendigo had tasted in weeks. Its putrid tongue entered Molotov's body through his new orifice and slapped up his meaty juices. Molotov convulsed uncontrollably. While he was being slowly devoured, Molotov talked to the kids.

"I'm never out of the fight," he said. With his one functional arm, he pulled his knife from his shoulder strap and stabbed the wendigo's hand. The wendigo dropped him painfully.

Half his torso gone, his legs dysfunctional, and the last of his life draining from his body, Molotov said, "You knock me down, I get back up, motherfucker!"

From the rise, Troy leapt into the air, his hunting knife in his hands. He landed on the wendigo and shoved the knife deep into its chest. The giant monster groaned, and then it fell over, dead. Troy pulled his knife from the monster's heart.

The second wendigo just stared at them astonished.

"Run," Molotov pleaded weakly. His face was pale as the nearby glaciers. His eyes rolled back, and he died.

Oran grabbed William and the travois. William was crying angrily. "Hey, stop that. We've got to go. Hurry!" Oran thrust a travois stick in his hands. "Run!"

Troy and the other children followed.

And they were off again. The cut they were taking soon caught up with the other group. He assumed that the lower cut that Ghost and the others took must have swept them wide and then reunited them. Together, they kept running.

Just when it couldn't get worse, right when the rest of the bulls had almost caught them, a tree ripped out of the ground and pounded down on one of the charging wendigos. Oran and the rest stopped behind a nearby pine to figure out what happened. Oran thought another gigantic-sized wendigo must be nearby.

"Did you see?"

"No."

In answer, the pine they were standing behind lifted off the ground and stepped toward the lesser wendigos. He was one of the largest wendigos Oran had ever seen in these parts of the country, over a hundred feet tall. The smaller ones raised their spears and stabbed at the tall, elk-headed wendigo.

Watching them fight was as epic as a gladiator battle between forest gods or like a grizzly bear fending off tigers. The elk monster flailed at the young wendigos as it roared at them, while Anuk and the other wendigos tried to circle around and take out its legs. Trees cracked and toppled. Oran honestly didn't know who would win. The larger wendigo had the strength and power, but not the numbers.

Several more wendigos rushed out of the trees and joined the attempt to take down the elk-headed goliath. They were all about the same size as the bison-headed wendigos that had been hunting Recon Team and the children. Seconds later, another large wendigo slid down the mountainside. This one, also elk-headed, crashed down the mountain like an avalanche, knocking over trees and sending up an enormous plume of dust that shrouded the fighting wendigos.

Oran had seen wendigos fighting before. Nobody knew what supernatural machinations drove the battle, and whether they fought territorially or over food. Their motives were as veiled as the creatures in the cloud of dust. From where Oran stood, only the monsters' shadows fought each other, their skeletal bodies exaggerated beyond comparison.

"We've got to go."

It was Kai. She had evaded the others, no worse for wear. Oran couldn't agree more. For once, luck was on their side.

"NO!" bellowed one of the wendigos.

From the monster battle emerged the same bison-headed monster that had pursued Oran all over the Rocky Mountains.

"Why won't he just die?" Oran growled.

The bison-headed monster grimaced. Exposed teeth grinded. The wendigo pointed at Oran, calling him out. For a moment, Oran thought he might have to go head-to-head against the titan of the Western United States, but then a massive fist reached out of the cloud and slammed down on the wendigo's giant body.

"I will find you!" Anuk shouted as he struggled under the weight of one of the larger, elk-headed goliaths.

"Let's go!" Kai insisted. This time, Oran ran with them. They raced all the way down the mountainside, and they didn't stop until they entered a deep coulee with plenty of cover. They collapsed on top of each other, exhausted and afraid and alone in the middle of the Montana wilderness.

And then the dead came.

# CHAPTER EIGHTEEN

Oran held his fist up. Both William and Wallace, who were crying, stopped. They held up their fists, tears still streaming down their soft cheeks, but they were quiet.

Within seconds, Crazy Dog Company was less noticeable than the wind. Ghost signaled that she was going to climb to the top of the coulee and scope around.

At the same time, Oran groaned. The pain in his leg and shoulder was getting worse. He pulled off his pack and sorted through it, searching for the autoinjectors. Kai came over, distraught.

"You're injured," she whispered, almost harshly. "Why didn't you say something?"

Oran showed her his fist, which in another lifetime would have had a very different message, but not here. Kai kneeled down next to him. She set her quiver and bow beside him, then helped him out of his jacket and shirt.

She stood back and examined Oran's naked chest. If there had been any question as to who he was, there was no doubting it now. Even Troy took note.

"Dang, brother. That's a lot of brass."

Oran reached for his shirt. He didn't like all this attention. Even the children had circled around him and pointed at his chest.

Where his heart should be was a tattoo of a very realistic heart, except this one was colored purple. Six more hearts were tattooed on his right pectoral, but they were all much smaller. A bronze star was tattooed on the left side of his chest, and his stars were inked below his neckline. This was definitely General Oran Old Chief.

"What are those?" Old Woman asked, a little scared.

He put his hand on her head. "Don't be afraid, Old Woman. The military cannot afford medals like in the past, but they want the world to know forever of your service, so this is how they recognize you."

"Do all the hearts mean you've killed lots of people?" Blood Clot Boy asked. Where Old Woman was frightened, he was excited. Such is how these things go with boys.

"They mean he was injured," Troy said. "The blue ribbon around his neck is the highest award that can be bestowed on a soldier."

"I want to paint you with more awards," Kai said. "Awards that recognize what you've done for these children. Kanontsistonties, wendigo, the Great Horned Serpent. Me."

"Hoorah," Troy said.

Oran scoffed. "I appreciate what you're saying, but I haven't done anything yet. We're pinned down in a ditch in the middle of hell. Don't thank me until we are in Browning. And even then, don't thank me."

He reached for his shirt, but Kai pulled it away. She signed for the children to move to the far end of the coulee. Then she bandaged his leg and tested his shoulder.

"It's dislocated," she whispered. "I will need to reset it."

Oran's eyes narrowed, and his jaw tightened.

"I hope that dirty look isn't for me. This has happened before, I take it."

Oran blinked. Any anger he showed was pure reaction. "Twice. Once in the service, and once growing up."

She took the hand of the disjointed shoulder and gently pulled it toward her. As she pulled, Troy leaned over him to make sure he didn't fight her. His metal tentacles plopped all around him.

"Why don't you cut those?"

"You kidding? They make me look more impressive."

"I am sorry about Molotov."

Troy blinked away a tear. "So am I. I'm not a believer like you, you know. All that Natosi crap." He glanced quickly to make sure none of the kids heard him. "I was born Catholic, but I haven't attended Mass in years. I don't believe in a higher power to help me. But right now, I hope there's something better out there for Molotov."

"At least he went out helping others," Oran whispered.

"I know, eh? That big badass acts like he's something else, but really deep down inside he's a softy." Troy sniffed. "You know, I can't. I tried. I'm sorry." Troy leaned back, tearing up.

"You need to be quiet," Ghost whispered as she came back into the ravine. She put her arm around Troy, and not for the last time, somebody was holding back sobs to keep quiet.

"What did you see?" Oran asked. He wasn't very good at signing with one arm bandaged up. Once he stopped crying, she signaled "two" "big" "moving away."

Oran signaled for the smaller wendigos, which was possible with one hand. She shook her head grimly. Then signaled "three" "dead."

Kai tapped him on the chest. He winced. She continued pulling his arm. He broke out in sweat from the pain as his shoulder ball rolled along his tendons. He knew he was supposed to resist the temptation to pull against her, but that was getting harder and harder with every second. Suddenly he felt the shoulder pop back into place.

An instant relief of pain washed over him. Kai wrapped his arm in a sling. By then the children had come back up to them. The children renamed Blood Clot Boy and Old Woman snuggled next to him, and he fell asleep.

He awoke from a dreamless sleep. It was dark outside, so he assumed it was sometime in the middle of the night. Wendigos would be about. He climbed out of the coulee. Troy had the watch.

"You make a lot of noise for an Indian," Troy said.

"Climbing with one hand will do that."

Oran sat down next to Troy. His legs dangled over the edge of the coulee. Troy offered his canteen. "It's cold coffee, but it's got caffeine."

Oran drank and winced. "That's strong."

Troy chuckled. "Just like I like it."

"How are you doing?"

Troy shrugged. "I really liked that Scottish bastard. I'd never met anyone from outside the States before I met him. He was always so much bigger than anything else, you know? His personality, I mean. It made up for how damn ugly he was."

Troy laughed at his own joke. Oran winked with his lips.

"The damage to his face, and his leg. God, it was horrible. His face looked like a dried up dog turd. A lesser person would've gone home, shut the door, and been too embarrassed to ever step outside again, and you couldn't blame them. But Molotov? Mother fucker embraced that shit. He would dare you to watch and laugh at you when you got sick from it. You don't just get over somebody like that in your life."

Oran nodded. He handed the canteen back to Troy. Troy closed the canteen and set it down.

"When are we going to talk about Browning?"

"Maybe two days from here, if we live long enough."

"I'm not worried about surviving the No Man's Land, Oran. Maybe I will live, maybe I won't. We all gotta die, there's no reason to be an asshole about it. If I die out here, at least I died helping to get kids to a better place, right? Doesn't that sound like something you could be remembered for? Not, he was a good businessman, or a good father, or even a good soldier. 'He died rescuing kids from No Man's Land.' I'm good with that. I believe that somehow, some way, you will get these kids to Browning. But between you and me, I've been there before. Browning's just another poor reservation town at the end of the world. Even before the Govern-not went away, it was hard up. My Indian Intuition says that hasn't changed. Browning barely has the resources to take care of itself. We've got twenty kids we picked up in that map dot town, plus the brothers from the cherry orchards. What're they going to do with 22 kids?"

# CHAPTER NINETEEN

"Something's wrong," Ghost said.

They were behind the children. Troy and Kai were leading them up front. Quiet One was back up and walking, so tired kids were taking turns on the travois. Oran had just told a straggler to keep up with the others when Ghost spoke to him.

She had a strange look on her very strange face. There was an emotion there, but he couldn't read it. Anger? Sadness? She didn't sound sad.

"Do you see something?" Oran asked.

She said, "No. It's not that. We've been descending this mountain all morning. We should be to the Hungry Horse Reservoir by now."

He glanced at the sky. "It's not dawn yet."

"It hasn't been dawn for a long time."

He stopped and thought about it for a second. "It was yesterday evening when we came to the lake."

"Since then, we've run down the mountains, slept for hours."

"I figured six."

"Right. So if we slept for six hours, that would make it maybe four a.m. when we woke. We've been descending for another four hours at least. Even in the shadow of the mountains, we should be feeling dawn coming. This is summer, not winter, but look around. It's pitch black."

Oran handed her his lance and climbed the closest tree. He got as high as he could and studied the sky, then climbed back down.

"No sign of sun or moon anywhere. That is strange."

"What do we do?"

"Well, what can we do? Either the sun and moon have stopped rotating, or the wendigos have some new magic they've conjured up. There is nothing we can do to change that, so we keep walking."

Even the children began to worry after a while. The two boys they picked up in the cherry orchards, Ryder and Coby, who were now Privates First Class Clark and Private Bruce, asked how much farther to the Hungry Horse. "It feels like we're descending Mt. Everest, and there's nothing that tall in the Swans," Clark said.

"I do not know," Oran said. "But we do not have a choice. We will keep going."

Troy called from ahead. "Hey, we're here!"

Something strange was going on, and nobody believed that there were any wendigos down where they were. It was like they had entered another realm. The humidity was thinner, the temperature colder. Some of the children had put their buffalo skins on for warmth. Yet despite the cold, the trees here were scorched, as if a wildfire had burned through not long ago. The air stank of cinder. Ash flakes floated on the wind.

The trees parted, and they came to the reservoir's inky black shores.

"I don't like it here," one of the children said. Oran touched the child on the shoulder to calm him, then moved through the children. He walked to the front with Troy and Kai. Troy's head was lifted to the sky, and Kai was looking at the ground.

"There are no stars in the sky," Troy said, his voice slightly cracking in trepidation. "On a cloudless night, in the middle of nowhere. We should be able to see the whole Milky Way from where we are. Where are we?"

Oran studied the sky, hoping to discover some clue that what Troy said was wrong, but he came to the same conclusion. There should be stars in that sky.

"Don't panic," Kai said, which made Oran consider panicking just on those grounds. "The pebbles of this lake are not stones at all."

"What?" Oran couldn't believe that, so he kneeled down and palmed one of the rocks. What he thought was a small pebble was a large, softball-sized rock. He rolled the rock in his hand. A grim skull smiled back at him.

Oran dropped the skull, and it rolled over the others. This was a lakebed of human skulls.

Immediately, everybody backed away. A girl screamed. She was pointing at the lake. There, where the waters lapped against the skulls, a ghoulish man stood in the black water.

"Who are you?" Kai called out as she armed her bow and pointed the arrow at the man. He had gray skin that was like very old wrapping paper pulled so tightly over a present, it no longer hides the gift. In this case, it was the man's bones.

The man stepped out of the water, hands outstretched. He wore deerskin and a ceremonial war bonnet with many eagle feathers. He was handsome and young, though frail.

Oran put his hand over Kai's arrow, lowering it. "He is a chief of the People."

The man addressed Oran in his native language. Everyone in the group had stopped to watch the interaction. They did not know what the man was saying.

The man coughed. Then he said, "You have forgotten the language, Old Chief, so I will speak in yours. I am Weasel Tail. I was once a chief of the South Piegan, long ago."

"I know you. I have seen your face in pictures, great chief."

"I wanted to be the first to speak to you. I wanted to tell you that you've made the Piegans very proud. You are the greatest Blackfeet warrior to ever live, and your stories will be celebrated for generations. I also wanted to tell you that there are many of us here at the shores of this lake. We would like to talk to you. We have messages for all of you," he said, now addressing all the children.

"Where are we?" Ghost asked.

"Can't you tell? You are in a place without pain. Your boy there. Quiet One. Does your arm hurt, child?"

The boy shook his head no, his face a mix of joy and utter terror.

"All your injuries are painless here. You can remove your bandages, Oran. You don't need them anymore."

Oran felt no pain in his shoulder or in his leg, but he didn't remove his bandages.

"You are unsure," he said. "It is hard to speak to ghosts. Perhaps an old ghost like me is making it harder." Weasel Tail motioned to the lake.

Three figures stood forward. Their skin was as gray as Weasel Tail, but there was no doubting two of them. Teller and Molotov stepped forward out of the lake. They were uninjured. In fact, they were better than uninjured. There was no metal or plastic in their bodies. Behind them was a third figure that only Oran recognized.

The children ran forward to Molotov and Teller, who kneeled down with open arms. William and Wallace hugged Molotov tightly. "Mah boys!" Molotov said, holding both the twins. Then he looked to Troy, who was in tears.

"I'm so sorry, Troy," Molotov said. The two men hugged each other tightly.

"I'm sorry, Mol. I should've stopped the wendigo."

"Aich! Don't say such things," Molotov said. "Ye're doing all that I want by taking care of these two little warriors."

"Troy killed a wendigo with his knife!" William said excitedly.

"Did you, now. You know, I always thought there was more to you than just some fool grunt."

Then two gray-faced people appeared behind Molotov, and the twins shouted out, "Mama! Dad!"

Ghost went to Teller. The children had many questions, but mostly they wanted to tell Teller everything that had happened in the brief time since he'd departed. Only Kai stayed by Oran's side when the third figure approached.

Oran choked up, taking a deep breath. The man standing before him was a mirror image of himself, but with a slightly leaner face, and a tad shorter.

"Dad," Oran said. And just like that, Oran was sobbing with joy like everyone else. He hugged his dad.

"You've been gone so long," Oran said. "There's so much I want to tell you."

"There is no time," Oran's father said. As Kai listened, she thought father sounded a lot like son in that regard.

"First, I keep tabs on you. I know what you are doing and what you have been through. Second, I have news of your family. They are in danger. Old Man helped Jodi and Daniel to get rid of those stupid men, but they will not stay gone for long. You must hurry if you are going to save your family."

Something dark appeared in Oran's periphery. His eyes wandered to it, but Oran's father grabbed his chin. "Don't look away, son! That is too dangerous. Look at me. Focus on your family, or you will stay here forever. The dead want nothing more than to be with the living. It starts innocent enough, like any addiction. But the more we stay near you, the more we ache for you. Your life draws us close. If you are to escape here, you must focus on what keeps you alive."

Kai tugged at Oran's arm, but Oran shirked away.

"There is more I must tell you, my sweet boy. There are still more dangers out there, but you are right about Natosi and the wendigo. The Sun was angry, so he unleashed them upon the world here as repayment for human's cannibalistic nature. Wendigos are man-eaters just as humans became man-eaters, consuming too much to sustain themselves and their world. They were eating themselves to death. So Natosi sent monsters to teach humans a lesson. There is nothing you can do for the people who have not learned this lesson, but maybe you and the children you have brought through the mountains will be the turning point. Maybe this new generation will learn to not devour."

Oran's father gripped the lance tightly. "Sacrifice and penance are your weapons, Oran."

Again, something was bothering Oran. Out of the corner of his eye, he spied tall poles.

"Oran," Kai said, somewhat alarmed.

Oran's father hugged him tightly. "This is the hardest thing I will ever do, Oran. You do not understand the sacrifice I am making right now, but you must leave now, before it is too late. There is a trail marked with fireflies. Follow it, and the trail will lead you out of here. There are still many dangers ahead of you, many monsters still to come. Beware the skin walkers, my son. Now go. Go!" and his father shoved Oran away from his tight embrace.

Immediately, his father grew grayer and sadder than he'd been moments ago. While he spoke to Oran, his voice had grown fuller and stronger. "Go!" his father said weakly.

Finally, Oran looked around. The poles he'd seen were scaffolds to hold the dead. These scaffolds were strung along the shores of the lake, and went on for as far as he could see, deep into a purple fog that banked at the far end of the reservoir.

The children smiled as the gray-faced men and women ushered them away. Oran knew these apparitions must be the fathers and mothers of the children. Only a few children, one being Blood Clot Boy, was not being taken. The spirits led the children into the lake water.

"Wait! Stop!" Oran yelled.

The ghosts turned on Oran. Where seconds ago, their gray faces had seemed blissful and content, they'd become seats of such dire hatred and jealousy. Their eyes were dark, and their mouths were full of tipi-shaped teeth.

"You cannot take them," Oran said. "These children have not begun to live, much less finished their lives."

"Aich," Molotov said. "Look what ye've gone and done." He, too, had a mouth full of triangular teeth. Oran thought of shark's teeth.

Troy pushed away from Molotov. "What happened to you?"

"Come with us, brother" Molotov said. "We just want to talk to you some more. You have no idea how lonely it gets here. A day here is like a lifetime of loneliness."

Troy unsheathed his knife. The spirit pulled away, keeping his hands up. "I won't fight ya, mate."

"Children, come back to me," Oran said. He held up his fist.

"I want to stay with Mama," William pleaded.

"This is a land of the dead. You don't belong here, William," Oran said. "One day you will return, but until then, your world is not here."

"But I want my world to be here," William said. Wallace agreed. Their mother, whose hands they held, smiled warmly at her two boys.

"I want you here, too, Georgie. You remember your action figures? You can play with them here. I have them, here in the lake."

The other children waited expectantly to see how this standoff ended.

"Really?" William, who was known by his mother as George, asked.

"Yes. Everything is here. All your toys, all your playthings. Everything from Sandyhill Point."

"Sandyhill Point?" William said, his voice a gurgle. "You died there."

"I know, Georgie, but we can be together."

"You all died. Mama, it was horrible!"

"It doesn't have to be horrible any longer, Georgie. If you'd come with me, I'd be so happy. We could talk forever." She pulled her boys to her.

Oran put his hand on William's wrist. At first, mother and son thought he was trying to pull the child away, but then they saw William's skin. His hand was completely gray, like ash. The ash was spreading up his arm.

"You're killing him," Oran said sadly. "Let go of him."

"But I want to go with her," William said. Oran ignored her. He begged the mother with his eyes to let her child go.

"I know it is a tragedy what happened to you."

"You have no idea!" the mother screeched. "My life, my CHILDREN, were stolen from me!"

"I know," Oran said. "Only you have the power to save your sons. Let them go."

"No!" Tears streamed down her cheeks. The gray spread to William's shoulder. Beside William, Wallace fell to his knees.

"I don't feel so good," Wallace said.

All around them, the same thing was happening over and over. Children fell over.

"I don't want to die," Wallace said.

"It is better for you here with me," his mother said.

Oran held the mother by the shoulder. Almost immediately, his hand turned ashen gray.

"The longer we stay here," Kai said, "the greater the dead affect us."

Oran's face turned gray, but he did not let go.

"You are stealing my children all over again!" the mother shouted. "You deserve every death. How dare you!"

Oran did not let go. He said, "Your pain for theirs. You know the sacrifice."

William and Wallace were now shaking their arms in their mother's grip. "Let go!" they shouted. "You're killing him."

Tearfully, Mama suddenly let go. She fell down to her knees, crying.

"We love you, Mama," William said. He and Wallace were pulling Oran away. Ash fluttered out of his throat as he coughed.

Reluctantly, children began pulling away from their parents.

"No," a young mother said as her five-year old pulled away.

"But you're dead, Mommy," the little boy said.

"But I'm your mother. I just want us to be happy and together." She pulled him back toward her. Her face was so dark, she looked more like a demon than a person.

Kai pushed the mother away gently. A glow, like the shine of gold in the dark, appeared from her hand. Oran stood next to her. The young mother looked down at Kai's hand, then let go of her child.

"You'll pay for this, Oran Old Chief," she said venomously.

"I don't doubt it, and when it happens, I won't regret it, either," he said. Molotov and Teller, now that they were away from Troy and Ghost and the children, just watched them mournfully.

"I'm sorry, boyo," Molotov said to Troy. "Keep care of them."

The demonic woman sobbed into her hands. Black tears drained from her cheeks and fell drop by drop into the lake.

Though none of the dead approached, Kai kept her golden hand held out to them. She shuffled the children behind her as they backed away from the shores of the lake.

The dead watched Oran and Kai sorrowfully. He wondered if they were just waiting for the right moment to sweep down and steal the children away.

"Where are we going?" Ghost asked.

"Look for a trail lit by fireflies," Oran said.

"Oh, I see that," a little voice said. It belonged to the five-year old boy whose mother Oran had to confront. Oran noted that he would rename the child Firefly once they were away from the lake.

The boy led the group to a path that was lined with fireflies. The path led up, and shortly after, the sun came out to greet them. It didn't rise from the east, but gradually appeared in the middle of the sky, as if the children were coming out of a deep well in the middle of the day.

"What happened to you in there?" Ghost asked Kai.

"I don't know. I guess I've just never liked death."

With a knowing smile, Oran said, "You're a Sky Person, right?"

Kai blushed. "I've heard that before."

"What's a Sky Person?"

"People who live in the sky," Oran said.

"Or very close to it," Kai added.

"I have had my suspicions for a while now. It explains why your hand glowed golden in the land of the dead. You have the power of the sun, which is the power of life. It also explains why you have no scars, yet you wear much less clothing than anyone else."

"You should be happy to play in the sun."

"Easy for you to say," Ghost said. "You don't get skin cancer."

"Do not try that," Oran said to Ghost. "Your cynicism will not work on Kai. She has lived all her life worshipping the sun, and living as close to it as anyone can."

The wayward group did not deviate from the path until the sun was warm on their shoulders. When Oran finally felt brave enough to turn around, he discovered they'd arrived at another bald peak.

"Where are we?" Troy asked.

"We've come through the Flatheads."

"That's impossible," Ghost said. "We were leaving the Swans last night."

"I think we've traveled further than we thought we did," Oran said. He pointed to a clear river and a small road. "That is highway 2. If we follow it, it will lead us out of these mountains."

# CHAPTER TWENTY

By the time the group actually left the Rockies, they were a changed people. Of the original five from Recon Team, only Ghost and Troy had avoided the grim reaper. Jack was gone, too, taken by the Great Water Serpent at Flathead Lake. The children fared much better, though one was minus an arm.

They had endured a lifetime of woe in the mountains of madness that were the Montana Rockies. They'd been chased by wendigos, attacked by dragons, and survived a gauntlet of flying skulls. They'd done it all on empty stomachs. The group that walked out of the mountains was gaunt, dehydrated, and always tired. From their exposure, most of the children had come down with sun burns. When they finally reached Browning, which was now fourteen miles across the open plains, the children would need to be checked over at the clinic, and some would need surgery to remove the cancerous growths jutting from their skin. So, too, would the soldiers. Only Kai avoided any skin damage. She appeared as unblemished as a cover model with a Photoshop pro hiding her scars. She alone seemed unaffected by the lack of food and water, as if these were baser needs that her body had evolved beyond.

Traveling the treacherous highway 2 took days because nobody in the party trusted the road, the mountains above, or the winding river that followed the road. They moved slowly, moving carefully in the day time when the wendigos were less likely to be roaming the mountains and searching for them.

The children had become as adept at camouflage as the soldiers. They huddled in their hiding spots at night so well that sometimes Oran had to search carefully to find all the children.

They communicated by sign language alone, having honed their signs during their mountain travails. Entire conversations about the weather, the road ahead, and the monsters, could be held without whispering a single word.

Of monsters, they had seen many, but always been able to maneuver around them undetected. Sometimes they waited hidden for hours waiting for a wendigo to cross the road. North of another derelict RV park, they discovered the nest of an owl-witch. The witch watched the roadside for any signs of travelers. Her giant nest was full of the bones of the travelers she'd eaten whole and then regurgitated. The only way to get around her was to crawl along the railroad tracks very slowly and hope to Natosi she didn't see them. At the worst point, she flew out of her nest and circled the area, twice flying directly over them on the railroad tracks, but the owl witch must have missed the group. They were curled up between the railroad ties so that they looked like the rocks beneath them. After she flew off to hunt for more people, everybody stood and ran down the tracks. They wanted to never meet her again. Her horrible face would haunt some of the children for the rest of their lives.

Their store of cherries ran out days ago, and all game had disappeared.

#

Oran lifted the pair of binoculars to his eyes and scanned the foothills below. He wore a hood over his head, and a bandana and sunglasses to shield his face. Ghost stood next to him. She didn't need binoculars.

They scanned the hills below. Oran located a small junkyard tucked behind some hills. He could barely make out the sign, "Nester's Neighborhood."

They watched the junkyard for the better half of an hour before one of the teens tapped Oran on the shoulder and signed a question. He then shook his hands back and forth in the air like he was turning an invisible steering wheel.

Oran nodded. There were five to ten cars that looked drivable. However, he kept his hopes in check. Nester's Neighborhood was a junkyard, after all.

There were thumbs up all around. The decision was made. The children would wait in the foothills with Troy, who was enjoying being out of the mountains. He was picking up all kinds of signals with his tentacles, and was working to establish communications with the outside world.

#

Oran and Ghost approached the junkyard indirectly, coming out of the hills to the far side of the office. They were watched over by Private First Class Janelle, who had been named Falcon for her sharp eyes and because she was often Teller's co-pilot. Falcon reported no movement from the junkyard's office.

The only movements were little dust devils being scattered by the wind. Oran and Ghost climbed over the chain-link fence surrounding the junkyard and walked between the folds of a wall of smashed cars. On the far side sat two old cars, a 1944 Ford F1 and a 1958 Chevy Bel Air. The Ford F1 felt alien to him with its bug-eyed headlights and round fenders. The sharp angles of the goliath Bel Air made less sense to him. Nobody had needed a stylish car in decades, and these two rust-colored monstrosities were a slap in the face to the modern world.

As he rounded the two classic automobiles, a closer examination left him inclined to think the cars were more or less intact. Somebody had rebuilt these dinosaurs, and he may be able to make use of that. This was the direct opposite to the other cars, which all appeared to have been scavenged for parts until they were nothing more than skeletons of their former self.

Oran and Ghost inspected the office, going in fast when they finally got to the door. Inside, they found the bones of the junkyard's owner, many years dead. A name badge identified the bones as belonging to the owner of Nester's Neighborhood.

Oran reported back to Falcon, then he and Ghost holstered their guns. While Oran went through the office searching for keys, Ghost wandered outside.

"Be careful," Oran cautioned her.

"I will be." The door closed behind Ghost.

Oran searched through the desk drawers and the open safe, but he didn't find anything. In the back of the office, he found a pegboard with a bunch of empty hooks. His heart sank. This was obviously where the keys were kept, and they were all gone, which meant that either the cars had the keys, or they were useless to them.

He walked outside, but didn't see Ghost anywhere.

"Ghost?" he called out. There was no real fear of there being anybody there.

"Over here," she said. A hand waved from behind a stack of old toilets.

"Did you find something?"

"I don't know. Come check it out." He noticed her voice was considerably lower than his.

He jogged around the wall of American Standards. Ghost was kneeling at a large fire pit built into the ground. Metal monkey bars, like from a children's playground, had been posted on either side of the fire pit. Blackened handcuffs hung from the ladder rungs.

"What is this?" Oran asked. He immediately felt an overwhelming sense of dread. Reactively, he scanned from east to west. Along with his dread came another feeling. They were very exposed.

"Falcon, do you see anything?"

"Nothing. Not even you. Where are you?"

"Oran," Ghost said, and it was the way she said his name without saying anything else that caught his attention. She was holding her knife in the ashes. As she pulled it up, a broken skull emerged from the ashes, an eye cavity resting on the tip of her knife. Despite being fragmented, the skull was obviously human.

He leaned down and held his hand over the ashes. "They are hot. We are not alone."

He and Ghost walked to either side of the pit, AR-15s drawn. Ghost entered the next area. Oran covered her. In this way, they moved from area to area, clearing it. Most of the areas were pits full of leftover junk. In some, they found old cars in disrepair. One of those areas had an old fashioned Hummer, a military juggernaut that had seen better days but hadn't yet been cannibalized for parts.

Oran signaled that he'd found no keys to the cars. Ghost nodded, then ran to the Hummer. She jumped inside and checked for keys, but found none.

She ran back next to Oran and very quietly said, "I half expected to see cannibals jump out of those trash piles. I was way too exposed."

"Are you seeing anything at all?" Oran whispered back.

She rescanned the area, then nodded.

Leaving the area, Oran went first, this time. Ghost caught her breath while she covered him. They moved around one of the giant junk piles. As they were leaving, Ghost glanced back. She thought she saw something, but it must be a trick of the brain. There was no way she could have seen *that*.

They rounded the pile of junk, mostly spare parts and corrugated siding. There was a wall of used tires and a stack of wheel-less trailers. Two more cars, too. A Toyota Celica and a Mitsubishi Galant. Neither had seats or a steering column or radios. These vehicles had been gutted. An old desk, like a teacher's desk, stood off to one side, covered in car parts. It seemed strange that a teacher's desk would be standing in the open air where the weather and sun could damage it, but this was a junk yard after all.

"This all feels very suspicious," Ghost said. Because of her metal face, Oran had a hard time reading any kind of reaction from her, visually, but he picked up on her concern by the sound of her voice. Her voice was clipped, and slightly higher pitched. However, she was a battle-tested soldier, and one of the best reconnaissance people he'd ever met. If something was fazing her, most people should run screaming.

Oran acknowledged her concern with a head nod. The owner was dead. Obviously, he died here many years ago, perhaps in the first years after the wendigos appeared. Somebody else was using the junkyard, had moved in and claimed it as their own, but who, and where were they?

Ghost pointed at the ground. Shoeprints led to the Celica, then disappeared. Oran and Ghost searched both sides. Ghost checked under the car while Oran put his gun in the trunk and under the hood. Nothing.

They finished clearing the area, then moved back in front of the trash pile. The trash pile was one of three piles that were the central hub of "Nester's Neighborhood."

Ghost studied the trash piles, then pointed to the next area. Oran charged in, weapon drawn and checking the corners. This time, Ghost jumped in with him. After he cleared the area, which was full of smashed cars, Ghost leaned in close to his ear. "I want you to go back out and tell me if you see anything off."

Oran circled back around her, his weapon drawn, as he poked his head out around the trash pile. There was nobody there. The only footprints belonged to the boots he and Ghost wore. There was nothing here.

Except the 1958 Chevy Bel Air.

Oran slowly pulled back around the trash pile.

"What is going on here?"

"I think they're hiding in the cars."

"But we searched the Celica and the Galant. There's no way anybody could have hidden in those cars."

Ghost shrugged. He had to admit, that was a compelling argument in a world of wendigos and flying skulls. He thought of the stories he'd heard growing up about dwarves and little people. Stories of little people were common among many of the tribal stories he'd heard from across North America. It was little people who helped a young boy create the first crazy dog society.

If it was little people, how would he spring their trap?

He motioned forward. This time, Ghost took the lead. In this section of the junkyard, they found stacks of old office tables. At the far end of the area stood the old Ford. Its headlights stared at them angrily. *What the hell?* Oran thought.

They backed up. As he turned, he discovered the Chevy Bel Air had somehow, impossibly, driven to this part of the junkyard. The cars were definitely moving, and more quietly than he could hear.

Oran faced the Ford. Ghost lined up against his back. The spikes on her vertebra pushed against his back, pricking his flesh.

The Ford F1 roared at Oran. Oran took a shooting stance, but did not fire. Behind him, Ghost shouted at the person hidden in the car, "Come out and fight us!" When the person did not, she fired her AR-15 at the Chevy's grill. The car made a whining sound, like its belts were tight, then it closed in on her.

The two cars' engines revved so loudly, neither Ghost nor Oran heard the Hummer coming over the trash pile. Suddenly, a half ton of metal dove down the side of the trash pile. Too late, Oran realized they'd been walled in between the driverless cars. Bullets cracked and muzzles flashed, dinging the Hummer that was coming at them like a mad rhino.

Ghost found an exit. She grabbed Oran and ran for it. They ran around the trash pile, the Hummer in chase behind them. She tried to duck into one of the smaller areas and regroup, but they were all walled off now, either with stacks of tires or with corrugated metal.

"They've trapped us," Ghost said. "Now they're just cattle being driven down a chute."

The "chute" back at the fire pit. Oran felt a plunging sensation in his gut. The Celica and the Galant were already there, waiting on either side of the pit.

The Hummer slid to a stop behind them. The Ford F1 and Chevy Bel Air edged in tight behind the Hummer. There was nowhere else to run.

"What do we do?" Ghost asked.

Oran shot the cars up, breaking glass and destroying mirrors and headlights. The cars didn't seem impressed. The Hummer pushed forward, crowding into them.

He shot their tires, but the tires didn't deflate.

The Hummer, deciding it had had enough, pushed into Oran, knocking him down.

"What devilry is this?" Oran asked. "If you are little people, show yourselves!"

The cars laughed, a sound akin to diesel fuel leaks and pistons accelerating.

Ghost helped Oran up. As soon as he was back on his feet, the Hummer moved forward, backing them up to the monkey bars.

"I know what they want," Ghost said. She climbed onto the Hummer's bumper, then reached into the monkey bars and snapped one of her wrists into the cuffs.

"No," Oran said. "We can't give up."

"We're surrounded," Ghost said. "We've got no choice."

Oran looked frantically from side to side. He felt his hopes of ever getting home slipping away with every second. The Ford F1 nudged him. The message was clear: lock yourself in the cuffs, or get run over. If it was one thing he'd learned in his time in Canada, it was that more time to think was better, and the battle was never lost. He climbed onto the Ford F1 and cuffed himself.

The cars revved their engines angrily. Oran and Ghost cuffed their other hand. As soon as they were fully cuffed, the cars pulled back gently, allowing them to hang from the monkey bars.

"Alright, you've got us. Now show yourselves!" Oran yelled.

The cars pulled back away from them, and then they went silent.

The sun wailed its fiery anger from above. In the open, Oran and Ghost had no protection from its cancerous rays. He was able to monitor the time that passed by the arc of the sun. By his guess, they had been cuffed around 4, during the heat of the day. With each minute, his joints hurt more. The weight of his body, his pack, and his rifle, were a burden on his shoulders and wrists. He felt like his arms were being pulled out of his socket.

The way Ghost kept adjusting, he figured she was having just as many problems, if not more. Her body was full of metal, after all. That was a lot of extra weight to carry around.

He swung back and forth, legs outstretched like a gymnast. Only, instead of trying to perform a perfect 10, Oran was trying to ease his pain. He would have to pay for it in spades. With each swing, his shoulders hurt more. His feet arched higher in the air. At the same time, he could feel his energy plummeting. It was hard to swing with fifty pounds of pack and rifle. He would only have one shot at this. If he didn't make it, he'd be stuck in his current position.

He kicked high and curled back. He felt his legs going above his head. Then the world flipped on him, and a spike of pain told him his legs had slammed down on top of the monkey bars. Slowly, grunting, he pulled himself upright on top of the bars. Now he could ease some tension. Immediately, he felt blood draining back into his arms.

Below him, Ghost began kicking out like he had. She quit after eight kicks.

Between deep breaths, she said, "I can't. It hurts too much."

"Try one more time. I'll grab you."

She nodded, took a few quick breaths, then kicked out as hard as she could. Her ankles cleared the bars, but not by much. Oran reached out with his legs and did a scissors cut maneuver to grab her legs. Her ankles slipped down his shins, but caught at his ankles.

"Okay," she said. "This is weird."

Oran laughed. He was sweating profusely. It was north of ninety five degrees outside, and gymnastics routines were meant to be done in spandex, not full battle armor.

He pulled her legs across the bars. Once her knees were up, she was able to pull herself the rest of the way.

They both lay on the bars now, legs dangling off behind them while they caught their breath.

In all this time, the cars hadn't moved an inch.

"What now?" Ghost asked.

"We wait."

Suddenly, his radio crackled to life, eliciting a high-pitched yowl, then went out. He looked to the cars, but if the people in them had noticed, he had no way of knowing.

A moment later, two sharp squawks burst from the radio. There was a pause, then a long squawk, followed by a sharp one, and then the long and short were repeated. Oran glanced to Ghost. Her robotic eyes darted from the cars to the radio. *So she has picked up on it, too*, he assumed.

Wendigos speak most languages, and the same goes for other monsters. But Morse code was an old communication system the military could still use that monsters did not understand. If these were monsters, they wouldn't know what they were saying to each other. If they were just human cannibals, which seemed more and more likely, then it was still unlikely that they would know Morse code.

He was just grateful that Troy had discovered a way to hack into Oran's radio and get it back on. (Oran had turned it off during the run to the playground.)

Short, short, long, then a pause. I, C, U. Troy was watching them from the hills and not moving in. Oran figured as soon as he had climbed on top of the monkey bars, they'd become visible again. With the hills behind him, he shifted his weight in such a way that he could show the cuffs to Troy. He then tapped his finger on the monkey bars, signaling "wait."

Troy sent back in code, "We will wait for your signal."

While they waited, Oran tried to figure out who his captors were. His guess was cannibals. He figured they were hiding out in their cars to keep out of the sun, which was burning bright in the sky above them. Once the sun went down, the cannibals would cook them. The only part of this that didn't equate was why they allowed him and Ghost to keep their weapons. They would be able to shoot the cannibals dead once they got out of their cars. Oran could not figure this part out, so he thought on it and prayed to Natosi.

A few hours later, the sun decided it was time to end their torture and slowly faded behind the jagged curtains of the Rocky Mountains. Even in its setting, the sun creeped along its axis, as if it had a personal vendetta against Oran. Sitting in the open, even with all their gear, Oran worried about the damage they'd received from the sun. Were the seeds of cancers now planted deep in the basal layer of his skin? Was he returning home only to find a carcinogenic death sentence? He had been away for five years now. If he was going back home utterly useless to his wife and son because he was too sick to work, what good was he? What purpose does a sick man have when he can't take care of his family?

This last thought really struck him. "A family man's only use in the world is duty to his family," he said to Ghost. "This is what battle has taught me. When I'm away, no matter how good I may be for the war, I am more important to my son and wife. Me being away, I didn't make the sacrifice. They did. They have lived on their own, a widowed wife and an orphaned son while I was away. If I go back, and I've gotten sick from cancer, I will be a burden on them. My wife doesn't need another child to take care of, and my son doesn't need a weak man in the house."

"I don't believe that you are sick. You are one of the cleanest men I've met. And even if the sun's rays did get to you this afternoon, if you got cancer, I think you have so much to offer your son and wife than health. You have a wisdom that your boy needs to hear. And he needs to see your devotion to your wife so that he will see how to treat a wife. Life kicks us when we are down, but that doesn't mean we can't get back up."

"Thanks," Oran said. "I needed that." Internally, he was thinking that he just whined about his perfect life to a woman with no face. What the hell kind of problems did he have?

The light of a small fire blazed orange and red on their faces, catching their attention. A tall man in bedraggled underwear was leaning over the fire pit. He had placed a few twigs down on the ground and doused them with gasoline. The tank of gasoline lay next to several large logs. While Ghost and Oran talked about their troubles, he lit the gasoline. The biting smell stung the inside of Oran's nose.

"Who are you?" Oran asked.

When the man stood, he was almost as tall as the monkey bars. He was lean, too, but had no cancer scars.

"Isn't it obvious? I'm the cook."

Oran didn't like having his fears revealed. "You cannot eat us."

"Why not? My family's been eating your kind for thousands of years." The lean man dragged some of the logs to the fire pit.

"Oran," Ghost said to get his attention. In the darkness, the other cars were standing up. They were reaching to fenders and tire walls and pulling them off. Auto body parts fell like leaves to the ground, then were swept away in the wind. Only the largest parts were too heavy to be lifted by the wind.

Underneath the leaves were tall people in very few clothes. Their faces and bodies were blackened from exhaust and grime.

"You are skin walkers," Oran said.

"Can't hide anything from you," a bald man said, smiling. His smile was full of sharp teeth, like a shark or a wolf.

"I always thought skin walkers changed into wolves and bears," Oran said.

"Like everyone else, we adapted. Wolf skins won't protect you from that sun's malignant curse. But Detroit steel? Shit, man. You can sit outside all day and nobody'd notice."

Oran watched the others pull their "skins" off. The Ford F1 had been the bald man. The Chevy Bel Air became a frazzle-haired, middle aged woman with a face as sharp as the lines of the Bel Air. The Celica became a short woman with a long, hawkish nose. She was maybe four feet tall. Compared to the seven foot tall giants, she was practically a baby. After the Hummer pulled his skin from his back, a bloated belly heaved up. He was a heavily obese man whose legs struggled to support his weight. That left the Galant, which Oran figured was the first man they met.

Except for the short one, they all had bulbous noses like hockey players or boxers.

"Damn, y'all are ugly sons of bitches," Ghost said.

"I will use your face as a plate for your meat," the fat skin walker said.

"What kind of seasoning do we have for them?"

"I have several marinades we can use," the cook said. He opened a refrigerator, which was as small as a microfridge next to him. The working fridge was stocked with trays of meat and milk jugs of marinade. "I was thinking the balsamic vinaigrette and red onion."

"You're trying to put me on South Beach diet again, aren't you?" the fat one asked.

"It wouldn't hurt, Baba. I want you to have a long life."

"How about we compromise? Barbecue?" the woman with the sharp features asked.

"Barbecue," the fat one said.

The cook shrugged. He grabbed two jugs of red barbecue sauce and strode over to Oran and Ghost. He popped the lid on one of the jugs and began pouring it down Oran's shirt, saying, "Don't fight me. You'll only make this worse." The sauce smelled tangy. Then he pulled on Oran's pants and poured some of the sauce down the front of his pants. "Okay, now wiggle."

Oran shrugged his shoulders.

"Come on, little man. You know how a marinade works. I need it all over you. And just so we're clear, either you can marinade yourself, or I can marinade you. Either way works for me."

Oran moved around on the ladder as much as the cuffs would let him so that the juices would run down his legs and his shirt. The skin walkers watched him, unblinking. He was practically brisket and ribs in their dreams already.

"That was really good. You're Blackfeet, ain't ya? South Piegan?" the short one with the upturned nose asked. "I can smell it in ya. Damn, I don't care what name you go by, you Blackfeet taste good."

Oran felt like puking. How many of his friends and neighbors had this backwoods family of skin walkers eaten?

The cook finished him off by pouring the last of the jug on his hand and slathering Oran's face with the vinegar. It stung his eyes and clumped in his hair. It was kind of like being slapped with a fat, tangy booger.

"Now, your turn, little girl," the cook said. "I know the girls don't like to be touched, but what's good for cooking the gander is good for cooking the goose, if you get my drift."

She sat rigid while he bathed her in barbecue sauce, his hands moving over the front and back of her torso. If she was appalled, her cold, robotic face didn't show it. However, as his hands moved along her spine, she gave a little twist to prick his fingers. It was enough for the spikes on her vertebra to draw blood.

"Christ on a skewer, that hurt!" The cook waved his hand as he dropped the gallon and sucked on his finger. He glowered at Ghost.

"She did that on purpose!" the fat one accused her.

The cook yelled, "You do that again, and I'll shove a stick so far up your asshole, it comes out your mouth, and then I'll cook you alive. I'll make soldier kabob with you, you hear me?"

Ghost gave her usual noncommittal response, staring back at the skin walkers blankly. Her nickname could have been earned by her ability to communicate absolutely nothing from her face. She was like the dead in that way: nothing to emote.

He approached her again. "Pull your trousers out. Now." She reluctantly pulled her pants button away from her body. The cook emptied the rest of the jug. "Now, wiggle like he did."

Ghost did a slow little wiggle. The juices ran down her legs and out the bottom of her pants. The cook lifted her by the ankle and sniffed at her calves. Then he gave her one quick lick.

"Hey!" the middle aged woman said.

The cook held his hand out to her while he thought about Ghost's taste. Then he said, "Oh, they'll be good ones."

"How much longer? I'm starving," the short woman asked.

"Quit your bellyaching. They haven't even begun to cook yet. I'm trying to decide to smoke them or to just sear them on either side."

"Searing locks in the flavor," the bald one said.

"True, but smoking gives that nice pink glow lining their meats."

"I suggest smoking us," Oran said.

The cook wrinkled his nose at him.

"I'm serious."

The cook said, "You think you're being clever, but let me tell ya a thing. If I sear you, you'll be dead inside of three minutes. Your clothes will catch fire, then you will catch fire and your flesh will blacken and crisp. But if I smoke you, you'll die slowly over the next sixty to eighty minutes. Your flesh will blister and sting, and you'll stop sweating because your body just doesn't have any way to cope with the heat any more. But what will kill you will be the smoke inhalation. As you scream to death, your lungs will fill up with some nice mesquite or hickory smoke. The air sacks inside will burst as they try to force your blood into oxygen. Your legs filling with blood, the capillaries bursting in your eyes, you still won't be dead yet, but if there's a god smiling down upon you, you'll soon blackout from the smoke inhalation. You won't really be dead for another five to ten minutes after that. So I'd better be careful what you ask for, Blackfeet."

"And I'd be careful what you ask for, skin walker," Ghost said. She pulled out her AR-15 and blew a cavity in the skin walker's head. While the other skin walkers howled at her, he spat his remaining teeth at her. As his head slowly grew back, he said, "You stupid stuckskin ass! Lead can't kill me."

"I'm not trying to kill you. I'm trying to distract you."

A single air zipped through the air and thunked into the small cavity remaining in the cook's re-forming face. The skin walker fell backwards. He was dead before he hit the ground.

Ghost jumped over to Oran. She shoved a narrow shim into the metal strand. The narrow piece of metal was all she needed to undo the handcuffs. She pulled on the strand and the bracelet came off. She quickly freed his other hand.

Oran rubbed his wrists quickly. He needed to get off the monkey bars. Laying six feet above the monkey bars, they'd gotten a little too warm for his comfort. Oran and Ghost jumped off the monkey bars and ran for a tire wall.

"Get them!" the bald one yelled. He pulled his skin off and fell to the ground, rumbling and growling and sounding suddenly more like a car engine than a human.

Arrows zipped overhead as Oran and Ghost did their best impression of recruits in BASIC climbing the obstacle course. They scampered over it faster than anyone could, then jumped down on the smashed cars beneath them. As they landed, the Chevy Bel Air crashed through the wall. Oran and Ghost leapt from the smashed car as it exploded to the side. The Chevy struck them in midair like they were levitating bowling pins.

Oran was lucky enough to hit another wall of tires. Ghost fumbled off of corrugated steel.

The Celica and the F1 came behind the Chevy, with the Hummer in the back. Oran barely had enough time to shake off the first hit before the Ford F1 was at him. He jumped to the side, and then when the F1 stopped, he hopped into the back of its bed.

The Celica fared better than the Ford. Ghost was phased and stumbling to her feet. She had a boxer's knees after being hit with a strong uppercut. She told her body to move, but the message wasn't getting through. By sheer luck she fell over out of the Celica's way.

The Hummer, though, it would not miss her.

Suddenly, Troy appeared out of nowhere and shot up the Hummer. The Hummer veered to the side. It was going for Troy now.

As Troy shot the Hummer, Oran grabbed his lance and jammed it into the creases between the metal of the truck bed. That didn't change anything.

Troy blasted the window of the Hummer, but the skin walker kept coming at the wall. Kai pulled him aside as the Hummer crashed through. He landed awkwardly on a car and rolled in pain.

"You can't stop moving, Troy," she said, dragging him to his feet as the Hummer burst into the area. She looked around for an advantage, but this was the open area with a single teacher's desk. She pulled him on top of it. He was holding his wrist. Kai could see that it was broken, but there was nothing she could do. She drew an arrow and aimed for the Hummer, which circled them.

Back with the other cars, the F1 veered sharply, flinging Oran off. He rolled into a trash pile and knocked over a bunch of old dirty diapers, falling behind a desk that had been hidden in the diapers. The smell was overwhelming. He glanced over the desk and noticed that the F1 had returned to the others. They were all now ganging up on Ghost.

Oran wished he had an answer, some magical cure-all that could end this, but he didn't. They were hopelessly outgunned and outmatched by the skin walkers. In car form, his lance and Kai's arrows were not strong enough to pierce their metal hides. So he prayed. "Natosi, please help me. I am stuck, and I have done everything I can to save my friends, but I have nothing more to give. If you can, send help. Please, Natosi."

He opened his eyes and hoped for some relief, but all around him were more horrors.

Ghost was back on her feet, but now she was cornered. The Celica, Chevy, and Ford F1 revved their engines at her. Together they looked like something out of a Stephen King nightmare.

The cars took turns feinting at Ghost. First one would come at her, and she'd jump with all of her might out of the way. It would be a pitiful jump because she'd twisted her ankle escaping the first car's attack. She wouldn't have long to feel guilty before a different car would feint at her.

"Come on!" Ghost shouted. "If you want me, come get me!"

The cars stopped. Like the four engines of the apocalypse, they lined up together and flashed their high beams on. Ghost put her hand over her metal eyes.

Oran felt a drop of rain on him. Rain was very rare in the plains, especially this side of the Rockies.

Another drop. And then another, and another. Rain dappled his skin, then a powerful lightning burst into the ground not far from the skin walkers. They pulled back instinctually.

Suddenly, a deluge of rain poured out of the sky. Thunder rippled loudly across the plains. The cars spun, but the dirt quickly turned to mud. They spun their tires faster.

Oran laughed. He thanked Natosi for helping him. He raised his eyes to the sky. Lightning cracked, and he could see the wave of clouds rolling through the sky. The lightning colored the clouds blue and pink. He'd never seen a more beautiful thunder storm in all his life.

A trick of the eye caught him. The clouds fluttered like the wings of a giant thunderbird. With each lightning blast, he was more convinced he was seeing the feathers of a giant eagle. From out of the heavens, something floated down to him. A small purple and blue feather landed in the open drawer of the desk. What he saw inside gave him hope.

Just as suddenly as the storm arrived, it disappeared.

"Stop!" Oran yelled. "Michael, Lewis, Angel, Sarah, and Daniel."

The cars spun out to face Oran. This was not easy in the mud. Oran stood before them, a car inventory book held up in his hand. The book had exactly five entries. Five names.

"The one thing that can always kill a skin walker," he said, "is saying their name out loud."

The car engines died. The skin walkers pulled their rusted hoods and white walled tires off their bodies and left them like dead flesh surrounding them. There was no wind to blow the leaves away this time.

On their knees, the skin walkers begged Oran not to say their names. "Please. We will do anything you want. Ask us any favor, but do not say our names."

"Let us go. Give us cars and gas, and do not follow us. If you do, I will shout your names to the sun and the moon and the four winds."

With each declaration, the skin walkers answered back louder and louder, "Yes!"

When Oran finished, they pulled out a long school bus that had been hidden behind a wall. "This will get you far. It is in good condition."

Oran didn't ask why the windows were broken and covered in blood stains. Kai and Troy helped Ghost into the back of the yellow bus. Oran showed the skin walkers the car inventory book with their names before climbing into the driver's seat. He dropped the thunderbird's feather in his parfleche. "All I have to do is say the names," he reminded them, then turned the engine on and drove out of Nester's Neighborhood.

# CHAPTER TWENTY ONE

The kids liked being in the bus. For the first time since Oran and Recon Team picked them up out of that hellhole behind the Cabinet Mountains, the children acted like normal kids. A quiet hum of excited voices rose from the back of the bus. For this group of kids, they might as well have been cheering at a concert, they were so loud, by Wendigo Road comparisons.

Oran didn't correct them. They deserved their happiness. Browning was not far away, and out on the plains, he was certain he'd see wendigos from a mile away. They should take advantage of the opportunity to talk and be like regular kids. They hadn't been able to just be kids in so long. They were always hiding or running or escaping. Quiet was a premium. They'd learned sign language and used it well. His quick glances in the rearview mirror told him many of the kids were still using sign language.

Troy and Kai wrapped Ghost's wrist. She definitely broke it during her fall. She groaned and shifted on the bus couch, trying to find the best position for not disturbing her arm. Troy gave her some morphine to help while they drove. The bus's struts were old and dirty. They left a lot of bounce in the old school bus, which was not kind to broken limbs.

After giving Ghost the morphine, her eyes closed and she fell into a deep sleep.

Troy said, "She should be okay. Does Browning have a doctor? I have been in contact with them, but I didn't hear anything about a doctor."

"You have been in contact with them?"

"Yeah. Once we cleared the mountains, these tentacles lit up like a reservation casino. They know we are coming, and that we are bringing twenty two children and a couple of haggard soldiers out of the mountains. They are making preparations for us at the old high school gym. But is there a doctor?"

"There was when I was there," Oran replied.

"Reservation clinic?"

"No, there is a whole hospital there. Doctors, nurses, techs, everything. But that was years ago, and a lot has changed since then, I am certain. The one constant out here is change."

"What do you mean?" Kai asked. She put her hand on his shoulder. Oran wasn't sure how he felt about that. Kai had always seemed closer to him than he was to her. He remembered legends of the sky people. Sometimes, sky people could be needy of humans. His situation dictated that he not stress that relationship. He needed her on his side. But he was going home to his wife. He wasn't intending to bring home a half-naked white girl to his wife. Oran leaned forward and away from her touch.

Her eyebrows knitted together in confusion, but she didn't say anything either.

"What I mean is that on the res, people go off to war every day, mostly kids. And while the town's never been attacked directly, the reservation is on the edge of wendigo territory, so the people there sometimes encounter monsters on the edge of the plains, like those skin walkers."

"Yeah, what was that about?" Troy asked. "Really? Skin walkers? I thought they were Transformers. Robots in disguise."

Oran smiled at Troy's reference. "I'd be guessing that, too, if I didn't see it with my own eyes. But they were skin walkers. Said so themselves. And I saw them pull the autobodies off just like skin. They said that like everything else, they'd adapted to the sun's radiation. Wolf skins didn't cut it anymore. They needed a skin that protected them during daylight hours."

"That's crazy," Troy said. "But I can respect that."

"There is something else needs asking," Troy said. "Now that we've got the time and nobody is trying to kill us every second of the day, do you mind telling me something?"

"Shoot," Oran said.

"Back in the Swans, I stabbed a wendigo. I killed it with my knife."

"You're wondering how you did that, and if you can do it again?"

"Well, yeah. I mean, I've seen Kai kill monsters with her stick arrows, and I've seen you take out wendigos with your lance, but all the time I've been in the fight, I've never seen a bullet or a bomb truly all-out kill one of those damn things. So what was different?"

Oran slowed the bus to maneuver around an 18-wheeler that was squatting in the middle of the two-lane highway like a long-dead dinosaur.

"The army tried to get me and a few others to start a school for wendigo slayers. We told them it wouldn't work, but they wanted us to try anyway. We tested them and shook them, and we got them involved in the war spiritually, but we never had better than a 15% success rate. We told them you couldn't train somebody to be a wendigo slayer. Either they were or they weren't."

"So what changed in me? I know I got angry, eh, but if all it took was anger, we'd be done with this FUBAR war by now, right?"

"I agree. It is not anger. But there is a purity there, and I think there is something in that purity. It was not just that you were angry at the wendigo. In that moment, you surrendered yourself to Natosi and he granted you the power to slay."

"But I don't really believe in any of that B.S. Like I told you, if anything, I was raised Catholic."

Oran shrugged. "Then maybe the white man's God gave you your powers. I'm not going to pretend I have all the answers. Like I said, we only had a 15% success rate. I don't think we did much to create new slayers."

"Will he be able to slay again?" Kai asked, cutting Oran off before he could say more. "I think that's the real question he wants to know."

"Maybe. I don't know. If he fights with the same purity as he did up in the Swans, then I think so. We had this exercise at the training school. Every soldier enlisted in the program had his own lance. And at the end of every week, each wendigo slayer candidate was told to stab a wendigo heart that the school had. Some people, no matter how often they hit that heart, and no matter how many classes they attended or how much spiritual training they received, they never could stab the heart. Others could stab it every time. And some could stab it, but only once. I'm afraid I don't have a wendigo heart for you to test your abilities against. Until then, you will just have to test it the way everything else is tested in the army: in the grand crucible of battle."

Troy pulled his knife out. "Is it holy?"

"As holy as you make it. If I give you a piece of mud and tell you it is holy mud with magical properties, does it matter if you don't believe in the mud?"

Troy leaned back in his seat. They approached the town from the southeast. Ahead, the sun was rising. There wasn't a cloud in the sky. The small town of Browning emerged along the horizon looking very much like the Promised Land. A halo of eastern light from the rising sun gave the little town a glow.

Seeing the town stirred up emotions in Oran. Browning had always been his home, and he didn't realize how much being away for five years would affect him. Browning was a small town, so every inch of it had a personal story for him. They passed an old, meaningless lot on the outskirts of town, but Oran saw the narrow dirt trail where he had raced his bike. Jumping Purgatory Creek was a rite of passage for all eleven year olds from Browning. They came to a round-about. Down the road to the south Oran saw the convenience store where he held his first job and the spot where he first met his wife.

If he turned east onto 89, his home was not far out of town. He could be there in ten minutes with his wife and child. His heart ached for them, pulling him south.

"Your family is that way," Kai said.

"Yes."

"We should go there first."

"No." His voice slackened and stiffened, all in one word. "Not until I have delivered you and the children to safety. Jodi and Daniel would have wanted it that way. Besides, knowing Jodi, she is probably already there helping to set up cots."

He rolled the bus around the round-about and headed west to the high school. A few blocks further, and they arrived. This was the school where he'd gone to school. It was a run-down building, but what wasn't since the wendigos emerged? Compared to the disaster zones he'd visited in wendigo territory, this gym was the Taj Mahal.

The construction firm designed the front entrance to resemble a tipi facing east, which was important to the South Piegans. Oran drove past the entrance and circled around to the school's gymnasium, on the far side. There he found old cars and young horses parked in the lot and people carrying wheelbarrows full of food and provisions for the children. They waved at the bus as it came to a stop at the curb.

Oran scanned the people for his wife or son. He told himself not to hope that they were there, that there was a good chance they hadn't received word of his arrival since they lived outside of town, but his heart couldn't help hoping. That's just the way the heart works. Even when the brain feeds it the logical explanation, the heart overrides logic.

He did not see Jodi or Daniel outside. Maybe they were inside.

As soon as the bus's brake drums REEEEEd their stop, a woman Oran knew named Dolores Little Owl climbed into the bus. She was a middle aged woman with a round face and a thick body, but she was always full of life. He had gone to school with her, and now she was a teacher.

"Oran!" she reached out with both arms to give him the biggest hug, and refused to let go.

"Dolores. It is good to see you. I have—"

"It is so good to see you. I can't tell you how glad I am that you've come back."

"Yes. I have brought the children with me." He pointed to them. Dolores pulled away. Seeing their disheveled, gaunt faces brought a tear to her eye.

"Of course, the children."

She addressed them, saying, "My name is Dolores Little Owl. I am a teacher here at Browning High School. We understand you are very tired and very hungry. You have endured so much, and we are so proud of you for making it here. What we are going to do now is bring you all inside the gym. There is plenty of food and drink, and cots if you need to sleep. We are going to take your names down and have a doctor examine you."

Ghost's bandaged arm caught Dolores' eye. "Oh, dear. We will bring you first to the doctor. We may need to take you to the hospital, my dear."

Ghost nodded groggily, though it mostly looked creepy.

"Does she need a stretcher? Cause we have one."

"I can walk," Ghost said. She stood from her seat, wincing. "I've walked this far. I can walk a little farther."

Dolores got back down out of the bus. Ghost, Oran, and Troy left first. There was a line of people waiting outside the gym. Some of them smiled and nodded and said, "Welcome to Browning." A few were kids holding little homemade signs. The signs were similarly worded, but in a child's hand, and often with crayons or markers.

Then Kai walked off the bus in little more than her bow and arrows, the reaction was immediate. Fathers (and mothers) dropped their jaws. A few scowled, and a few blushed. Mostly, they tried covering their children's eyes before they could see anything. The damage was already done, though. Children were gaping. Some of the older ones were trying to peek around their Mom and Dad's hands.

Not that Kai noticed. She was too busy directing kids off the bus. Sure, the crowd was silent, but she was accustomed to long bouts of silence, so she didn't think it was odd nobody said anything.

One woman glared at her husband, arms akimbo, until he stopped staring.

Another woman said under her breath to her friend, "Honey, I didn't even know they could come like that."

"Excuse me," a taller woman said after she stopped waving when she saw Kai step out of the bus. When nobody from the bus reacted, she said more loudly, "EX-CUSE me."

Everybody stopped.

"Does she know she's naked?" the tall woman asked. Oran recognized the accuser as Betty Magee. She was an older woman, not yet 60. She used to work in his warehouse, sorting foods and wrapping palettes for shipment.

"This is Kai. She did not grow up in our world," Oran said. He thought of stories of people who fell in love with the sky people.

"You got that right." This was the same woman who didn't know a woman's body could look like Kai's.

"She..." and he thought about telling them the truth, that this woman was one of the Above People, like the stars, and she had come down to be with them. He did not think they were ready for this story to become reality. He said, "She is from up high in the mountains. She saved our lives many times."

Betty chirped, "And now she's in Browning. We have societal rules."

Oran said, "The white man wanted to dress us like him. He stole our People's ways by telling us how to dress, how to eat, and how to pray. After all that, I am not going to tell this woman how she is supposed to dress. This is the way her family lives."

"You might as well be comparing apples and oranges, Oran. That happened hundreds of years ago. That world is dead. But some things are true. You simply do not walk around bare-assed naked through town in front of children."

Kai said, "I have walked around this way for the past week, bringing these children safely through Wendigo Country. It was good enough for surviving those mountains, and it is good enough now. If you spent less time fearing the sun and more time celebrating him, you would dress like me, and Natosi would smile down on you and grace you. To me, you are all the indecent ones because you're ashamed of your bodies and hide them from the sun. I am not embarrassed. Perhaps that is why you are all covered in scars and not me."

Dolores stepped forward. "Why don't we talk about this later, Betty? These people have survived an ordeal. We can discuss this at another time, okay?"

"I hope for your sake, you do, Dolores. You've already lost your husband once to the Old Chiefs. You don't want it to happen again."

Oran wondered what that meant, and if his dreams had more to tell him than he thought.

The last of the children out of the bus, they walked into the dilapidated gym. Decades of disrepair had taken its toll on the gym but the roof still stood, and the floorboards were straight and polished, a small miracle.

The gym was separated into four areas: registration, supplies, rest, and medical. All the adults had been ushered into medical for immediate review, as well as Private Quiet One.

A line of tables along the far side of the gym had everything a person could want. It was like a hurricane evacuee center. There were clothes, towels, toiletries, lemonade, water bottles, homemade chocolate chip cookies, fresh hotdogs and pizza, and fry bread. A few of the kids were gawking at the pizza and lemonade like fine wine. These were the kids who'd already been processed. They excitedly collected a slice of pepperoni pizza and a lemonade and sat at picnic tables that had been brought in for them.

At another row of tables, which were near the bus entrance, men and women were taking down names and basic information about the children. What were their parents' names and where were they born? What tribe were they, or were they white or Hispanic?

But for Oran, there was only one question, and it had yet to be answered. He searched the faces of the volunteers. None of them were Jodi or Daniel. He'd hoped he would catch the eye of his son or wife, and maybe they would go running up and hold each other. He didn't know if he would laugh or cry when he saw them. Right now, though, he was getting very antsy. Where were they?

"Dolores," Oran said, holding on to her hand tightly, "Where are Jodi and Daniel? Are they back at the house?"

Before she could answer, Oran heard one of the volunteers talking angrily. "No, I need your real name," the man said. Oran knew Milton Decker. He was one of those kids growing up who was 15 going on 50. Even as a kid Milton walked tightly, head stooped like osteoporosis was setting in. Now that he was a 40ish year old, he was older than dirt, and just as compassionate.

"I gave you my real name."

"Don't lie to me, son. No white kid's named Blood Clot Boy."

"Private Blood Clot Boy," the child emphasized.

Oran guided through the children, parting them like a kayaker parting the waters of a lake in autumn. He put his hand on Blood Clot Boy's shoulder.

"Tell them my name is Blood Clot Boy," the child said. "I don't want any other name."

"Hey, they need the name you used before you met me."

"But I don't want that name."

"You will not be forced to use it. To me, you will always be Blood Clot Boy," Oran said, parting the child's hair. "But Milton here needs to know your original first and last name for record keeping. It is in case any family members try searching for you. You would not want them to get confused, would you?"

"I guess not, but I don't have any parents anymore, so does it have to matter?"

"Yes, Private Blood Clot Boy. It matters. It may sound strange, but one day people will look back on these horrible years, and they will want to know what life was like and what we did. They will want to know all about you: your adventures, your love for stories, and your feats of strength. Without giving these nice volunteers your information, they will not be able to record you."

"Oh," Blood Clot Boy said despondently. "Well, I guess, then. If it helps people to remember where they came from, I guess it is important."

Milton glared at Oran crossly. Oran said as coolly as he could, "Wait till you get to Private Go Fuck Yourself."

"You're joking."

Oran just smiled at him. Perhaps it was a bit toothy of a grin, but Oran was pleased with himself.

He returned to Dolores. Before he could say anything, she put her hand up in his face. She was handing out Oreos to the kids.

In front of them were the bleachers where he used to make out with his wife back when she was still just his girlfriend and the war seemed so far away.

"Dolores, I need to find my wife and son. Do you know where they are?"

She eyed him carefully, like a cat trying to decide what to do with the mouse between her paws.

"I need to tell you something," she said.

Oran looked away. He looked down. He looked for a chair. He looked for them one final moment. "No," he pleaded.

"It's not what you think," she said. "They are alive."

"Oh, thank God," he said.

"Don't be thankful just yet. You remember Ernest Upham and Greg Falcon Runs? They took Jodi and Daniel away."

"Away? Where?" Oran started moving toward the door.

Dolores pushed him back with her hand. "Back to the Sawtooth Mountains."

"I will sow the mountains with their blood."

She stopped him again. "Hold on. There's something you should know. You remember Marrow Bones' son Horus? He's not more than fourteen now, but he followed them as far as he could. He turned back when he caught sight of Ernest and Greg meeting with a wendigo. Horus says it was the biggest one he's ever seen. Taller than two pines standing end-to-end."

"I've made a living killing monsters. I don't care how big or hungry this undead creature is. Ernest and Greg could've made a deal with a hundred wendigos, and I wouldn't care. I will kill every monster that stands between me and my family."

"We want to help."

Oran scanned them. Troy, Kai, and the children of Crazy Dog Company stood ready for battle.

Oran studied them for a moment, his eyes as hard as iron. "I cannot ask this," he said, his voice choking as the weight of their gift affected him.

"You don't have to," Private First Class Bruce said. "You saved me in the orchards and got us through the mountains. We all owe you a debt we can never repay. Let us do this for you, General."

He scanned the crowd of children, aged 5 to 17. All of them were gaunt, malnourished, and dirty as stray dogs. "I am humbled by your gratitude, children, but no. I did not bring you here just for you to die in the mountains saving Old Chiefs. If you want to repay me, stay here, regain your strength, and make something of your lives. Be good people, serve your communities, raise families, cause that's how we'll beat this thing. Don't hate people because they're different."

Oran picked up a chocolate chip cookie and handed it to the little girl he'd first told the Blackfeet creation story. Her name was Private Old Woman now. He smiled at her and ruffled her hair, then he shook hands with Troy. "Look after these kids while I'm out."

"I can kill for you," Troy said.

"You are needed here. Ghost needs you."

Troy handed Oran an old walkie talkie. It had thick nobs and a fat antenna, like a relic from the Vietnam War. "I'll be listening."

To Kai, Oran said, "I need someone to watch over the kids while I'm gone."

"Are you ordering me to do that?"

"I don't give orders any more. I just ask real nicely. Please watch over them."

With that, he walked out of the gym and went to go get his wife and son.

# CHAPTER TWENTY TWO

Anticipating his needs, and as a partial apology for what happened with his wife, the elders had retrieved his pickup from his home and brought it to the gym. They did not mention why they felt so guilty and wanted to apologize to him, and Oran left it alone. His dreams had been real, he knew now without a doubt. He had bigger problems than the elders, but when he came back, he would have to address his wife's treatment.

The red F-250 Highboy was an early 70s monster with a lean body and a front-side wench. It was high enough to drive over his land, yet sturdy enough to last forever. Family legend had it that Grandfather Old Chief won it on a horse bet.

Oran put his boot in the stirrup and climbed into the driver's seat and drove home. There, he gathered his rifle and went to the fire pit in the backyard to start a fire. He removed the thunderbird feather from his parfleche. He hadn't really taken the time to study the feather. It was a true thunderbird. It felt slick and smooth in his hand. The colors of the feather were like staring at a sunset that never ended, purple and blue and rose in between.

Oran held the feather over his head and squeezed, like he was milking a cow. Water flowed into his mouth, much more water than the feather could possibly hold. He cleansed his face and hands, and then placed the feather on a porcelain dish on the ground.

Oran kneeled down before the fire. "Natosi, I thank you for delivering me and the children to Browning. I have one last request. Help me defeat my enemies and take back my wife and son."

He sat in silent contemplation while the fire burned bright in front of him, then he took the thunderbird's feather from the plate and placed it in the fire. Strangely, the feather did not fly up into the air. He'd feared the thermal energy coming off of the fire would blow a flaming feather back into his face. The feather stayed in the fire where he placed it. Dapples of water and oil surfaced on the feather, and then it burst into flames.

Oran placed his lance into the back of the Highboy and drove away from his home.

Along the highway, he spotted a familiar face. Kai stood in the open with all the sun shining down on her. He pulled up alongside her.

"You shouldn't be here."

"I'm exactly where I need to be."

"But the children."

"There are more than enough people in Browning to take care of those children. You didn't order me not to go."

"I asked nicely."

"Something happened in those mountains. I can't explain it. I haven't wanted to talk about it. We talked to the dead. I met my grandmother. She told me many things, but the most important thing she told me was to always be here, so you need to know that I will always be here."

"Always?"

"Just as you escorted those children through the mountains, I will escort you. You can't make me stop that any more than you could make Molotov or Ghost not escort those children."

Oran opened the door, and she slid in beside him.

Up the road a bit he regarded something that stirred in him a familiar feeling of dread. He slowed down in front of the road block. A Chevy Bel Air and a Ford F1 cut off the highway.

Oran reached for his parfleche, which carried the car inventory book.

The Ford F1 ripped his metal skin off and approached the Highboy in a path of rust-colored petals.

"I'm not here to start trouble," the bald skin walker said, smiling mischievously. Oran didn't trust a mischievous smile, especially one full of serrated teeth.

"Then why are you blocking my path?" Oran asked.

"I wouldn't be, but a voice came over all the radios at Nester's Neighborhood. It was so loud, it was like it was coming from somewhere inside us. The voice told us to meet you here and guide you north to Chief Mountain and help you get your wife and child back."

"Whose voice?" Oran asked, but he had a good idea.

"I don't know, but we're here."

Oran nodded. "If they are going to Chief Mountain, these men and this wendigo are taking my wife and son back up to Canada. We must hurry."

The three cars drove west, then turned north. Up 89 they drove. They drove all day. By nightfall, signs told them they were now on Chief Mountain Road. A giant block of granite jutted out of the ground like the Earth's tooth. It blocked out the stars.

"How do we get there?" the bald skin walker asked when they stopped on the side of the road. "I've driven all these roads. No street takes you up to the mountain."

"We will have to drive along the creek. That will lead us to Chief Mountain."

"That is dangerous driving at night. We should wait until morning."

"You can all wait. I'm going."

"That's foolish," the bald skin walker said.

"If they escape to Canada and I lose my son and wife to them, then that is foolish. At night, they will not be able to see us."

"Wendigos are awake at night," Kai cautioned.

"Then we will have to be careful."

#

The cars cut along the edge of the creek, winding back and forth toward Chief Mountain.

"Why do they call it 'Chief Mountain?'" Kai asked.

"The Blackfeet called it Nínaiistáko. White people gave it different names, but they settled on 'Chief Mountain' as a kind of a compromise on the name. I'm skipping a lot of history there, but that's the gist of it."

Ahead, the F1 and the Bel Air rolled to a stop. Oran pulled up next to them and cut his engine.

"Road ended," Oran explained.

In front of them, the two giants pulled their skins off. The way the metal popped off their hides like bones being wrenched from sockets made Oran wince. He didn't care if their skin did transform into some kind of leaf, the sound was gruesome.

"We are entering sacred land," Oran said to Kai and the skin walkers. "My people have been taking pilgrimages here for centuries to hold rituals at the base of the mountain. The top of Nínaiistáko is a place where gods dwell. This world and the world of the gods are very close there. Gods can move back and forth between the realms of existence there."

"That is where we will find them, isn't it?" Kai asked.

"I think so."

The skin walkers grimaced, as if the idea of a sacred place left a bad taste in their mouth. They led the way, and Oran was not going to stop them. Even if they were on his side, he preferred being able to see them at all times.

They walked for several miles through forest, the strong face of Chief Mountain towering over the trees whenever they came to a clearing.

"Are there any other stories of Nínaiistáko?" Kai asked.

"Many," Oran replied. "But most are of great chiefs and warriors climbing its peaks to seek out great medicine and spirit journeys. They would use bison skulls for pillows." After a moment, he said, "There is this one, though."

"What's that?"

"It is said that during the end of days, a great white god would appear on the mountain. And upon the god's departure, the mountain would crumble. This would signify the end of the days of the Blackfeet."

They walked through the night, circling around to the south side of the mountain. As they walked they would pass painted bison skulls and bundles of sweet grass. Closer to the mountain, they discovered burial sites. They were careful to always keep a respectful distance from the burial sites.

At the southern base, Nínaiistáko rose 1500 feet. It was not as sheer as the northern face of the mountain. This side was a steep slope to the top of the mountain.

"Ancestors, give me strength," Oran said.

"There," the skin walker woman said. She pointed to a spot not far ahead on the slopes. Hidden in the night among the rocks was a wendigo. As she pointed, the monster stood. Oran recognized the angry bison wendigo that had chased them throughout the mountains. The skin on its arm was tattered, flapping from his bones like an old flag fluttering in the summertime winds.

Kai drew an arrow.

"No, Kai. Not yet," Oran said. He gripped his lance and walked toward the bison. It crossed to him in three steps.

For a moment, the two warriors stood there, sizing each other up. They were like stone gargoyles, ugly and fierce.

"Natosi sent me," the bison wendigo said. His voice sounded like the deepest hollows of the Earth.

"Why?"

"I'm not going to tell you."

"Fine. Are you going to kill me at the summit?"

"No. I'm going to help you kill a wendigo, and then I'm going to leave."

"Fine. But if you even look at me the wrong way, I'll kill you."

"You toss that little stick my way, and I won't kill you. I'll just eat your family."

Oran didn't say 'Fine.' He waved to the other three, and they came over. The bison wendigo was almost twice as tall as everyone else, should they have somehow formed a four-person/monster piggyback.

Together, they climbed the mountain. The wind swirled the dust around them as they ascended the southern side. The skin walkers had the hardest time with the first ascent, which was all steep slow. They didn't have the humans' small size or the undead bison's weight, so they struggled to stay on the mountain.

At one point, the bison wendigo reached out and steadied the woman skin walker.

"Hungry," she said.

The wendigo nodded.

Oran didn't hear them.

A large crashing noise shook the mountain. At the top of the peak, a greater wendigo appeared. The creature was hugging the mountain. It was two or three hundred feet tall and easily the tallest wendigo any of them had ever seen.

A magnificent crown of antlers sat upon the monster's skull. Long tendrils of fur or hair or moss dangled off its body. It reached with its long arms around the side of Chief Mountain, using its claws to keep its purchase on the mountainside. It opened its bony maw, which was full of long, triangular teeth, and screamed.

"A world ender," Oran said with finality.

Even Kai was taken back. "How do we kill that?" she asked.

Nobody in the party answered her. They pushed on. Eventually, the wendigo crawled to another side of the mountain, but surely it must have seen them. They were too tall and conspicuous not to be seen.

"This isn't like the skin walker way. They can see us coming if they haven't already. We should wait and move slowly, camouflaged," the bald skin walker said.

"We don't have that kind of time," Oran said.

They continued climbing.

During the second stage of their ascent to the top of the summit, they encountered a few hundred feet of sheer face. This was the hardest, scariest part of the climb. The rock wall defined Chief Mountain as a prominent geological landmark and a fixture of beauty. It was so prominent that the face could be seen from Canada miles to the north. But for Oran and his team, they would be at their most vulnerable.

"Expect them to attack us here," Oran said. "We need to get over these rocks as quickly as possible, but if they know we are coming, which I would bet they do, they know that on this sheer cliff we are defenseless."

They scaled the side of the mountain, the strong wind's pitch echoing in their ears as they anticipated the attack to come. Oran's head swiveled on his neck every time a raven cawed or a small rock fell.

Suddenly, a giant hand reached out and swatted Oran off the mountain. It came so quick, Oran didn't have a chance to react. All he could do was fall and die.

# CHAPTER TWENTY THREE

The mountainside fell out and away from Oran. The world ender had reached down and smacked him into the air like an ant. Now the monster, too, was falling out and away. He didn't want its ugly skull head to be the last image in his eyes.

Oran did not fall far before the bison wendigo plucked him out of the air and shoved him back onto the mountainside.

"Grab something!" the wendigo bellowed. Oran was already scrambling for any kind of purchase. This part of the mountain was so sandy, it was hard to find a hand or foothold. Suddenly, the safety net of the wendigo's hand was gone, and Oran's feet were scuttling on the edge of the mountain. Thankfully, something took, and he was saved a second time from falling to his death.

The giant creature screamed. Its wail was like a banshee, sharp and hissing. Its eyes were like two pale moons bearing a false light on their souls. Oran felt weaker in the dead thing's cold gaze.

He fought hard to keep climbing. Kai, too, pushed up the mountainside. With no way of using their weapons, Oran and Kai were useless in this fight. The only way they could help would be to get to the top of the mountain and the monster.

This close to the world ender, though, Oran learned that what his eyes told him was moss hanging off the monster's skeletal frame was actually long cords of human bodies and bones.

The skin walkers grabbed onto one of those tendrils as the monster climbed around the mountain at them. The skin walkers used the flying tendrils to bring them crashing down on the giant monster's body. They bit and clawed at the creature's ribs.

The world ender ignored the skin walkers. It focused on the creature responsible for Oran's safety. The giant elk wendigo crawled around the side of the mountain like some sick version of an undead gecko and snapped at the bison wendigo.

The bison wendigo leaped out of the way, stabbing the slope with its feet to keep itself upright. The world ender tried again to take out the wendigo, but this time it began bashing the sides of the mountain, dropping large rocks and layers of sediment down on the monster.

The bison wendigo was not a creature of retreat. It was the kind of creature that pursued its hunt for hundreds of miles. So it jumped at the world ender and latched onto his bony ribs. The wendigo reached for the monster's heart.

The world ender screamed in fear. It brought its fists down on the wendigo like a hammer, but the bison-headed wendigo gripped onto his ribs tighter and wouldn't let go.

The bison-headed wendigo began pummeling the monster's plump, red heart with its bony fingers. Agonizing, the world ender retreated to the far side of the peak. The last thing Oran saw, besides its feet scraping past, were the two skin walkers still clutching to the cords of human corpses.

"Climb!" Kai shouted. She and Oran raced up the final feet of the side of the mountain. As if charging up the sheer face of a mountain peak wasn't hard enough, they had to do it while the peak shook from the monster fight going on out of sight. Oran would reach for a crevice only to find the crevice shaking and moving. He thought that was impossible. It was more likely that he was shaking and moving, but it sure felt the other way around.

"Hurry!" Kai shouted again. She was already at the top. As soon as she hooked a leg over the ledge and pulled herself up, she reached back down for Oran. He took her hand, and she pulled him the rest of the way up.

Oran didn't have time to be impressed with Kai's strength, but he was still impressed.

They seemed to be alone on the summit, and Oran worried that Ernest and Greg were on a lower section of the mountain on the north side. He'd placed so much faith in his belief that they were here, he didn't know how to accept it if they weren't.

Thunder boomed overhead. Oran thought it was more of the wendigo fight, but after the second shuddering boom, he noticed the pewter sky. The wind was strong up here, blowing his hair around his face. Arrows and lances would be pointless here.

He glanced over the side of the mountain peak just as the world ender climbed up. Oran was taken aback by the sheer size of the gargantuan monster. As it crawled up on top of Nínaiistáko, its body was large enough for its legs to sit on either side of the narrow summit.

Oran and Kai stood back.

The world ender held the bison wendigo in its bone-white hand. Later, the size of the two creatures would leave Oran flustered with amazement. Here was the bison wendigo that, just a few weeks ago, men had slid under. Now it was the size of an action figure in the world ender's long claws.

Seeing the way the bison wendigo punched relentlessly at the wendigo's hand suddenly took Oran back to another time somebody had stabbed at the hands that were holding him. Just like Molotov, this bison was not going down without a fight.

The world ender placed the bison in his mouth, ready to pop off his head like a tough stick of bison jerky.

"Come on," Kai said. "There's nothing we can do." She pulled him back up the narrow spine of the peak. Oran hesitated to follow her. He did not want to leave a brother in combat, even one who had, up until recently, been his enemy.

The skin walkers had not given up the fight. They swung wide and came around on the world ender's face. At the last second, they pulled their skins off. Detroit steel slammed into the wendigo's skull. The skin walkers burst into fragments, but their collision was powerful enough to get the wendigo's attention. It slapped them as they fell. Hunks of steel went spinning into the mountain, then rolling hundreds of feet down the long slope. Doors went flying, and Oran was pretty sure he saw a bumper fall off, too. He didn't know the first thing about skin walker anatomy, but he was pretty sure they couldn't survive that fall.

Lightning zapped the mountain peak's high ridgeline, illuminating the undead monster in glory and electric vapor.

The world ender hurled the bison wendigo into the night sky. Oran neither saw nor heard it land.

At that moment, Oran shouldered his rifle and shot the wendigo. The monster knocked the rifle out of his hand, and nearly knocked him off the ridge, too, if not for Kai grabbing him.

Oran jumped back up. Lightning slashed the skies again. The wendigo cackled. Its white skull and pale eyes loomed over him. The world ender pointed at Oran, saying, "Devil of Tecumseh."

Its voice was like a thousand hissing snakes. The monster laughed. "Vengeance!"

Oran pulled back and hefted his lance at the creature. The lance curled in the air, but only seemed to gather speed. The wendigo moved to bat it out of the way, but the lance was too fast. The lance, decorated in sacred beading and eagle feathers, plunged deep into the wendigo's heart. The wendigo cried out in pain, arching its head backwards. At that same moment, a thunderbolt streamed down from the clouds, striking the lance, and through it, the wendigo.

A torrent of blood gushed out of the wendigo's mouth. The gigantic monster fell forwards, the full weight of the monster raining down on the peak. The mountain shook, knocking both Oran and Kai to the ground. For a moment, Oran thought this was it, this was the moment when the white god departed and the mountain crumbled, but the mountain stood strong.

After about twenty seconds of shaking, Oran and Kai tried to stand.

"Stop where you are!" Greg Falcon Runs came over the top of the high peak. He wore buckskin pants and a bison-horn cap. He showed them his bone club. "I have the high ground."

"Greg, look behind me. Do you see the world ender you made a deal with? Who do you think killed him? I have travelled from Alberta, crossed the Rocky Mountains mostly on foot, and fought countless monsters just to be with my wife and son. Do you really think you can stop me?"

"You are defenseless."

"A person with friends is never defenseless."

Behind him, Kai drew an arrow.

Greg was flustered. Whatever the plan was, it wasn't working. Oran walked toward him.

"D-don't do that, Oran. Stop!"

"I am not scared of you, Greg. And it is not because one of the best warriors I've ever met has my back or because you are just a fool who stayed on the res stirring up trouble while I went to war against the wendigo."

Oran walked up the side of the peak.

"You are not going to hit me because that's not your style. You strike at people who can't hit back. You cannot imagine fighting me. You are a coward, Greg. But that is not why I am not scared of you, either."

"You should be."

Oran stood face-to-face with Greg now. Oran's countenance evinced his pity. Kai was full of anger. The shaft of her arrow was over Oran's shoulder, the arrowhead inches from Greg's face.

"This is Chief Mountain, Greg. But it is Old Chief Mountain. I've never felt more at home or at ease than here, walking with the gods, knowing they are watching over me. And not you."

Oran took the bone club from out of Greg's hand. "Go away before I kill you, Greg."

Greg was so embarrassed by Oran's words, he lost control of his bladder, which embarrassed him even more. He ran away, his head in his hands.

Oran Old Chief walked over the crest of the peak. Below him sat his wife and his son, both tied up with hemp rope, their mouths duct-taped.

"Keep away, Oran," Ernest Upham said. The old man, like Greg, was dressed in ceremonial garb. A crown of feathers adorned Ernest's painted face.

"What are you doing, Ernest?"

"I'm going to make great medicine with them, and then nobody will be able to stop me from doing whatever I want."

Oran's face scrunched up with disgust at the obscene idea.

"You're an elder. You help run the town. You are respected, rich, and can go as you please. What else do you need in this life?"

Ernest answered with his eyes. Oran had seen that look many times back on the front, and during his travails through wendigo country. The bison wendigo had those eyes when they met them in the Swan Mountains. He'd seen the same look in the skin walkers while they were preparing to cook him and Ghost. It was an addiction to consuming. Monsters had come to this world as a cure for humanity's dissatisfaction with what life had to offer. People wanted more luxury, more refills, more super sizes. More clothes, more games, more channels, more models. More drugs, more love, more blame. The worst word in the English language was "more."

Ernest wasn't satisfied, and he never would be.

Oran thought of mercy. Killing skin walkers didn't stop them, and warring against wendigos hadn't prevented wendigos from taking control of almost half the land in Canada and America. If he killed Ernest, there would just be another like him to take his place.

Oran opened his parfleche and pulled out his medicine bag. The bag was decorated with a medicine wheel made of beads and porcupine quills. "This is my medicine bag. It is the most powerful medicine I know. It's kept me alive and brought me great satisfaction with my life. I will trade you this powerful medicine for the bad medicine you are trying to make."

"I don't want your medicine. It's not part of my plan."

It took less than a look over his shoulder. The arrow flew fast, all the stored energy of the bowstring unleashed on Ernest. The arrow ran through his eye and out the back of his brainbox.

Ernest fell backward and gasped. Another arrow cut off his windpipe. The old man choked and fell to the ground. Another arrow slid between his ribs, through his heart, and severed his spine. Ernest fell over and rolled off the mountain.

Oran ran to his wife. She was already struggling with the lashings and burst out of them. She ran to him and jumped into his arms, the tape still over her mouth. She didn't care. Daniel ripped the tape off enough to say, "Dad."

It was a powerful word.

Oran threw his arm around his son, who cried unabashedly. They were together. Though the miles had separated them, and he had fought many battles to get here, none of it mattered any more. He was home.

They hugged each other desperately, sobbing. It felt so good to have them in his arms again. He had missed their smell, their touch. To feel their weight against him.

"You've grown," Oran finally said to his son when they pulled apart to look at each other. Tears were in Oran's eyes.

Jodi pulled the tape off her lips.

Oran said, "You haven't changed. You are just as beautiful as the day I left." He kissed her passionately. They held each other.

"I'm sorry I've been gone so long."

# EPILOGUE

On the way down the mountain, they passed Ernest Upham's body. All his want dribbled out of his head.

Farther down, the Old Chiefs crossed the site where the skin walkers had fallen. Broken and bent auto parts lay strewn everywhere. But what Oran took notice of was the lack of cars, and the footprints leading away.

Oran settled back home. Ghost recovered. True to her word, she and Troy returned to the front. They joined an army convoy that was traveling around the mountains, through Idaho and Oregon back to the front.

Some of the children went east to other families, but most were adopted to families in Browning. They would visit Oran from time to time, and when they did, he addressed them as their military names. When Private First Class Falcon/Janelle fell in love with a South Piegan boy she met, she asked Oran to walk her down the aisle, which he did gladly. He enjoyed his life with his wife and his son, who was almost old enough to start his own life.

He prayed thanks to Natosi, made many offerings, and served his community. He lived in peace.

Yet on some days, he found his eyes wandering to the mountains out west. He was troubled by the mountains, but more by a bitter question it left growing like an infection in the back of his mind. Jodi would say a darkness fell over him when this happened.

Then one day, a visitor came to his porch. The boy was older now by a few years, and he had a metal arm.

"Quiet Child, what brings you here?" Oran asked. (His wife and son had learned to leave Oran when any of the Crazy Dogs came around.)

"The mountains."

"What of them?"

"I want to go back."

"You lost an arm to them. Why would you want to go back?"

"The mountains took, but I gained."

Oran thought this was very astute for a child. "That's the thing about journeys. They change you. You leave one person, but you come back another."

"What about you?" Quiet Child asked.

Several thoughts passed through Oran's mind. His first thought was, *I'm South Piegan. The mountains don't change me, they are me.* While true, the boy wasn't asking about Oran's culture (he damn well knew better than most whites about the Blackfeet now that he'd lived with them for several years), so to answer that way would be fraudulent.

"I went to war to kill wendigos, and by killing wendigos, I hoped to ensure the continued existence of my family and my people. And while I did kill wendigo, I also gained many friends, and I learned about so many other peoples. And then when I decided I was done, I intended to find my wife and son back home. And I did. But I also found twenty brave children hiding in buildings and two more hiding in orchards, and these children continue to inspire me every day because they changed who I was and made me better. If I hadn't come across them in the mountains, I don't know what kind of man would have returned to my wife and son. I don't think he'd be half the father I am today. I needed time to relearn how to act in a family. So the answer is yes and no. They changed me for the worse by turned me into a hardened warrior, a wendigo slayer, and a general in the timber armies. But then through you and the other children, they helped transform me back into a person again. So the answer has to be yes. I think the journey was meant to happen the way it did."

"Me, too." Quiet Child's voice changed as disjointed as his shift in topics. "Remember when we were walking through that village in the mountains, and it seemed like somebody was watching us?"

Oran made a sound in his throat. He remembered it. "We secured the area but did not find anyone."

"I think that's because they were hidden so well. But not too well. I saw somebody."

"Who?"

"A child. There's still more children out there. I know it. They are hiding and waiting because they don't know what else to do. Their parents are gone, and most people are dead. Someone has to go find them."

Oran had a good idea who that person would be.

Photo by Sam Shepherd

**Thanks for Reading**

If you enjoyed Wendigo Road, please leave a review on Amazon. Like most authors, I depend on reviews and word of mouth referrals of readers, so anything you can add would be greatly appreciated.

I am also the author of:

**Severed Press Books by Doug Goodman**
Dominion
Kaiju Fall
Kaijunaut
Shark Toothed Grin

**Zombie Dog Series**
Cadaver Dog (Book 1)
Dead Dog (Book 2)
Zombie Dog (Book 3 available for preorder)

My website is dgoodman1.wordpress.com. Feel free to email me at douggoodmannet@gmail.com. To sign up to be notified of new releases, giveaways, and other book news, check out my website or click here to sign up for the mailing list.

In case you are looking for a few other ways to reach me…

Facebook:  Doug Goodman
Twitter:  @DougGoodman1
Instagram:  42Trails or TexasGeekDad
Pinterest:  douggoodman

# CHECK OUT OTHER GREAT CRYPTID NOVELS

## BIGFOOT WAR
## by Eric S. Brown

Now a feature film from Origin Releasing. For the first time ever, all three core books of the Bigfoot War series have been collected into a single tome of Sasquatch Apocalypse horror. Remastered and reedited this book chronicles the original war between man and beast from the initial battles in Babblecreek through the apocalypse to the wastelands of a dark future world where Sasquatch reigns supreme and mankind struggles to survive. If you think you've experienced Bigfoot Horror before, think again. Bigfoot War sets the bar for the genre and will leave you praying that you never have to go into the woods again.

## CRYPTID ZOO
## by Gerry Griffiths

As a child, rare and unusual animals, especially cryptid creatures, always fascinated Carter Wilde.

Now that he's an eccentric billionaire and runs the largest conglomerate of high-tech companies all over the world, he can finally achieve his wildest dream of building the most incredible theme park ever conceived on the planet...CRYPTID ZOO.

Even though there have been apparent problems with the project, Wilde still decides to send some of his marketing employees and their families on a forced vacation to assess the theme park in preparation for Opening Day.

Nick Wells and his family are some of those chosen and are about to embark on what will become the most terror-filled weekend of their lives—praying they survive.

STEP RIGHT UP AND GET YOUR FREE PASS...

TO CRYPTID ZOO

# CHECK OUT OTHER GREAT
# CRYPTID NOVELS

## SWAMP MONSTER MASSACRE
## by **Hunter Shea**

The swamp belongs to them. Humans are only prey. Deep in the overgrown swamps of Florida, where humans rarely dare to enter, lives a race of creatures long thought to be only the stuff of legend. They walk upright but are stronger, taller and more brutal than any man. And when a small boat of tourists, held captive by a fleeing criminal, accidentally kills one of the swamp dwellers' young, the creatures are filled with a terrifyingly human emotion—a merciless lust for vengeance that will paint the trees red with blood.

## TERROR MOUNTAIN
## by **Gerry Griffiths**

When Marcus Pike inherits his grandfather's farm and moves his family out to the country, he has no idea there's an unholy terror running rampant about the mountainous farming community. Sheriff Avery Anderson has seen the heinous carnage and the mutilated bodies. He's also seen the giant footprints left in the snow—Bigfoot tracks. Meanwhile, Cole Wagner, and his wife, Kate, are prospecting their gold claim farther up the valley, unaware of the impending dangers lurking in the woods as an early winter storm sets in. Soon the snowy countryside will run red with blood on TERROR MOUNTAIN.

# CHECK OUT ANOTHER GREAT CRYPTID NOVEL!

## REPTILIAN
## by **John Rust**

The South Carolina Lizard Man had always been considered a local legend, a way to draw tourists to rural Lee County.

Until a local man shoots and kills the beast.

Jack Rastun, Karen Thatcher, and their team from the Foundation for Undocumented Biological Investigation are called in to collect the Lizard Man's corpse. When they arrive, they find the man who shot it torn apart, and the creature's body gone.

This is only the beginning. More lizard men emerge from the swamps, stalking and killing townspeople. Rastun, Thatcher, and the FUBI wage a desperate battle to try and end the bloody attacks.

But deadly reptilians are not the only threat. A former Marine is convinced the lizard men are part of a vast global conspiracy, and has a plan to deal with them, one that could mean disaster for the entire county.

With thousands of lives at risk, Rastun and Thatcher are faced with a difficult question. Who is more dangerous? Monster or man?

Made in the USA
San Bernardino, CA
08 November 2019

59611584R00112